I0598202

A DECADE ABORNING

The CASA Chronicles – Vol 4

Keith Julius

Published by Keith Julius

Temperance, MI 48182

Copyright © Keith Julius 2023

All Rights Reserved

First edition - January 2023

www.KeithJulius.com

ISBN: 978-0-9969607-9-3

Printed by KDP Select

Cover Design - twenty4hrdesign on fiverr

This book is dedicated to all the wonderful CASA volunteers everywhere. Without your dedication and commitment to the children you serve the world would truly be a sadder place.

I want to express my gratitude to Jeff Ferris of REACH IN WORD for his enthusiasm toward my writing and his diligence and attention to detail in helping me to prepare this manuscript.

Keith Julius

Chapter One:

SHE WAS going to jump.

There was no question in his mind, considering her appearance and demeanor.

She looked scared. She must have been intimidated with what she was facing. But there was a certain something, a grim determination, that presented itself in the teenage girl standing at the edge of the bridge, braced against the blue metal railing that served as the boundary between the roadway and the emptiness of space.

She held her body rigid. Unyielding. Intent on her actions. Her course was set, and even the occasional gust of wind that blew across the structure was unable to sway her.

He only hoped he had time to intervene before it was too late.

Officer Gerald Dickens was halfway through his morning shift when he turned onto the High Level bridge. The metal and concrete span crossed the Maumee River and connected the city of Toledo with the southern suburbs of East Toledo and, just beyond that, the cities of Oregon and Rossford. He traveled the route daily, all part of his normal routine.

It had been an ordinary shift so far, with nothing more significant than a few minor warnings. Traffic had been congested earlier, during the morning commute. But now things moved at a moderate pace. It was approaching lunchtime, and time to consider where he would stop to eat that afternoon.

Such thoughts deserted him when he reached the center of the bridge.

He nearly missed the young girl as he passed by, his attention focused on the cars in front of him. But he managed to catch a glimpse of her with his peripheral vision.

He instantly swerved to the side of the road, turned on his flashers, and made a hurried call to dispatch.

"Officer Dickens. Car 3409. On the High Level bridge heading north. Teenage girl, sixteen or seventeen, on the side of the structure. Looks like a possible jumper. I am responding immediately. Back-up and emergency assistance required."

He stepped from the squad car. Several vehicles approached from the other direction. They failed to yield to the uniformed officer, who swore under his breath as he waited for them to pass. He crossed to her side of the road, easily vaulting the concrete divider between the opposing lanes of traffic, taking in the sights around them as he crossed the roadway.

The view from the bridge was scenic. On certain days it could have almost been tranquil. Today, with the crisp taste of early autumn in the air and thick gray clouds hanging on the horizon, the moment struck him as ominous.

One side of the structure faced the city proper, with Toledo's skyline encroaching on the banks of the river. The city, as with so many other urban pockets, was attempting to rejuvenate the downtown area. Swanky apartments and local eateries, most catering to the young clientele that frequented the downtown area, predominated. Cars vied for space on the busy thoroughfares of the city.

On the river a few motorboats hugged the coastline, searching for a place to tie-up, adding their nautical congestion to the setting. There were less boats than there had been even a few weeks earlier, when the weather was still balmy and fishermen and pleasure seekers alike crowded the waterway that was the Maumee River. The season was winding down now, and soon the river would be deserted save for the squawking gulls that patrolled the area constantly, regardless of the season.

The other side of the bridge faced the newly developed Middlegrounds Park, an oasis of green in the concrete surrounding it. A picnic fire smoked beneath the wooden pavilion, its wispy tendrils floating on the breeze toward the river. Several people meandered through the twisted paths of the park, walking their dogs and enjoying the weather.

All seemed unaware of the drama taking place on the bridge above their heads.

The bridge was wide, with two lanes of traffic crossing from each direction. A pedestrian walkway paralleled the roadway, protected from the drop-off along the water's edge with a metal railing, barely chest high, where the bridge crossed the water. The view of the surroundings and the upstream area encompassed the river as it twisted its way alongside concrete grain elevators and railroad tracks, middle-income houses and boarded up abandonments. One of the grain elevators was painted with huge sunflowers, the golden colors of the adornment seeming to mock the scene with its cheerfulness.

Officer Dickens sprinted over, decreasing the distance separating the two of them, then slowed to a quick walk as he drew nearer.

Traffic had stopped by now, and silence gripped the scene. Previously each passing car had elicited a loud THUMP of a sound from the roadway, caused perhaps by the expansion joints of the structure sliding past one another in protest. The absence of the structure's complaint aroused the girl's attention. She turned, and became aware of the officer's presence.

"Don't come any closer!" she warned.

Dickens reduced his pace.

"I mean it." Her voice cracked, lending it a hysterical lilt. "You come any closer and I'll jump."

"You don't mean that."

He kept his voice calm, but came to a halt in difference to her words.

"Why don't we talk about this?" the officer suggested.

She shook her head. It was a violent back and forth motion as she turned away from him. "There's nothing to talk about."

"At least tell me your name."

"Why should I?"

"I just want to know who I'm talking to. That's all."

Her answer was slow in coming. Finally, when the words arrived, they were in a quieter tone.

"Pamela. My name's Pamela."

"Hello, Pamela. My name's Gerald. But my friends call me Gerry."

There was no reply.

"You can call me Gerry, if you like."

"Why should I? We're not friends."

"But we can be."

"No."

More head shaking.

"You want to stop me from jumping. You want to get in my way."

"Maybe I just want to understand why you're here? Why you think you need to do this?"

The reply came with no hesitation, delivered with the near-hysterical tone she had exhibited earlier. "Because my life is a mess, that's why."

"It can't be that bad?"

"How would you know? How would anyone know what my life is like?"

"Then why don't you tell me about it?"

He took another step forward. She failed to notice, so he moved yet again, emboldened by her lack of attention.

"Suicide is a drastic step, Pamela. There's no turning back from something like this."

"I don't care!"

8

She started to cry then. The tears were slow at first, but as she continued it was as though she finally was allowing herself to break down.

"I hate my life, and all the crap I have to put up with."

Her words were slurred, garbled due to the increasing flow of her tears, as she continued with her soliloquy, the approaching officer forgotten now.

"I thought things had gotten better. I thought all that trash was behind me. But I was fooling myself. It will never be behind me. I have to live with those memories for the rest of my life."

Her voice quieted with the last words, as she drifted further into painful recollections.

Dickens kept his voice distinct and clear. "We all have to put up with things, Pamela. That's part of life."

The police officer took another step. He was close enough that he could almost touch her now.

Off in the distance a siren blared, the sound growing louder as the emergency vehicle approached. The strident wail of the ambulance permeated everywhere.

Maybe there's still time, Dickens thought. I just need a few more seconds.

The teenager chose that moment to turn and face him again. "You have no idea what my life has been like."

As she spoke her face became more animated, as she noticed the figure that was almost upon her.

"No!"

She stood abruptly, panic washing over her.

"I told you to stay away from me!"

She shifted position, lifting her leg over the railing in a move that immediately threw her off-balance. The loss of footing disturbed her more than she had expected. She grabbed for the railing, missed, and started falling backward, toward the emptiness beyond the edge of the bridge. A scream escaped her lips.

Dickens lunged, throwing his arms around the girl's thin

waist. She was much smaller than him, but the suddenness of her weight pulling against him caught the officer by surprise. He lost his footing, slammed against the metal railing. His right knee took the brunt of the blow, tearing his pants and scraping a layer of skin. He gritted his teeth against the shock but managed to retain his grip on the girl.

She was still screaming. Panic gripped her, as she flailed with her hands for any purchase she could find. Her fingernails clawed against the officer's chest, grabbing hold of his shirt pocket. She refused to let go. Her eyes were tightly closed, shutting out the images around her, while her chest heaved up and down.

Her body shook, the tremors uncontrolled. She became a dead weight to the officer, a screaming shaking figure of uncontrolled emotion unleashed.

Dickens heard footsteps. He didn't dare relinquish his grip, even to look around him. But he knew help was at hand. It would only be a few moments more and the girl would be safe.

Seconds later other arms reached out.

Pamela was pulled off the railing, onto the safety of the pedestrian walkway.

She collapsed to the ground.

Officer Gerald Dickens allowed his heart to start beating again as he breathed a sigh of relief.

Chapter Two:

ANGELA WATKINS stormed into the room like she was looking to start a fight, with a determination of purpose propelling her forward. Her husband Tim followed closely behind. His manner betrayed his aggravation as well – his pensive examination of the environment as well as the stiffness in his demeanor, both denoting how uncomfortable he was with the current situation – though he seemed more composed than his wife.

"I'm looking for Patrick Zimmerly," Angela announced, addressing the three people gathered around the conference table. They were all nicely dressed in casual business attire. Two of those present were women, so it was hardly surprising when the lone man in the room rose to his feet.

"I'm Patrick. You're Mrs. Watkins?"

"Yes I am. Now what's this all about? Where's my daughter? Where's Pamela?"

Tim rested his arm lightly on her shoulder. "Now Honey –."

She shrugged the gesture off without even facing him. "Don't *Now Honey* me! I want to know what's going on with my daughter."

"She's been taken to Toledo Hospital for observation."

"Observation? I thought she was okay. You said nothing happened to her."

"She hasn't been hurt," Zimmerly assured her. "Physically. But emotionally she's been through a lot."

"This is all crazy," Angela remarked. She paced back and forth as she talked, her nervousness driving her actions. "I just don't understand what's happening here."

One of the women at the table spoke up. "Please sit down, Mrs. Watkins, and we can talk about what's going on." Her voice was soothing; intended to calm.

Angela hesitated, unsure what to do. Her husband pulled a chair out from the table, and though she seemed not to notice the gesture she sat down nonetheless. She maintained a steady glare at the woman speaking to her. "And you are?"

"Shantel Monaghan. I'm a Supervisor here at Children's Services." Shantel gestured toward Tim. "Please get comfortable, Mr. Watkins."

"I prefer to stand."

"As you wish."

Patrick Zimmerly sat once again, and as papers were shuffled around the table Angela took in the bare adornments of the tiny conference room. She thought back to the phone call she had received that morning, and the conversation that had led to this moment.

The caller had a professional, no-nonsense tone to his delivery. He had identified himself as Patrick Zimmerly, from Lucas County Children's Services. "I'm calling in regards to your daughter, Pamela," he had announced.

Angela found herself immediately on the defensive. "What's this about?"

"Have there been any problems in regards to Pamela? Anything going on in her life that would cause her excessive stress?"

"No. Of course not. Pamela's just fine."

"Any recent mood changes? Modifications in her behavior?"

"You're starting to scare me, Mr. Zimmerly."

"I'm sorry. That's certainly not my intention. But there has been an incident."

"What's going on?" Angela practically screamed into the phone. "What happened to Pamela?"

"She was observed on the High Level bridge late this morning. She appeared to be contemplating suicide."

A stunned silence answered, as the connection went dead for the space of several heartbeats while Angela Watkins digested the information.

"No."

Her tone was a cross between disbelief and outrage.

"No. That's ridiculous. Not Pamela. Why would she be thinking about suicide? There must be some mistake. You sure it wasn't somebody else? My daughter's in school right now."

"Pamela told us she couldn't face going to school today, but she didn't mention anything more specific. Have there been any issues lately at school?"

"No. Everything's fine. Pamela's fine."

Then, as an afterthought, she spoke the question she was dreading to hear the answer to.

"Is my daughter okay? Is she hurt?"

"She's fine. Nothing happened, Mrs. Watkins. She's in a safe place and being taken care of."

"I want to see her."

"Of course you do. But there's more we need to talk about first. Can you and your husband come down to Children's Services so we can discuss some things?"

Angela refused to be persuaded. "I want to see my daughter first."

"I assure you, your daughter is in good hands, Mrs. Watkins. And I promise we won't take up any more of your time than is absolutely necessary. But there are things we need to talk about, and the sooner we can have this discussion the sooner you will be able to see Pamela."

She nearly said more, then realized the futility of arguing. The man on the other end of the line seemed determined to have his way.

So she capitulated.

"I can reach Tim at work and we can be down there right away."

"Good. Give your name at the Security checkpoint. They will contact us and let you know where to come once you get here."

And so here she was, sitting in a cold and empty office, being scrutinized by three people from Children's Services, while her daughter languished at Toledo Hospital.

None of it made sense to her, and the longer things dragged on the more upset Angela felt about the situation.

"This is a waste of time. I want to see my daughter."

Shantel spoke up. "That will have to wait, Mrs. Watkins. Due to the severity of the circumstances, we need to do an investigation, to determine what's going on here."

"Can't we do this later?" Angela's voice was beginning to rise, as if by speaking louder she could sway the trio confronting her. "My daughter needs me, and all you can think of is asking your questions and keeping me away from her. She needs to come home."

"We understand how upset you are," the social worker offered, in an attempt to placate the distraught mother. "But something prompted this action on your daughter's part. Home may not be the best place for her right now. We need to be certain she's in a safe environment."

"So now you're saying my home isn't a safe environment?"

Tim's hand reached out, rubbing his wife's shoulder in a supportive motion. She shrugged the motion aside.

"Who do you people think you are? I want to see Pamela. My daughter needs me, and I need to be there for her."

"We're only asking for a few minutes of your time. This is important."

"My daughter's well-being is important!"

Angela stood, her chair scraping against the linoleum floor as she pushed herself away from the table. She looked at her husband, speaking in a tone that brooked no discussion.

"We're going to see Pamela. Right now."

Silence greeted her.

"Are you coming with me, Tim?"

He ignored the question as he turned toward the others.

"So what happens now?" His voice was calm and rational, almost soothing with its cadence. "How do we move forward in Pamela's best interest?"

Patrick Zimmerly answered.

"Your daughter will remain in the hospital for the time being. For observation. Most likely it will only be for a day or two. We would like to have her stay with someone else for a while, after she's released, rather than returning home immediately. Can you recommend a relative that could take her in?"

Angela stormed back toward the table.

"You won't even let us take her home?"

Tim, his voice steady, spoke up before a response could be offered. "Brian. My brother Brian."

Angela shot her husband an incredulous look, an expression he chose to ignore. His attention was focused on the business at hand as he continued.

"I can give you his phone number and address. Pamela knows him. And is comfortable around him. I'm sure he can take her for a while."

"Thank you, Mr. Watkins."

Information was exchanged. A few other details were covered. And the meeting was terminated.

Tim continued to keep his voice calm.

"Can we see our daughter now?"

"Of course."

Angela and Tim walked down the hallway away from the conference room. Her heels clattered unnaturally loud in the vacant corridor, a staccato rhythm that expressed her aggravation and accented her urge to remove herself from the premises. She refused to look at her husband, and not a word was spoken until they reached the elevator. After punching the down button Tim reached his hand out toward his wife.

"I'm sure it's only for a few days."

She shrugged off his gesture.

"I'm not talking to you. After what those people are doing to us. You didn't need to be so nice to them."

"They're concerned about Pamela. And what's best for her."

"And I'm not?"

"Of course you are. I am too. But once you calm down you'll see this is all for the best."

She shook her head, refusing to see the sense in his assessment of the situation.

"This is all just a load of bureaucratic nonsense. That's all it is."

She turned to face the elevator, refusing to look at her husband as she continued.

"And why'd you give them Brian's name?"

"They're going to put her somewhere. At least it's with family."

"She needs to be with us."

"She will be. Just give it some time."

Chapter Three:

IT WAS dark in the little room. The shades had been partially drawn earlier, in difference to the afternoon light spilling through the window, but now that the sun had set the room seemed dismal and depressing.

Considering the circumstances, it was an appropriate setting for the three people in the room.

Pamela Watkins was sleeping peacefully, the blankets on the bed covering the flimsy hospital gown she wore. Tim Watkins sat in a chair beside her, reading a book. Occasionally he would look up to glance at his daughter. Once or twice he reached over, to rest his hand on her arm, as if to reassure himself that she was only slumbering. She looked so relaxed, so still, that he needed to be certain.

His wife stood at the window, staring off into the distance. There was a world of activity just outside the hospital window, the hustle and bustle of an active city. It was doubtful if she was even aware of the cars hurtling pass on the nearby interstate, and they certainly were oblivious to her situation. They had their own lives to contend with; the plight of a teenager in trouble didn't concern them.

A Life Flight helicopter, its body aglow in the darkness, perched on a platform across the street from the medical center. A bevy of floodlights was trained on the mechanical bird, while its flashing red light imparted a tone of urgency to the setting. It had landed a few minutes earlier. Angela had briefly wondered what crisis the arrival of the metal contraption indicated, but the thought had fled her mind immediately following the occurrence. She had enough to worry about already.

The sound of a Med Cart in the hallway disturbed them for a moment, a squeaking wheel and the padding of soft-soled shoes announcing its passage. Then the room was plunged once more into a silence interrupted only by the steady beating of the monitors connected to the form on the bed, the metronomic cadence a constant reminder of the setting.

When Angela spoke the words came slowly, addressed to the darkness outside.

"Why do you think she did it?"

Tim closed his book and set it down on an end-table by the bed. He said nothing, allowing his wife the time she needed to continue.

Angela turned to face her husband.

"What could be so bad in Pamela's life that she felt the only solution was to....?"

She struggled, unable to complete the sentence. She felt a sudden chill, just from the thought of what had nearly happened that afternoon. It was difficult to come to grips with the concept.

"I don't know what I would have done if she had actually gone through with it."

"Don't go there, Angie."

"I can't help it. It's all I can think of. Doesn't it make you wonder?"

"Of course it does. But there's nothing we can do now but be there for her. She needs our support, Angie."

"But what did we do wrong? I feel like we failed her, Tim. Like this was a cry for help. She needed us, and we weren't there for her."

A new voice intruded on the conversation.

"You didn't fail her."

Angela addressed the new arrival. "Who are you?"

"Dr. Antonio Bargalony."

The man was dressed in a white lab coat, which failed to conceal his portly appearance. He had a superior air to him, like he was used to asserting himself and expected respect from those around him. His demeanor was a cold one. Perhaps he had seen enough pain and suffering over the years that he was no longer able to empathize with those under his care.

But his eyes, upon closer examination, revealed a softness, or possibly a weariness, beneath his demeanor.

"Mr. and Mrs. Watkins?"

"Yes. I'm Tim. This is my wife, Angela. Have you spoken with our daughter?"

"Yes I have. I'm a Psychiatrist practicing in conjunction with the hospital. They called me, shortly after Pamela was admitted, and assigned her case to me."

"What did you mean?" Angela asked. "When you said we didn't fail her?"

"Parents naturally think they're to blame," the physician continued. "That's a common reaction from family members in these types of circumstances. They can't help but assume the fault lays with them. There's nothing to be gained in thinking those types of thoughts."

"Then what was it? What caused her to...?"

Once again Angela couldn't even say the word.

"I don't know," the physician admitted. "I talked to Pamela at length, following her arrival, but it's far too early for me to reach any conclusions regarding her situation."

The doctor took a step further into the room, as though attempting to bridge the gap between himself and the parents of his patient, though his demeanor remained professional as he continued with his recitation.

"I did detect a certain erraticness regarding her answers to my questions. It was as though she was rattled, and not thinking clearly. Which goes without saying, in these types of circumstances. Her brain is confused right now, sorting through a myriad of conflicting emotions. She needs time to heal, and come to grips with whatever issues are controlling her thoughts and causing her to act in such an irrational manner."

"That doesn't sound like Pamela," Tim offered. "She's generally pretty level headed about things."

"We never saw this coming," Angela added.

"Have you noticed any mood swings lately?" Dr. Bargalony inquired. "Has she mentioned anything that's been bothering her?"

"Nothing. Everything's been fine."

Angela looked at her daughter, watching the teenager's steady breathing beneath the hospital blankets.

"If I could just talk to her, I'm sure everything would be better."

"Your daughter was extremely agitated when she was brought to the hospital, Mrs. Watkins. We gave her some midazolam to help her sleep. I don't think she'll be doing any talking this evening."

"How long will she have to stay here?" Tim asked.

"A day or two, anyway. I'd like to observe her further. And talk to her more, once she's settled down. Until then, there isn't much you can do for her. It may be better, for all of you, to just go home. I'm sure things will look better in the morning."

"Can't we stay? Just a bit longer?"

"Of course, Mrs. Watkins. No one's going to make you leave. I'll be back, first thing tomorrow, to see how Pamela is progressing."

Angela moved toward the bed, her hand reaching out to touch her daughter. The motion halted several inches short of the target. Without a word she turned away, facing the window once more.

"We'll take good care of her, Mrs. Watkins."

Tim answered for his wife.

"Thank you, doctor."

The physician left, leaving behind him a more oppressive atmosphere than that which he had intruded upon moments earlier.

Tim walked over to Angela, placing his arm gently around her waist.

"Everything will be okay, Angie."

"How do you know that?"

The tears had started, streaking down her face.

"We don't even know what's wrong with her. Our little girl was crying out for help, and we don't even know why."

"These people are experts, Angie. They deal with this sort of thing all the time. I'm sure they'll get to the bottom of things."

"But what if it's not over? What if she tries this again?"

"We won't let her."

The logic failed to appeal to the distraught woman.

"We can't be with her 24 hours a day, Tim. So what do we do?" She glanced around the room, as though seeing the antiseptic environment surrounding them for the first time. "Do we keep her locked away, in some place like this, so she can't do any harm to herself?"

"You're overreacting."

"I just want her to be safe. I just want our little girl back."

Chapter Four:

Beverly FONDLED the scarlet chrysanthemums carefully, being certain not to harm the delicate petals of the flowers, as she lowered the plant into the hole she had dug in the dark black soil. She pushed new dirt over the roots, then added water from the purple and blue watering can by her side. Rising to her feet – brushing aside an errant leaf that had clung to her pant leg – she stood back to admire the results.

She smiled, pleased with the way things were looking. The mums had joined a dozen or so other plantings in a carefully arranged grouping at one end of the flower garden, adding a splash of color to the setting.

Beverly enjoyed working outdoors. Especially in the mornings, when the air was crisp and clear and the entire day stretched ahead of her. The potential for what was to come always seemed endless with the beginning of each new day. She relished the time she was able to spend in her backyard, planning the arrangements just right to attract the birds and butterflies she loved to see come visit her little corner of the world.

She wiped her hands together, removing some of the dirt from the gloves she wore, and contemplated the flower garden some more. The brick supporting wall, three layers tall, wound through the backyard. It encircled a large tulip tree and several small bushes. It still looked in pristine condition, after being there for twelve years.

Little wonder, she thought. Russell had done an excellent job with the project, digging the trench and laying dozens of bags of gravel, stamping the loose stones into place, then carefully positioning and leveling each block as he worked around the perimeter of the garden. It was the way he did everything. Meticulously planned and executed.

She missed him immensely.

The garden had been completed the summer before the accident that took his life.

She still marveled that Russell had been gone for twelve years now. At times it seemed like an eternity since she had last held him; since she had last had a conversation with him; since she had last shared time with the man she had been married to for forty-one years.

But on other occasions it seemed an instant only since she had last heard his laugh. And seen the sparkle in his eyes when he grew enthusiastic about something. His enthusiasm had always brightened her spirits, and just thinking about him again brought a smile, albeit a sad one, to her lips.

There was still more to be done, so Beverly shook herself from her reverie. Even though she had been retired for years now, she still tried to keep to a schedule. Mornings were for yard work, or errands, or anything active to keep her going. There were plenty of flowers still left to go in the ground, which meant there was more work to be done.

Before she could continue with her chores she was disturbed by the shrill chiming of her cellphone. She had left it on the back deck, close at hand in case anybody needed to get hold of her. Jennifer kept in touch constantly. It was nice that her daughter was so concerned, but sometimes it was a bit of a nuisance.

Then again, it could also be a call regarding her CASA work.

"Hello. This is Beverly."

"Hi, Beverly. This is Becky Poole, from the CASA office."

Beverly had been involved with CASA for nearly ten years now. The program, set up in conjunction with the Lucas County Juvenile Court, was a volunteer program. Along with over one hundred people in Lucas County alone – and thousands of others across the United States – Beverly proudly served as a Court Appointed Special Advocate.

CASA volunteers represented children in cases of child abuse and child neglect. In her role as a CASA volunteer Beverly conducted investigations. She wrote reports, detailing her findings and the time she spent on each case. She visited every month with the children entrusted to her guardianship, providing support and stability during the often turbulent times the children found themselves in. She interviewed family members, friends, professional people involved with the children and their parents, and anybody who could be considered pertinent to the case.

She also attended court hearings.

Court was disheartening to Beverly at times. As you entered the courtroom you couldn't help but notice how many different people were involved in the proceedings. There were the representatives from Children's Services, the caseworkers and attorneys. Each parent was in attendance, along with their attorneys, and due to the bizarre familial ties in some of the cases she worked on there were often several fathers present. The magistrate and court clerks were there as well, presiding over the hearings.

And way in the back sat Beverly, in most cases feeling like a casual observer to the events.

She knew she could make a difference in a child's life. She had seen it happen firsthand. And her opinion was always solicited, and considered, during the proceedings. But sometimes it just didn't seem like enough.

As much as she did for these children, it seemed there was a constant need to do more. There were so many of them out there, children being raised in troubled families, struggling through desperate situations, longing for someone to be there for them in their time of need.

It was nearly overwhelming when you stopped to consider the sheer numbers of children that needed assistance.

She pulled away from these thoughts and returned to her phone call from the CASA office.

"How are you today, Becky?"

"Overloaded with work. As usual. We just had a new case open up that I thought you would be interested in."

Beverly hesitated, stumbling over her answer. "You know, I just finished a case. And I know I should jump at another. But I was hoping to get a breather for a few weeks. Before starting all over again."

"I understand. But this one is special. It's in regards to a seventeen-year-old girl named Pamela Watkins."

"I'm sorry. That name doesn't mean anything to me."

"Wait a minute." The distinct sound of rustling papers came through the receiver. "Perhaps this will help. It was ten years ago, and the child's name was Pamela Sutter. She was six at the beginning of the case, and ended up being adopted by the foster parents. Angela and Tim…."

Beverly completed the sentence. "Watkins. I remember now. It was my very first case after becoming a CASA. I remember how happy I was that she was adopted by such a loving couple."

"Well, she's back in the system."

"That's too bad. What happened?"

"Pamela, who's seventeen now, tried to commit suicide."

"Oh My God!" The words caught in Beverly's throat.

"We don't know the details," Becky offered. "All I can tell you is the young girl is being placed with a paternal uncle. I can give you the contact information if you want to take the case."

Beverly hesitated. For a few seconds she reflected on the many cases she had handled in her ten years as a CASA volunteer. She had met and worked with dozens of children during that time, and at some point had felt an intense attachment to each and every one of them.

One of the hardest things about the program, at least from Beverly's point of view, was saying goodbye when the case was eventually resolved.

She had often wondered what happened to her young charges once she was no longer involved. There had been some cases where things hadn't gone as anticipated; where Beverly had disagreed with the outcome but was helpless to do anything to change the magistrate's decision. All she could do then was hope and pray that everything worked out all right in the end, and tell herself the children were being loved and cared for and that's what really mattered.

She had never worried about Pamela Sutter. Rather, Pamela Watkins. Her case had resolved itself exactly as Beverly had hoped it would. Though vague on the particulars, she recalled enough about it to remember the adopted parents as being a loving couple that welcomed the youngster into their home.

But a lot can happen in ten years. People change. Situations develop. Things happen.

"Yes," she responded at last. "I'll take the case."

"Good for you. There's an Emergency Hearing at 12:30 this afternoon. Do you think you'll be able to attend?"

Beverly glanced at the display on her cellphone. It was after 11:00 already.

"That doesn't give me much time."

"Sorry I couldn't give you more notice. These things happen quickly at this stage. You aren't required to attend today. Especially since you haven't been officially assigned to the case yet. But considering your history with the family, and your willingness to take it on, there's no reason why the magistrate wouldn't allow it."

"I've never attended an Emergency Hearing before. Is there anything I need to know before I get there?"

"Not really. Monica can fill you in on the details when you arrive."

Monica Perry was the staff attorney for Lucas County. Beverly had worked with her in the past, on quite a few of her cases.

"I'll try my best to be there," Beverly responded.

"That's all we can ask for. If you can't make it I'll email you all the information we have. Though your background should be an advantage to working through this one."

"I hope so. At least I've met the adopted parents. And Pamela. Though I suspect she may not even remember me."

"You'd be surprised. Sometimes kids have phenomenal memories. This was during a very traumatic moment of her childhood. She may well remember all of it."

Beverly thought back on the case. Though not fresh in her mind, she did remember some of the key elements involved. In particular, she recalled why the biological parents had lost custody of the child.

"I hope she doesn't remember all of it," Beverly commented at last. "What that girl went through….. Some things are best left forgotten."

Chapter Five:

Mommy AND DADDY were fighting again. It seemed to happen every day.

I got so tired of it.

Why didn't they get tired of it?

Mommy always sent me to my room when Daddy got home from work. She always told me that it was safer that way, and that I had to understand that's why she did it.

I always just nodded my head. As if I understood. But I didn't. Not really.

Why was it safer in my room?

Daddy would never hurt me. He loved me too much. He took care of me. We played games together, when Mommy wasn't feeling good. And he read books to me, using funny voices for the diff'rent animals in the stories. He even did the sounds. Like the elephant trumpeting. Or a pig going oink-oink-oink. It sounded a bit silly. And I guess I was getting too old for it. But it was always funny, and we both ended up laughing and giggling.

But Mommy said I should go to my room. So I did. I went to my room. I closed the door, and picked up my dollie, and pretended not to notice the way they talked to each other and the way they yelled at each other and the bad things they said to each other.

It just didn't make sense to me.

I heard Daddy's voice. His voice was always loud, but 'specially when he was angry. Daddy's voice was loud that day.

He told Mommy she was drinking too much. Which was silly, 'cause Mommy knew she was drinking. She did that every day.

Mommy said it wasn't any of Daddy's business. She used her angry voice. She got that way a lot. 'Specially in the morning, when she had a headache and wasn't feeling good, and she wanted me to go play and leave her alone.

Daddy called her Stef then, even though her name was Stephanie, and said the drinking was no good for Pamela. He always called me Pamela, though Mommy called me Pammie.

Like when she said Pammie was okay. Mommy said Pammie was okay, and she took good care of me.

Daddy didn't believe that. Daddy said Mommy didn't even take care of herself. That she didn't even keep her clothes clean.

Mommy told Daddy he was wrong, 'cause she was always home when I got home from school and she was looking out for me. And that's the truth. Mommy always was home when I got home from school, but sometimes she would be asleep on the couch and I knew I had to be 'specially quiet 'cause if I woke her up she would be angry with me.

Daddy said Mommy was always home 'cause she was drinking too much and couldn't leave the 'partment. But that wasn't true neither. Mommy did leave the 'partment, to go to the store on the corner and get more stuff to drink.

Sometimes, if I was home from school, she would let me go to the store with her. But usually she left me home by myself. She said I was getting to be such a big girl that she could leave me home by myself.

Though sometimes, when she did leave me home alone, it seemed like she was gone for such a long time that I would get scared, and I would begin to wonder if maybe something happened to her. I was always glad when she got home, 'cause then I knew she was okay.

I also worried 'bout what Daddy would think if he got home and Mommy wasn't there. He would be mad. Like he was that day.

So I hid in the room, and I listened through the door, and they kept on yelling at each other. And then I heard a crash. Maybe it was a dish. Or it might of been a glass. They threw things sometimes when they were mad at each other. Sometimes Mommy didn't clean it up, so I would have to clean it up later. But I didn't mind. Mommy just needed some help once in a while, that's all.

Mommy's voice got more quieter then. I think she was starting to cry. She told Daddy she was a good mother.

Daddy didn't say nothing.

Things got even more quieter after that.

I leaned closer to my door, and held my dollie tighter, but I didn't hear nothing. For a long time I didn't hear nothing.

Then I heard footsteps, coming to my door. I backed away, closer to my bed. There was a knock on the door. It was Daddy, asking if he could come in.

I didn't answer, but he came in anyway. He looked sad. Daddy seemed to look more sadder and sadder every day.

He used to look happy all the time. He used to laugh, and Mommy used to laugh, and we used to have a lot of fun together. We used to go on picnics together. Or to the zoo. One day we even took a whole weekend and went to a big amusement park together. We stayed overnight. And we got to use the swimming pool at the hotel and everything.

I missed when Mommy and Daddy were happy.

Daddy asked me how school was, and he called me Sweetie. I liked it when he called me Sweetie.

I shrugged my shoulders and told him it was okay. I didn't really like school. Not really. Except when it was reading time. I liked reading time.

Daddy scrooched down on his knees and held his hands out. Then he told me how pretty I looked.

He always told me I was pretty. And that I was his special angel. It usually made me happy, but I didn't feel like smiling.

He asked me if I was hungry. I had some cookies when I got home from school, so I really wasn't very hungry. But after he asked me if I was hungry I decided that maybe I was hungry after all. I guess him just saying something 'bout eating must of made me hungry.

Then he asked me if I wanted to go out to get something to eat.

I asked if Mommy was coming with us, but I knew what the answer would be.

He said no. it was just gonna be me and Daddy.

I said okay.

When we got to the front door I asked why Mommy couldn't come with us.

Daddy looked at the kitchen. I could still hear Mommy in there. She was still crying, but it was a real quiet crying.

Daddy just looked back at me and smiled.

Then Daddy gave me a hug and we left.

Chapter Six:

IN HER ten years as a CASA volunteer Beverly had never attended an Emergency Hearing at the Juvenile Court.

This wasn't that unusual, considering the steps typically undertaken during these types of disputes.

Each case that came before the Juvenile Court started pretty much the same. Once an allegation had been made, regarding either neglect or abuse involving a minor, Children's Services launched an immediate investigation. The caseworker conducting the investigation would interview participants and determine a logical interim solution.

This could be as simple as placing the child under protective supervision. This was done in circumstances where they felt there was no immediate risk to the child, who would remain in the home of the current parent or caregiver. During the subsequent months Children's Services would conduct periodic visits with the family, to determine that the situation was under control and no new issues had developed.

This option was often taken in cases of Domestic Violence. Once the perpetrator of the violence was removed from the environment, with court orders not to visit or return to the scene, then the rest of the family could resume their lives with a minimum amount of disturbance. This was particularly important for school age children, so they could continue their education with no alteration to their classes and the normal procedures they were accustomed to. As long as nothing developed to corrupt the situation then the protective custody order would remain in place.

More often, however, the child would be removed from the home, to isolate them from the circumstances that had resulted in the allegations and ensure they were residing in a safe and healthy environment. Finding a family member willing to take on the responsibility of caring for the child was always the first choice for such moves. This was easier for the children involved, and generally resulted in a less disruptive experience for everyone.

In the case of Pamela Watkins – Beverly's current case – the family had suggested her Uncle Brian. Before the decision could be finalized a background check would be made of the candidate, as well as a home study where the investigative caseworker would visit the residence to determine if it was a proper setting for the child, or children, involved.

If a suitable family member could not be found then the child would be sent to a foster home, a certified placement that had already passed the necessary scrutiny required by the agency and had been deemed a safe haven for children. Foster parents were properly trained to work with children, as well as being equipped to handle any special needs or situations involved.

At all times during the process what was best for the child was of primary importance.

Of necessity, all this happened quickly. Within 48 hours of the allegation coming to light an Emergency Hearing needed to be held at the Juvenile Court. It was necessary for everything to be in place by then so the magistrate could make the proper ruling.

The rapid response of the court system generally prevented the assignment of an advocate this early in the case. It was following this initial hearing, after the children involved were in placement and the parents or caregivers had been introduced to the system, that the CASA office reached out to the area volunteers. Only then was someone solicited who would be suitable for the assignment of dealing with the family and its concerns.

Beverly showed up at the Juvenile Court, wondering what to expect from this new experience. She was curious as well regarding how familiar the participants would be to her, considering the decade that had passed since her previous involvement with the family.

She remembered Angela and Tim Watkins the moment she laid eyes on them.

For the life of her she couldn't have recalled their faces earlier. She distinctly remembered the case. Or, at least, certain aspects of it. And Pamela's image, as a young girl of seven, was vivid in her memory. But the faces of the two people who had adopted the young girl had remained elusive to her.

It all came back in an instant. A wave of remembrance flooded her. So many of their conversations, even the inflections of the voices, returned as soon as she set eyes on them again.

It felt nice to have something familiar in a case, instead of starting from scratch. It was intimidating at times to keep track of the different members and allegiances presented by some of the families she became involved with, so this experience of reviving an old case was a welcomed one.

She saw Tim Watkins first, sitting by himself in the hallway outside the courtroom.

"Hello, Tim."

He gave her a puzzled, *do I know you?* type of look.

"I'm Beverly Johnson. I was the CASA for Pamela ten years ago. Following the removal from her family and during the adoption proceedings."

"Of course." He stood up and offered his hand.

"Where's Angela?"

He motioned toward an approaching figure.

"Here she is now."

Angela started talking before she even reached the two of them.

"This is ridiculous."

"What's the problem?" her husband asked.

"They're treating us like a bunch of low-lifes. Like they're all superior or something, and they can look down on us as if we don't mean anything."

Beverly spoke up. "I'm certain nobody feels that way, Angela."

She exhibited confusion with the greeting, similar to that experienced by Tim only moments earlier. By the time introductions had been completed she had calmed down slightly.

But only slightly.

"What's the matter?" Beverly asked.

"I was just talking to my attorney. She said they'll want us to go down for a urine test, to check for drugs." She shot her husband a scathing look, as though the whole thing was his fault. "Both of us. Right after court today."

"Why would they do that?" Tim asked.

"Because they think we're both losers. Not fit to take care of Pamela."

Beverly was quick to jump into the conversation.

"I assure you, Angela, that's not what's happening here. Routine drug testing is standard with any case that comes to the Juvenile Court.

"Please try to understand this from the county's point of view. So many people come in and out of these doors every day. A lot of them have a problem with drugs or alcohol. It clouds people's minds. It tears families apart. Believe me. I've seen it first hand.

"So, to err on the side of caution, they check everyone involved in every case. It's routine. Because if they can determine there are drugs involved, that could certainly have contributed to what happened with Pamela. They just want to be certain there aren't any issues at home they need to be aware of."

"There aren't any *issues* at home," Angela interrupted. "Pamela is fine. Her home life is fine. Why don't they just leave us alone?"

"They're only looking out for your daughter. And doing what's best for her."

"What's best for her is to be with her parents."

"Now, Angie," Tim began, attempting to soothe her. "We don't really know what's going on with Pamela, do we? Maybe a change in routine is what she needs right now. To get her thinking clearly about things. It might be a good thing to get her out of the house for a while."

"Why do you have to be so logical all the time?" his wife asked.

"It's a curse."

He smiled, hoping to alleviate some of the tension.

Angela took a deep breath, then sat down in a chair beside her husband.

"I just want this whole thing to go away," the distraught woman admitted.

"We're all concerned," Beverly informed them. "That's why we're here."

Both parents smiled but said nothing, at a momentary loss for words.

"So have you seen Pamela?" Beverly asked. "Since this happened?"

"At the hospital," Tim offered. "Last night and this morning. She was pretty out of it yesterday, but today we did manage to talk a bit."

"Did she give you an idea about what was bothering her?"

"Not a word," Angela provided in reply. "All she said was that she didn't want to talk about it. We were uncomfortable pressing her any further."

"Give her time. And keep your spirits up."

At that point the CASA volunteer became aware of approaching footsteps. She looked up and recognized the woman walking down the hallway toward them.

"Please excuse me," Beverly said to Pamela's parents. "This is Monica Perry, the staff attorney for the CASA office. I have to check in with her. But we can talk again after court, if you'd like. And I'll be stopping by your house, periodically, to see how things are going."

Angela's voice returned for a moment to its sarcastic tone of a few minutes earlier.

"Checking up on us, you mean?"

Beverly merely smiled and walked away.

Monica escorted Beverly to a room in back.

"There are several Emergency Hearings being considered this afternoon," the lawyer advised, as they walked down another hallway. "So everything you hear back here won't be pertaining to your case. But just bear with us and we'll get through it."

"Will I need to say anything?"

"Most likely not. Since you knew the parents before, during the adoption proceedings, there may be some general questions addressed to you. But nobody expects you to be up to speed on what's been going on with the girl."

"That's good. It has been ten years, you know."

"Ten years?" Monica paused for a moment, considering the fact. "Has it been that long since you've joined us?"

"Yes it has. As a matter of fact, Pamela was the first child I represented when I began serving as an advocate."

"Wow. Where has the time gone?"

They reached their destination – a large, scantily decorated conference room in back – and were greeted with a scene of organized chaos. The dozen or so people in the room were mostly employees with Children's Services. Beverly recognized one or two of them.

There were also several attorneys present, each there to represent their client and to present him – or her – in the best light possible. To hear the testimonials offered, as various conversations competed with one another around the room, the lawyers represented the salt of the earth.

Those warrants were for infringements incurred several years ago. My client has been clean since then. These past offenses have no bearing on the current situation.

He freely admits using marijuana on a daily basis. It's not like he's strung out on heroin or something hard. Besides, marijuana is legal in Ohio now, so what's the issue here?

The fact that she's lost custody of three previous children is no reflection on my client's moral character. She assures me things are different now, and she's a model mother to the child.

It was a familiar litany Beverly had heard many times in the past. To hear the attorneys talking, there wasn't a single parent out there who was at fault for anything. It was merely a matter of unfortunate circumstances, or a mistake by someone at the agency. It seemed there were as many excuses as there were cases.

Beverly realized this was all part of how the system operated. Each parent did have a right to be represented, and no one wanted to make the mistake of removing a child needlessly. But the safety of the child had to come first.

Eventually each case had been discussed, with the caseworkers and attorneys reaching a consensus on the best option for each matter that was going before the court that day.

Six cases had been examined, involving six mothers, nine fathers, and a total of fifteen children. The youngest child considered that afternoon was a newborn suffering from withdrawals, due to the copious amounts of illegal drugs the mother had poisoned herself with during the course of the pregnancy. They weren't even certain the infant would survive to make it home from the hospital.

The oldest child was Pamela Watkins.

As they were leaving the conference room Monica spoke to Beverly in an aside.

"And today was just a typical day."

The concept surprised the CASA volunteer.

"Really?"

"Really. Sad to say. Everyday it's pretty much the same thing. We keep fighting for these kids, advocating for their rights, finding homes and families for them that are suitable, and the system keeps spitting more of them out. It's a never-ending battle."

All that was left at that point was the hearing itself. It lasted barely ten minutes, with the caseworker presenting what little evidence they had regarding Pamela Watkins and her suicide attempt.

The magistrate agreed with the recommendation offered by the county. Pamela Watkins would be removed from her home and sent to live with her uncle until further notice.

Chapter Seven:

BRIAN WATKINS drove home from work early. He attempted to concentrate on his driving – he prided himself on his caution behind the wheel, having never been stopped for a traffic ticket and having zero accidents to his name after over a dozen years behind the wheel – but even so, he couldn't keep his mind from wandering.

What was going on with his niece, Pamela?

Was she in some kind of trouble?

And why were they removing her from Tim and Angie's place?

Maybe the right question was, what was going on with Tim and Angie?

It just didn't make sense. He knew his older brother. Tim, much like him, was sensible in the way he dealt with things. They had both inherited their logical tendencies from their father, who as a civil engineer had learned early in his career to take things one step at a time and not sweat the details. Details always had a way of working themselves out if you gave them enough time.

No, he was sure it had nothing to do with Tim.

Was it Angie, then?

She did have a bit of a temper. Never afraid to speak her mind, she could be pretty opinionated about things. As much as he liked his sister-in-law, Brian was pretty sure he wouldn't have wanted to live in the same house with Angie. Had she done something wrong? Or said something to Pamela that upset the teenager?

Upon further consideration, Brian refused to believe that as well.

He didn't know why Children's Services was involved with the family. All he really knew, from the meager information the caseworker had provided, was that Pamela was being removed from her home and needed a place to stay. They would prefer it was with a relative, Patrick Zimmerly had stated, but if need be they would locate a foster home.

Brian didn't want to see that.

Family was important.

If there was something he could do to help then he was of course happy to open up his home. Even if it did feel a bit awkward, to think of his seventeen-year-old niece moving in with him. He was used to being on his own – keeping his own schedule, coming and going whenever the mood struck him. It would be a definite adjustment.

For both of them.

He glanced at the dashboard clock once again. It was close, but he should be there before Pamela showed up with the caseworker.

He had been home for less than ten minutes when the doorbell announced their arrival.

The young man on the front porch presented a brief smile before introducing himself. "I'm Patrick Zimmerly. From Lucas County Children's Services. We spoke on the phone."

"Yes. Of course." Brian stepped out of the way. "Won't you come in?"

Behind the caseworker, lingering on the sidewalk, Pamela seemed a bit bewildered, like she was uncertain where she was. Or, more probable, what was expected of her. She examined the pavement at her feet with downcast eyes, refusing all the while to make eye contact with her uncle. Eventually she moved forward, with slow, shuffling footsteps that seemed out of place considering her usual nature.

Brian sought to lighten the mood.

"So. If it isn't my favorite niece."

It was an expression he used often. It usually brought a smile to the young girl's face, but not today.

She responded in a matter-of-fact voice. "I'm your only niece, Uncle Brian."

"Doesn't matter. You're still my favorite."

She attempted a weak smile, then entered the house.

For a few moments the three of them stood in silence in the confines of the front hallway. Pamela broke the mood.

"Can I go to my room now?"

"Sure, Pamela. Whatever you want. It's the guest room down the hall."

He made a gesture, indicating the direction, which she ignored.

"I know where it's at."

"Sorry about the mess back there," he commented. "I can move some of the stuff around if it's in your way."

"It don't matter," she responded.

She slouched past them, entered the designated room, and closed the door, slowly, behind her.

"Is there somewhere we can talk?" Zimmerly asked.

Brian led the way to the living room, and once both men were seated the conversation resumed.

"So what's going on here?" Brian asked. "What's the deal with Pamela? Is she okay?"

"Your niece tried to kill herself, Mr. Watkins."

For several long seconds nothing was said, as Brian attempted to absorb the information just presented by the caseworker.

"How? I mean, what happened?"

"She tried to jump off a bridge. Luckily a policeman happened by in time to prevent her from carrying through with it."

The only response he could manage was a weak one. "I don't believe it. I know suicide is a real thing. But I never expected it with anyone I know. Certainly not Pamela."

"Unfortunately, it isn't as unusual as you would think. Many people aren't aware of the fact, but suicide is the second-leading cause of death for ages fifteen to twenty-four in the United States. Over 9% of the people in that age group have actually attempted suicide. That's a sobering statistic when you stop to think of it. One out of every ten teenagers in this country has gone through what Pamela is experiencing right now."

"Wow!" Brian shook his head in disbelief. He had never considered the enormity of the matter before.

"I never would have thought that. But…. I mean…." He stumbled with his phrasing. "But, why? What does a teenager have to feel suicidal about?"

"These are trying times, Mr. Watkins. The teenage years are never easy. Their bodies are changing. They're becoming aware of so many new things. There's the ever prevalent drugs. And sex. And the need to feel like part of a crowd."

"You just described my teenage years. Everybody's, for that matter. But I don't ever recall this being a problem when I was in school."

"Times are different now. Social Media has a lot to do with that."

"Social Media?"

"Of course. Peer pressure has always had a huge affect on the way teenagers feel about themselves. With Social Media, that pressure can be blown way out of proportion."

"But why? I mean, why Pamela? What, specifically, is she going through that she would even consider something this extreme?"

"We don't know. So far she refuses to talk about it. She's scheduled to see a therapist next week, to start counseling. That may help."

"Was something going on at home that I need to know about? Is that why you removed her from Tim and Angie's?"

The caseworker was quick to refute the suggestion.

"Not that we're aware of. No accusations have been made against your brother and his wife. But we want to be cautious until we understand more clearly what's going on."

"So what can I do?"

"Providing a good, safe environment for your niece is a good start."

"What do I say to her? I mean, I shouldn't bring up her suicide attempt. Should I?"

"On the contrary. Feel free to talk about it. It needs to be out in the open. Trying to hide it isn't going to solve the problem. Or remove the issues that are bothering her. She knows what she did, and there's no denying that she's bothered about something. Maybe she'll open up to you about what's going on."

Brian hesitated, considering how he could approach the issue. The thought of talking so openly with his niece, about such a difficult subject, seemed awkward, to say the least. It seemed, as well, to be such an invasion of her privacy.

He had always felt close to his brother. They had talked often in the past regarding family. Tim and Angie had tried for years to have children of their own. Unsuccessfully, as it turned out. They had become foster parents to fill the void in their lives.

When the opportunity came to adopt Pamela they had jumped at the chance. She was seven at the time, a gorgeous, precocious, sweet little thing that had somehow survived through a difficult childhood. She had brought so much to their lives, and the entire family welcomed the new addition to the Watkins household.

Brian and Pamela had spent time together in the past, of course, sharing the typical family events. Holidays and birthdays. An occasional picnic or zoo outing. The two of them had always gotten along well, though their relationship was basically a superficial one.

It was easier that way. Brian was single, and pretty set in his ways. He was comfortable with his house and enjoyed his lifestyle. He had sown his wild oats a long time ago, and was content to go to work, putter around the house, and follow the Detroit sports teams. Tigers. Lions. Red Wings. Pistons. It didn't matter to him. He watched them all.

So his time with Pamela had been a series of brief encounters only, spending a few hours together then each going their separate ways. And as much as he wanted to be there for her – and assist in any way he could – he couldn't help but question whether he was up to the task.

Patrick Zimmerly, failing to notice Brian's hesitation, stood, putting an end to the conversation.

"Just do your best, Mr. Watkins. And give her time. When Pamela is ready she'll talk about it."

Pamela stayed in her bedroom the rest of the afternoon. With dinner time approaching Brian went to her room, rapping lightly on the panel.

"Pamela? May I come in?"

"You might as well. It's your house."

She sat on the bed, knees tucked under her, reading a book. HARRY POTTER AND THE GOBLET OF FIRE. She failed to look up as he entered, concentrating instead on the written adventure in her hands.

Brian paused a moment, taken aback with her appearance. She was dressed in dark colors – faded black jeans, a dark blue pullover, even her sneakers were black. Her hair was uncombed, loose strands tumbling everywhere. Her fingernails were painted a deep purple, though the polish was chipped and faded in spots. She looked like an adult, not like the young teenager he was used to. It was like his niece had disappeared and someone else had taken her place, someone with deep dark secrets hidden inside.

He wasn't sure if he could relate to the new Pamela, but he knew he had to try.

"Is that a good book?"

No response.

"I've seen the movie. Even have it on DVD. We can watch it later if you'd like?"

She continued to ignore him.

"Are you hungry?"

"Not really." She shrugged with the answer.

"I'm not much of a cook, but I could throw some burgers on the grill. There might be some french fries in the freezer."

"Whatever."

"I could order pizza if you want."

"I don't really feel like eating right now. I just want to be left alone."

"Listen, Pamela. I feel bad about what you're going through. If there's anything you want to talk about…?"

"There's nothing to talk about."

"We both know that isn't true."

"I said I don't want to talk about it."

"That's fine. We can talk later. When you're ready."

She held the book down for a moment, to stare back at him in exasperation, then resumed her reading. She failed to comment further.

"All right, then."

He left the bedroom, closing the door behind him, and paused for a moment to reflect.

You're off to a great start, Brian. Could you have been more lame?

Chapter Eight:

IT WAS noisy in the locker room.

The boys had finished the dodge ball game late, due to a reluctance to put an end to their high-spirited competition, and they were rushing now to finish their showers and get their clothes on so they could make it to the next class. The metal doors of the lockers slammed intermittently, the sound echoing off the cinder-block walls of the cavernous room to be lost amid the racket of teenage voices. The ever-present splashing noise from the running water in the shower area covered everything else, like a blanket of sound. It was reminiscent of a heavy rain in the summertime, muffling the rest of nature with its cadence.

Garry Debrue slip-slided his way across the damp floor, making his way to Bobby Beard.

"Hey B-B? Did you hear the latest?"

Bobby was tying his Nikes. He finished the task and flung back his hair, the wet strands cascading down his back. He stood and grabbed his shirt from his locker before facing his friend.

"What's up, Garry?"

"This is really good. You won't believe it."

"So out with it already."

"It's about Watkins."

Bobby's motion suddenly halted. For the space of two seconds he was frozen in time, all animation gone as the words hit him.

Though Garry, intent with the information he so anxiously wanted to announce, failed to notice.

Recovering quickly, Bobby pulled his shirt over his head, wrestling the material across his moistened torso and slipping his still damp arms into the sleeves of the garment. He maintained a flippant edge to his reply, though an attentive listener would have detected a strained quality to his tone.

"What about Watkins?"

"You won't believe it." Garry laughed, the type of laugh a co-conspirator might use.

"Out with it, man."

"She nearly bit the big one."

"What are you talking about?"

"On the High Level bridge, dude. Can you believe it?"

Matthew Cody, standing at the locker across from Bobby, chimed in.

"No. It's true. They said she nearly jumped."

"What are you two clowns talking about?"

"Pamela Watkins," Matthew informed him. "They say she tried to commit suicide a few days ago. Almost took a leap off the High Level bridge. Can you imagine that?"

Garry, warming to his topic, faced Matthew. The two seemed to forget Bobby as they continued their discourse. Their conversation was casual, nearly irreverent, as though they were discussing nothing more pressing than the latest weather forecast.

"I heard some policeman stopped her. Grabbed her 'round the waist and pulled her back just in time."

"Probably copping a feel at the same time. Get it? A policeman *copping* a feel?"

Garry chuckled at the joke. "Can you blame him?"

"Can you imagine what something like that would be like?"

"I bet she peed her pants," Garry smirked. "I know I would have."

Bobby, looking down at his sneakers, pushed his way past the two of them.

"There's nothing funny about any of this, guys."

Without another word he exited the locker room, ignoring the stares from the two boys he left behind.

The hallways were crowded as always between classes, but Bobby failed to notice as he joined the ever-shifting queue of students competing for space in the corridors. He made his way to his Algebra class, grateful it was final hour and he'd be going home soon.

He couldn't concentrate.

His mind wandered.

What should he do? Should he try to contact Pamela? See if she was okay?

No. She must have been okay. The guys wouldn't have been so flippant about it if she was really hurt. She must have been okay.

But still…?

Somehow he made it through until the end of the day. The walk home felt excruciatingly long. His mind wouldn't relax, as he replayed in his head the last time he had seen Pamela, and the events of their afternoon together.

It wasn't his fault, he reasoned. It couldn't be his fault. He didn't do anything wrong. She had been all eager and anxious, too. Just like him.

It must have been something else was bothering her.

It had to be something else.

Yeah. That was it.

By the time he got home and walked in the back door he had nearly convinced himself that he was blameless of any wrongdoing.

His stepfather Alec sat at the kitchen table, munching on a sandwich and nursing a beer. A portable television on the counter displayed a game show, which seemed to have the older man captivated by its antics.

"How's it going, sport?" Alec had a deep voice. It was like he didn't know how to speak quietly. It used to be intimidating to Bobby, back when he was younger and Alec had first taken an interest in his mother, but with time the tone had come to be accepted as normal.

"It's going," Bobby replied, not bothering to slow down as he walked through the kitchen.

He was in the dining room by the time Alec spoke again.

"Don't forget. Tonight's garbage night."

"I know."

"Don't forget the bag out back this time."

"I won't."

"Like you did last time."

"I said I'd take care of it."

Bobby rounded the doorway and headed up the stairs, brushing past Hannah as he did so. He didn't seem to notice his little sister.

"Watch where you're going!" she snapped.

Bobby made no reply. He headed for his room, slammed the door shut behind him, threw his book bag on the floor, and threw himself on the bed. He buried his head in the pillow, trying to control the thoughts running through his head.

It couldn't be his fault.

There was nothing wrong with what they had done.

Sure, Pamela had been a bit awkward about the whole thing. Bobby suspected it might have been her first time with a guy. It's like she didn't know what was expected of her.

But who better to show her the ropes than the captain of the football team. Right? She was learning from one of the best.

It wasn't his fault that she freaked out the way she had. And over nothing.

Maybe there *was* something wrong with her, after all? Something he hadn't picked up on at first, due to the casual nature of their acquaintance. They didn't know each other that well. After all, he hadn't been interested in a relationship with

Pamela. He certainly wasn't looking for anything long term.

Bobby rolled over. He noticed his football on the nightstand behind him. He reached over to grab it, then stretched out on his back.

Throwing the ball into the air, he watched the lazy spirals it performed as gravity brought it back to him. He repeated the motion over and over again. It was a lazy sort of movement, and it served to calm him down. Relax him. Take his mind off his problems.

Eventually he stopped thinking about Pamela Watkins completely.

Chapter Nine:

"Bobby? DINNER'S ready, Dear."

"Okay, Mom. I'll be right down."

It was later in the day, and Bobby had put away the football and turned his attention to his video games. He had become absorbed in the activity and, consequently, had forgotten all about Pamela Watkins and the revelation that had been revealed to him earlier in the day at school.

He quickly saved his game and bolted down the stairs. As usual, he was the last to reach the table.

Alec shot him a scathing look which he ignored. It seemed no matter what Bobby did his stepfather was never happy about it. Their arguments had been plenty in the eight years Alec had been part of the family. The teenager no longer paid attention to the constant criticisms. He couldn't please the guy. There was no sense in even trying.

His mother was more forgiving, though her words betrayed her irritation.

"Nice of you to join us," Lisa Sutter commented.

"Sorry, Mom." The words left his lips automatically.

His mother placed her hands together in blessing, with the rest of the family following suit. Her voice was animated with the benediction she delivered. It was doubtful if she even noticed the less than enthusiastic response of the rest of the family.

"Bless us O Lord, for these Thy gifts, which we are about to receive, from Thy bounty, through Christ, Our Lord. Amen."

A lackluster "Amen" followed from the others.

For several moments nothing was said, as bowls of food were passed around the table and plates were filled. Once they all started to eat the normal routine followed, with Lisa leading the discussion.

"So how was everyone's day?"

Hannah, as usual, was the first to speak.

"We're supposed to go on a field trip next month." Enthusiasm colored her words.

Bobby shot his sister a glare, the typical expression a teenager would use around a younger sibling. Hannah, at seven years old, was still at that disturbing age where school was an adventure and learning was fun. Bobby wondered if he had ever been that naive. And decided that couldn't have been the case.

"We're going to the pumpkin farm," Hannah informed the gathering. "Right before Halloween."

"That's nice," Lisa replied. "Are you dressing up for it?"

"Not for the field trip. But we get to dress up for school on Halloween."

"And have you decided what you're going to be?"

Alec, though appearing not to pay attention to the conversation, chimed in. "I bet you're going to be a unicorn."

"Nope. A fairy. With beautiful wings and everything."

"Is that so? And does your mother know this?"

"Mom?" She displayed her best puppy dog look, a pleading expression cultivated to elicit sympathy. "Can I be a fairy?"

"We'll go costume hunting when it's closer to Halloween and see what we can find."

"Goodee."

Lisa took a bite of her food, then addressed her son. "How about you, Bobby? Are you going trick or treating this year?"

"Get real, Mom. I'm seventeen."

"You were almost seventeen last year and you went."

"That was just because some of the other guys were going. That's all."

Alec jumped in once more. "Maybe your mother can find matching outfits, and you can go as a fairy like your sister."

"That's pretty lame, Alec."

"That would be funny!" Hannah giggled as she talked. "Bobby would make a good fairy."

The laughter abated after a few minutes, followed by an awkward silence.

Lisa began anew.

"I heard something disturbing today, Bobby. I think it was about one of your classmates. Do you know a Pamela Watkins?"

Bobby, fork in hand, instantly became still, his attention caught by his mother's words. Alec, on the other side of the table, paused as well, taking care not to miss what his wife had to say.

All eyes were on Bobby as he muttered a reply. "Yeah. I know her. She's in some of my classes."

"I heard the poor thing tried to kill herself. Tried to jump off a bridge, they said. Do you know anything about it?"

"No. Nothing."

"What a shame. Imagine what her folks must be going through right now. Do you have any idea why she would do something like that?"

"No."

"It's just that, with her being in your class and all, I thought...."

"I said no!"

Bobby threw down his utensil and stood up, nearly upsetting his chair as he pushed away from the table.

"Just leave me alone."

His footsteps pounded up the stairs, followed by the slamming of his bedroom door.

"Now what was *that* all about?" his mother wondered aloud.

Alec, a concerned look on his face, slowly rose from the table.

"I'll go talk to him."

As he left the room Hannah resumed the conversation, launching into a lengthy explanation of what she had done at school that day.

Alec didn't bother knocking on the door. Instead he stormed into Bobby's room, an angry expression on his face.

"What's going on here, young man?"

Bobby sat at his desk, playing a video game, his fingers punching the buttons on the controller. "Don't you know how to knock?"

"It's my house. I don't have to knock."

"But it's my room. And I don't want you in here right now."

"What do you know about this girl Pamela?"

"I don't know nothing about her."

Alec grabbed the arms of Bobby's chair, spinning him around so they faced one another, then grabbed the video game controller and threw it on the bed. He leaned in close, inches away from the young man's face.

"She was here. The other day."

Bobby shrugged in reply. "So what? So she was here. So what? Nothing happened."

"She was here one day, and the next day she tries to kill herself. Doesn't that sound suspicious to you?"

"Leave me alone." Bobby tried to spin the chair away from his stepfather, but the man's grip prevented the action.

Alec said nothing. He continued to contemplate the teenager in a threatening manner.

Bobby finally withered under the stare.

"We made out. That's all. We made out, she left here mad, and that's all I know."

"Why was she mad?"

"I don't know."

"Did you ask her?"

"No. I didn't ask her."

"And why not?"

"Because I haven't seen her since everything happened, that's why not. I didn't even know something was going on until one of the guys said something to me in the locker room."

"What did you do to her?"

"I didn't do nothing. I already told you that."

Alec relaxed slightly, drawing away from the boy.

"I imagine you did more than just make out with her?"

A malicious grin crossed the teenager's face. "Maybe."

"How stupid can you be, Bobby? In your mother's house? How do you think she'd feel if she knew what you were doing up here?"

"Don't go playing the holier than thou attitude on me. Mom's no saint. It don't take an Einstein to realize you guys had only been married for seven months when Hannah came along."

He never saw the slap coming.

Alec hit him across the cheek, causing the chair to swivel from the blow.

Bobby was startled. The blow didn't really hurt him. Even if it had, he never would have admitted it. Not even to himself. His self-image prevented any such admission.

He jumped from his seat and moved away from his stepfather. He said nothing; just stared in wonder.

"Don't ever talk about your mother that way."

"I'm sorry."

"You should be."

"I said I was sorry."

"And I better not hear you had anything to do with that girl's problems. Understand?"

"Yes, Sir."

Keith Julius

Alec could hear his wife in the kitchen, cleaning up after their meal.

She called in to him as he entered the dining room. "I left your plate on the table. You rushed off so quick, you didn't get the chance to finish."

He sat down, picked up his fork, and played with his food for several moments.

Then he pushed away from the table and walked into the kitchen.

"I'm not hungry," he announced.

Lisa turned to face him, drying her hands on a dishrag.

"So what's up with Bobby? Is he okay?"

"I think so."

"It's hard to believe anyone could even think of doing something like that. Committing suicide and all."

"I don't want to talk about it."

He left the room, and she returned to her tasks.

Chapter Ten:

ANGELA SAT on the back porch, watching the darkening sky as the evening sun made its leisurely descent into the treetops. A glass of ice tea sat on the table beside her. Occasionally she would take a sip, swirling the glass a few times so the ice had a chance to melt further, chilling the amber liquid.

A photo album sat opened on her lap. Pictures of a young girl, most of them with a serious expression on her face, graced the pages. Angela moved her hand across the photos, as though she could reach out and grasp the images portrayed there. But that's all they were. Images from the past. The solace she was expecting to find, the comfort she needed, failed to materialize.

"Angie? Are you home?"

She heard Tim's voice from the front of the house, but she refused to answer. He would find her. Eventually. She was enjoying the isolation and hated to see it come to an end. Caught up in the memory of Pamela's childhood, and the reflections of the family times they had shared together, she was content to allow the rest of the world to pass her by.

It was a false comfort, and she knew that, but it was the only comfort she could find at the moment.

The sound of the door sliding open, then shut, behind her announced her husband's presence. He hesitated, eyeing the two-seated swing and the empty space beside his wife. Instead he decided to sit on a chair off to the side. It was one of those Adirondack type contraptions, done in a fake plastic that resembled wood. He sat down and looked out over the backyard. Their chunk of the Earth, he liked to call it.

A massive wooden structure, weathered from the elements and the countless storms that had swept over it, occupied the space he looked upon. The contraption featured three swings, two slides – one on either end – and a climbing wall in the middle. The second story of the edifice was adorned with fort-like walls, complete with a plastic cannon that had cracked and faded, over time, to a dirty white in color. A rope ladder hung from one side, though the fibers had weakened years ago and it clung to the structure now with only the thinnest of strands.

The entire play-set looked like it had been long since abandoned, which wasn't far from the truth.

"What was I thinking?" Tim asked at last, a grin on his face as he reminisced. "What eight-year-old needs that big of a jungle gym?"

Angela remained silent.

"She did like it though, didn't she?"

His wife refused to be drawn into the conversation. Instead, she took another sip from her drink.

Tim continued, his voice betraying his enthusiasm as he warmed to the subject.

"Do you remember how excited she was when I was building it? Every piece I put in place, she'd run over to check it out. *Oh Tim,*" he exclaimed, doing his best to imitate the shrill tone of a young girl. "*This is just 'bout the best thing I've ever seen.* And she'd laugh, and go on in that non-stop way she had of asking question after question.

"It's like everything was new to her. Her whole life an adventure. It made you realize how good we had things, compared to what she grew up with."

He looked again at his wife, who still remained silent.

"How good we *still* have things."

A dog barked, from somewhere in one of the neighboring yards. Tim looked around but failed to spy the offending creature.

He turned back toward his wife.

"What are you thinking?"

"We shouldn't have let them take her away."

"We didn't have a choice, Angie. You know that."

"We could have contested it. Spoken up in front of the judge or something, I don't know. She should have stayed with us."

"And what good would that have done?"

"We'd still be a family."

"We still *are* a family. We're just going through some hard times. That's all. Besides, maybe Pamela needs some space right now. To sort things out."

"What things?"

She shifted in her seat, facing him for the first time.

"What kinds of things does Pamela need to sort out?"

"How would I know? I've never been a teenage girl. Maybe she's having trouble at school? Or there's a boy she likes that isn't paying any attention to her?"

Angela looked down at the photo album in her lap. She flipped through a few pages, but didn't bother to take time enough to notice the pictures.

"She was such a sad little girl," she commented at last. "It was like pulling teeth to get her to laugh."

"Can you blame her? Considering the life she lived? The family she had to deal with? That would suck the life out of anyone. Especially a young child."

His wife flipped a few more pages before continuing, though it was a reflex action only. She didn't bother looking at the pictures. Instead her eyes held a faraway expression.

It was like she was looking at the past.

"She always was a bit odd."

Her words surprised Tim. "That's not a very nice thing to say."

"But it's true." She leaned forward slightly, bridging the gap that separated her from her husband. "She was behind in so many things. You didn't see it, the way I did. You were always away at work."

"I had no choice, Angie. You know that."

She chose to ignore his rationale. "I was the one that had to deal with her temper tantrums. I was the one that had to be the tough guy, making her tow the line, teaching her the difference between right and wrong."

Angela paused to consider, reflecting on her memories of the past.

"And she was so awkward around other people," she continued. "With no social graces at all. Like she'd been raised by a bunch of apes or something."

She slammed the book shut, rested her hands on the cover, and addressed her husband once again.

"Remember the first night she was here? And she took a bath...."

He waved the matter off. "That was nothing."

"Nothing? She walked in the living room buck naked, like it was the most natural thing in the world. What kind of behavior was that for a six-year-old?"

"She just didn't know any better."

"Well, she should have. Especially at that age."

"And how would she have known better? Remember what her mother was like. Stephanie had a drinking problem. One so bad she lost her child over it. What kind of attention do you think Pamela received from someone like that?"

"Probably no attention," Angela conceded.

"Exactly. Sounds like the father was off on his own a lot, too. The poor kid was left to fend for herself most of the time. It's surprising she didn't end up more screwed up than she did."

"So you admit there was something wrong with her?"

"No. That's not what I meant. There was nothing wrong with her. There *IS* nothing wrong with her. She was just a confused little kid, thrown into a rough situation, and expected to come out well-adjusted and ordinary. There's bound to be growing pains."

"So what about now? Suicide. She tried to kill herself, Tim. Our Pamela tried to kill herself. Is that more growing pains?"

"Of course not."

"Then what is it?"

"I don't know what it is. But I do know if she needs our help, then we need to be there for her."

He stood and took a step closer, towering over his wife. "This isn't about us, Angie. This is about her."

Angela nearly blurted something out. Then, thinking better of it, she took a deep breath to steady herself.

"I know that, Tim. I know that. But I can't help thinking this is all our fault. Regardless of whatever that doctor at the hospital has to say about it. We failed her."

"We didn't fail her."

"How do you know that? Maybe, if we had done things differently, then maybe none of this would have happened."

"We can't possibly know that. And it serves no purpose to second guess ourselves at this point. What's done is done."

She nearly responded, but he didn't allow her the opportunity.

"One thing I do know, Angie. We can't give up on her. Not now. Not ever."

She brushed back a single tear. "I wouldn't think of giving up on her. She's my little girl. I fell in love with her the moment I met her, and I still love her. But it's just so hard. Knowing what to do."

He sat down beside her, placing his arm lovingly across her shoulder. She jolted, as if shocked from his touch, then relaxed against him.

"Maybe this is the best thing for her," Tim continued. "Being away from us for a while. Maybe she'll come to miss the way things are with us. She'll come to appreciate the good things in her life."

He cupped Angela's chin in his hand and lifted her head slightly, then delivered a kiss to her forehead.

She tried to smile, but found she couldn't manage the gesture.

"Pamela will be okay," Tim reassured her. "I just know it. Our little girl will be okay."

Her tears came in full force, then, as she buried her face in his chest.

Chapter Eleven:

IT WAS pretty scary when the policeman came to the 'partment.

Daddy was mad at Mommy, 'cause she was the one that called the police, and he said she shouldn't of done that, but she did it anyway even though he didn't want her to, so that's why Daddy was mad.

But Daddy was mad even before the policeman came over.

He was mad 'cause there was still dirty dishes in the sink when he got home from work. I told him it was okay. I told him I would wash the dishes for him, 'cause Mommy was too sick to do it.

But he didn't want to listen to me. He just wanted to yell at Mommy.

Usually Mommy didn't say much when Daddy yelled at her. But she started yelling back at Daddy.

And that's when she used the nasty words. And called Daddy something really bad that she shouldn't of said.

Then Daddy really got really angry and pushed Mommy really hard. She fell on the floor. I ran over, to try to help Mommy to stand up. She was crying, and I noticed her shirt was torn, and I felt really bad for her, so I just hugged her and told her not to cry.

I think Daddy felt bad, too, 'cause he just turned and walked away from us.

When Mommy stood up, she looked really mad.

But she didn't say a word.

Mommy took me by the hand, and together we walked to Mommy and Daddy's bedroom, and she locked the door so Daddy couldn't come in.

That's when Mommy called the police.

Lots of people came to the 'partment after that. They asked lots of questions. They talked to me a lot. They asked me if Daddy was ever nasty to me. Or if Daddy ever hit me.

I told them Daddy would never do that. He loves me too much to do nothing bad to me.

They made me leave Mommy and Daddy and go in a car with a man and a woman I didn't even know. But they let me take some of my fav'rite clothes with me, and even one of my books.

The woman seemed pretty nasty. Like she was mad 'bout something. She wouldn't tell me what it was. But the man was real nice and kept asking me if I was okay.

I told him I was.

But I really wasn't.

I couldn't understand why they took me away from Mommy and Daddy. They said that since Mommy and Daddy was fighting so much they didn't want me to get hurt. But Mommy and Daddy fight all the time. And I never get hurt.

They took me to a big house then, and that's when I met Angie and Tim. It was their house. Her name was really Angela, but she said I should call her Angie. She wore a real pretty dress, and her hair looked real pretty too. I guess she was pretty.

But not as pretty as Mommy.

Tim said I would be staying with them for a little while. They took me to a room with yellow walls and a bed with pretty flowers on it and pictures of animals on the wall. They said this was gonna be my bedroom.

I told them I already had a bedroom. With Mommy and Daddy in our 'partment.

But they said I would be staying in this room instead.

The house was really big, with lots of rooms and a big backyard. There was even a basement. We didn't have a basement, 'cause we lived in a 'partment and there wasn't much room. There was lots of neat stuff in the basement. There was a television with video games. And a ping-pong table. Tim said he would teach me how to play. That sounded like fun.

They made spaghetti for dinner, which is one of my fav'rite meals. But it wasn't like Mommy's spaghetti. Mommy's spaghetti had her special meatballs in it that she got from a bag in the freezer. And the good sauce in the red jar.

It felt funny when it was time to go to bed. Angie and Tim had both been real nice to me. Tim even read me a bedtime story.

But after they left the room, and the lights were off, and I was all alone in the room with the yellow walls with the animals on them, I felt real alone.

And a little scared.

I never spent a night away from Mommy and Daddy before. It just didn't feel right. I felt cold, even though I snuggled up under the blankets and hugged them tight 'round me.

I really missed Mommy and Daddy.

Angie said I would be seeing them in a couple of days. She didn't know when. But she said it would be soon.

Angie said she would drive me to my school the next day. But then she told me I would have to start going to a diff'rent school pretty soon, 'cause my old school was so far away from where they lived.

And she was right. In a couple of days I did have to start someplace else. I didn't know any of the kids there, but there was a little girl named Jessica that seemed real nice and we played together at recess, and we got to be really good friends.

But it felt funny to go home after school and Mommy and Daddy weren't there.

Chapter Twelve:

FOR FOUR days Pamela sequestered herself in her Uncle Brian's spare bedroom, attempting in vain to fight back the memories that overwhelmed her.

For years she had fought against the images that had disturbed her so much. After ten years she had managed to suppress them, to lock them away where they could no longer harm her. They might have belonged to another person. They certainly belonged to another lifetime. As the days turned into weeks and the weeks were swept away by years, the memories had ceased to trouble her. Pamela had moved on with her life.

Then, the afternoon before the fateful day on the High Level bridge, the dam had burst open. The memories had flooded back into her head, released by the equally disturbing event that precipitated the torrent.

She wanted to scream.

She wanted to hide away somewhere.

She wanted so much to tell the world what was bothering her.

But it was all too shameful. All too embarrassing. The thought of talking about it – to anyone – brought a queasiness to her stomach. She knew it was something so personal that she alone had to deal with it. Even thinking about it was an ordeal. It led to so many self-doubts, and so many conflicting emotions, that all she could think of was finding a way to escape from the pain.

No matter what it took. But how? That was the question she kept asking herself. How?

It was a Wednesday evening when Pamela started her new living arrangements at her uncle's house. She couldn't face going back to school right away, and nobody questioned her staying home the rest of the week. Uncle Brian took the following days off from work as well, to be with her. During the next four days he never left the house, remaining ever vigilant in case she would need him. Even though they seldom interacted – a result of her self-imposed isolation – it comforted Pamela to know that someone was looking out for her.

From time to time she would hear his phone ring. Then the muffled sound of his voice, conversing in hushed tones, would penetrate to her room. She couldn't make out the dialogue, but she was certain it was about her. What else could it be about?

There were no visitors during that time. She suspected that was Brian's doing, to allow her the time to think things through, but whether her time in isolation contributed to a solution or not was debatable.

So for four days it was just the two of them.

Pamela kept to her room, venturing out only for bathroom breaks and to grab an occasional snack. By the second day she left her self-imposed sanctuary to get something more substantial to eat. She couldn't stomach the thought of food before then. Her uncle would say a few words to her when she made an appearance, idle chit-chat in an attempt to get her talking. But she refused to cooperate.

He didn't push it. He allowed her space. He gave her time. But on Sunday evening, as she sat across from him in the small kitchen they now shared, he became more assertive.

"I think you should go back to school tomorrow, Pamela."

"I don't know if I can."

"But you have to."

She made no reply. Instead she stared at her plate, stirring her food around with her fork as he continued.

"I can't begin to understand what you're going through. Believe me, if I could chase all your problems away I would. But I can't do that. Life doesn't work that way. Things happen, and you find a way to deal with them.

"You can't hide from life, Pamela. You need to get back out there and deal with it."

The idea seemed preposterous to her. "Why should I? I don't need school. It's such a waste of time. What does it matter to me who fought in the war of 1812? Or any of that other nonsense they try to jam down our throats. That's ancient history, anyway."

"There's more to school then history," he pointed out. "There's a lot to learn out there, and it can't all be found on the internet."

"I get by just fine the way I am," she informed him, as if that ended the discussion. "Besides, in another year I'll be eighteen. Then nobody can tell me what to do. I can get a job. Go somewhere where I can be happy."

"You can't run away from your troubles."

"How would you know!"

She screamed the words as she pushed herself away from the table. She was in tears when she got to her room.

But somehow, whether through her uncle's perseverance or her own determination, Pamela decided he was right. Maybe being at school, and with people her own age, would at least get her mind off her problems for a while.

So on Monday morning she went back to Whitmer High School to resume her classes.

She could feel the eyes staring at her everywhere she went that day. In the hallways, between classes. In the lunchroom, when she sat down all alone at an empty table in the corner. It was like she was an outcast, and no one dared to be associated with her.

Classrooms were the worst. As she approached she could hear the typical noises resulting from a roomful of teenagers crammed together in an environment against their will. There were conversations, dozens of them occurring simultaneously, with an occasional random word escaping from the clutter of voices. Young girls giggled and young boys laughed. Sometimes a chair would scrape across the floor, or a pencil would drop. It was a constant din of audio sensations.

But it would all cease the moment she walked in the doorway. It was like some master mute button had been employed to deny her hearing anything. Some faces would turn away. Some students looked at their desks, or suddenly opened a book. Those that didn't turn away looked on in wonder. Or shock. Or simply disbelief.

Pamela would pass through the gauntlet of questioning onlookers until she reached her seat, then do her best to be forgotten. She took to rushing through the hallways to arrive at her next class as early as possible. This allowed her to avoid some of the embarrassment, anyway.

When she entered her third period Science class Mr. Thorndyke met her at the door, motioning her aside and addressing her in a whisper.

"Miss Watkins? You're to report to Mrs. Jarecki's office. She wants to talk to you."

Mrs. Jarecki was Pamela's guidance counselor. They had spoken several times about the teenager's plans for after high school. Pamela's grades had always been decent. Never exceptional, but decent enough, according to Mrs. Jarecki, to get her into college.

Tim and Angie had always pushed for a college education as well. Tim especially would stress the importance of having a degree to get ahead in life. *It opens a lot of doors*, he would advise her.

Pamela, still undecided regarding the decision, had yet to pursue the idea any further.

The hallways were devoid of life, with an emptiness that mirrored her own troubled thoughts. By the time she reached her destination Pamela had reached the conclusion that this meeting wasn't going to be about college choices.

"I'm glad to see you this morning," Mrs. Jarecki began. "I think it's good for you to get back into the normal routine of things."

Pamela remained silent.

"We're all concerned about you, Pamela. And what you're going through. If there's anything we can do…."

"I'm okay," she interrupted. "Things are good."

The counselor's look expressed her disbelief regarding the comment, but she failed to respond to it as she continued.

"Toledo Public Schools maintains a staff of grief counselors. To help students through trying situations like this. If you want, I could set up an appointment with someone."

"No. Thank you. I'm okay."

"It would help to talk to someone. Someone more experienced in dealing with these type of situations."

"I have an appointment later this week with a therapist."

"Good. I'm sure that will be beneficial."

"Is there anything else?"

"No, Pamela."

"Okay."

As she turned to leave Mrs. Jarecki spoke up again.

"I'm here for you. If you ever need anything. I'm always here for you."

The second day back seemed a repetition of the first, minus the visit to the counselor's office. The third started off much the same, though something changed at lunchtime.

She was picking at her food when she became aware of someone standing on the other side of the table, looking across at her.

"Mind if I sit down?"

It was a boy's voice, though she didn't recognize the speaker. Nor did she bother to look up to see who it was.

"Do what you want," she managed in reply. "It's a free world."

She returned to her food, ignoring him in the process. But she couldn't shake the feeling that he was watching her. Glancing up, she noticed his attention.

"What are you looking at?"

"Nothing." He set his tray on the table, straddled the bench, and resumed talking once he was seated. "You don't look crazy to me."

"Is that supposed to be a joke?"

"Well, yes. I guess it was. But it didn't turn out like one, did it? Sorry."

"Doesn't matter. I'm sure that's what all the kids are saying anyway."

"Some of them are," he admitted. "Some of them feel bad for you. And they should. They can't imagine what you're going through."

"But you can?"

"Maybe. I've been through some tough stuff myself. It can be hard. You feel all alone. And unique. Like it's something you have to face alone.

"Sometimes it helps to talk things over with someone."

She gave no response.

He leaned toward her, in a conspiratorial fashion.

"At least, that's what my therapist says."

He paused, and Pamela found herself looking at him, really looking at him, for the first time. He was a couple of years younger than her – probably a sophomore. But he was tall for his age. And he somehow looked older. Like he had been through a lot, and was experienced about things.

"You have a therapist?"

"Sure do. Been seeing him for about seven years now."

"Wow. That's a long time."

"And I know what you're thinking." His voice remained flippant, as though they were discussing something unimportant. "This kid must really be screwed up. To spend seven years in therapy…."

"No, no." she interrupted. "I wasn't thinking that at all."

"Because it's okay if you were thinking that. Because I *was* screwed up. Big time. Did some crazy stuff. But that was in the past. I feel I get better and better every day."

"That's good."

"It's true."

He paused, to dunk a few of his fries in the glob of ketchup on his plate. He devoured them all at once, then resumed talking as he swallowed.

"I'm Aaron, by the way."

"Pamela. But you knew that."

"Yes I did."

"And you stopped anyway."

"Yes again."

"Why?"

He answered immediately, as though the entire conversation had been a prelude to this point.

"Because you shouldn't be alone through this."

Before he could continue another boy arrived, bumping Aaron purposely on the shoulder to get his attention. The new arrival looked amazingly similar to Aaron, though his physique was a bit chunkier.

"Hey, Aaron. What's up?"

"Nothing bro." He indicated the young girl across from him. "This is Pamela."

"Pamela." The boy's hands were occupied, balancing the tray he held, so he merely nodded in greeting. "I'm Evan."

"Are you two brothers?" she asked.

They replied simultaneously. "Twins."

Evan turned back to his brother. "Are you joining us? The guys are waiting for you."

"Sure. Just give me a sec."

Evan walked away, and Aaron returned his attention to Pamela. "Sorry about that."

"No. That's okay. If you need to go with your brother....?"

She hesitated. She didn't want him to leave. It was nice having someone to talk to. But she didn't want to appear too demanding. Or, even worse, too needy.

He smiled, sort of apologetically. "I do need to talk to him about something. But listen. I want you to know. I was lucky. I had my brother around. And my mother and stepdad. They're what pulled me through. It made me feel less alone."

She made no response, so he added a parting thought.

"Talk to people, Pamela. It really helps."

Then he got up to leave.

As he turned around she blurted out his name.

"Aaron?"

He turned to face her.

"This crazy stuff you talked about. Did it include....?"

She found she had difficulty forming the words. He came to her rescue.

"Suicide?"

Pamela nodded.

"No. I never tried killing myself."

He leaned closer, almost to her ear, and whispered. "I did burn my Grandparents' house down, though."

"You're not serious?"

He kept a smile on his face as he used his finger to mimic an X on his chest. "Cross my heart, I did."

She wasn't sure how to respond, but it didn't matter anyway, since he didn't allow her the opportunity to say anything more.

"See you around, Pamela."

"See you, Aaron."

Pamela failed to notice it, but the smile on her face was the first one she had worn in over a week.

Chapter Thirteen:

BEVERLY HAD no problem finding the house, even without using the GPS. She had spoken to Brian Watkins the night before, and he had given specific instructions for where to go. The place was actually in the same subdivision where Beverly's son Joey and his wife Teri lived. She even considered stopping by to visit with the kids, if she had time afterward, but then decided against it. Chances are both of them would be at work anyway.

Maybe she would be able to visit with the grandkids? She couldn't believe Andrew was fourteen already, and Stephanie was sixteen. Where had the years gone?

Stephanie was sixteen. It struck her suddenly that she was on her way to visit another young girl, practically the same age as Stephanie, who had found her life to be so tragic that she had considered – and even attempted – suicide.

What could possibly be so dismal in a young girl's life that she felt the only way out was to kill herself?

For a moment Beverly was lost in reflection, as she remembered herself at that age. All she could think of back then was having fun with her friends, or maybe getting to know a few of the boys in her classes better. She hadn't started to date yet at sixteen, but as she recalled she was really looking forward to it.

Along with her girlfriends she would go swimming in the summer, riding their bikes to the community pool four blocks away, then investing countless hours soaking up the sun as they worked at perfecting their tans. In colder weather they would listen to their records – actual records, not compact disks or digital downloads – and play board games together.

She had felt then like her entire life stretched out in front of her. She couldn't wait to get older, and start enjoying all the things adults get to do. Like driving a car. And going to work. What fun that must be.

She couldn't help smiling to herself. Boy, was she wrong about that last one.

Things just seemed so different anymore. Children were growing up so much quicker than in her day. They were exposed to so much information, bombarded with a constant media barrage of useless facts and inconsequential statistics. Celebrity lifestyles were glorified and spectacularized to the point where a normal life couldn't help but seem unfulfilling.

And, as Beverly well knew, many young people lived a life that was far from what could be considered normal.

Still, she was excited to be meeting with Pamela Watkins again, even considering the circumstances. Beverly was certain she had been a positive influence on the girl a decade ago, when they first met, and she was proud of the role she had played in the young girl's life.

She could only hope the current case would have a satisfactory resolution as well.

It felt good to be visiting a nice neighborhood for a change.

Beverly found it hard at times not to be judgmental in her cases. She often found herself thinking how glad she was that she didn't have to live in some of the places she visited. Her CASA responsibilities took her to portions of the city that she not only wasn't familiar with, but where she felt uncomfortable and, at times, unsafe.

When these thoughts occurred to her she would do her best to rein herself in. Many of these people had no choice but to live where they did. Poverty was a hard reality of life, and families made do with what they had or they simply did without. Their circumstances didn't need to be a reflection on the type of people they were. There was good and bad everywhere, regardless of the neighborhood.

Still, for the sake of the children involved, she needed to be aware of her surroundings and any inherent issues that might arise due to their current living conditions.

Beverly was satisfied with the house Brian Watkins lived in. It was, after all, in a good location. Her son Joey would have settled for nothing less. It was a working class neighborhood, many of the houses dating back to the sixties, but all of them seemed to be well-maintained and cared for. Brian's house was one of the smaller structures on the block, but for a single male it most likely served the purpose.

Beverly parked her car, hung her CASA identification tag around her neck, and walked to the front door, where she was greeted by Pamela's uncle.

"I'm Beverly Johnson. From the CASA office."

"Certainly. Please come in."

Brian led her through a hallway to a comfortable sitting area that looked out over the front porch. Once they were seated he resumed.

"I'm afraid I'm still a bit unclear on why you're here, Beverly. The caseworker was in earlier this week for a visit. Isn't this sort of repetitious, to have two of you checking up on us?"

"That's a common misconception that could use some explaining," she told him. "Though I work with the caseworkers, and we do share information and opinions, we represent two different agencies with two different agendas.

"The caseworker you met earlier, from Children's Services, will assist with services and appointments – setting up doctor visits, home studies, assisting the families in a multitude of ways. You can consider them the watchdogs of the entire process. They deal with the child, but they also handle the parents' issues and make certain everything is being followed through and services are conducted properly.

"I am of course interested in the parents as well, but in a more superficial capacity. I need to know the issues, and gauge the progress as the case moves forward. But my primary concern is for the children involved. Are they safe? Are they being taken care of properly, and are they in a suitable environment? Are their needs being met?

"In order to fulfill my obligations, both to the child and the court system, I will be visiting with Pamela at least once a month. I am entitled to stop in unannounced for a visit, but that typically doesn't happen unless I feel there are major concerns."

Brian Watkins looked around the room, as though trying to assess the environment from the CASA volunteer's point of view.

"I hope you don't feel there's anything wrong here," he managed, with a smile on his face.

"I'm sure there isn't, Brian. I'm not here to cause any problems, for you or for Pamela's parents. So please don't think of me as your adversary. Like you, I only want what's best for Pamela. You're obviously concerned about your niece, or you wouldn't have opened up your house to her."

"I do want what's best for Pamela. That's all. Have you met her?"

"It's funny you should ask that. Ten years ago, when your brother and his wife adopted Pamela, I was the CASA on the case. So yes, I have met her. But gosh, that was a decade ago now."

"I'm sure you'll find she's changed a lot since then."

Beverly nodded in agreement. "Obviously. A child changes a lot between seven and seventeen. The physical alterations alone are enormous. But we need as well to consider the emotional changes. I assume you've seen her regularly over the last ten years. Has her mood changed? Does she seem like something's been bothering her lately?"

Brian considered a moment before replying. "That's a tough question, Beverly. Sure, we've been together a lot over the years. But generally it was at holidays. Birthday celebrations. Things like that. There's always been a lot going on. And everyone's generally in a good mood. Pamela always seemed fine."

"And now?"

"I just don't know." He shook his head, considering how best to voice his apprehensions.

"She's so quiet," he continued. "Withdrawn. Patrick Zimmerly – from Children's Services – told me I shouldn't hesitate to talk to her about her suicide attempt. But I just don't know how to approach it with her."

"I know Patrick. He's a good man, has a lot of compassion for the people he works with. And he's certainly correct. We can't just ignore things, and pretend like nothing happened. Something is bothering the girl. So much that she felt the only way out was to take her own life. I've been through some rough times in my life. Believe me. But I never felt like that. I never felt so depressed about what I was going through that I would even consider such a drastic measure as suicide. It's hard to relate to."

"It's certainly a difficult subject to discuss, Brian. And I understand your trepidation. But somehow we have to get through to this young girl. You. Me. Her parents. We all need to work together and try to make things right."

"And I'm onboard with that. Believe me."

"Can you tell me anything about her family life? With Angela and Tim. What's it like for Pamela at home?"

"I can't really say."

He paused, embarrassed with his answer.

"I'm not trying to be evasive here, Beverly. But I never saw any issues with Pamela's home life. Everything always seemed to be fine. Sure, Tim and Angie bicker once in a while. What couple doesn't? But it's never gotten out of hand, as far as

I know.

"I do know they've always provided for Pamela's needs. They've been supportive. Attended school functions. But I guess you never really know what goes on in someone else's house, do you?"

"There's a lot of truth to that, Brian. I've been doing CASA work for ten years now. Pamela was actually the very first child I advocated for. Some of the things I've seen in those ten years...."

An awkward silence filled the room as Beverly paused, lost in the recollection of the families she had been involved with since becoming a volunteer. There were a lot of triumphs to consider.

But there was also the occasional tragedy.

And those were the ones that really stuck with her, and made her all the more determined to do whatever she could during her advocacy for the children that were entrusted to her oversight.

She dismissed these thoughts to continue with her questions.

"So has Pamela opened up to you at all about what happened that day? Or about what's bothering her so much that she would even consider something like suicide?"

"No. She hasn't. She's been keeping pretty much to herself. I leave for work right after she goes to school, so there haven't been any problems with that. She gets home right before I do and she's always in her room when I get here. We have dinner and she goes back to her room. It's like I hardly even know she's around.

"She does have an appointment tomorrow, though. With a therapist. Maybe that will help."

"Do you have the doctor's name?" Beverly pulled out a pen and notebook, to record the information.

"Let me see...." Brian consulted his cellphone, where he apparently had all the information entered.

"Dr. Antonio Bargalony. Her appointment's for 10:00 tomorrow morning, so Pamela will miss a few hours of school. I'll have to go in late to work, but at least that hasn't been a problem. My office has been very supportive of what we're going through here."

"I know Dr. Bargalony," Beverly informed him. "He was working with one of my clients in a case a few years ago."

"How was he? I mean, did he help your client?"

Images floated through Beverly's head, of a young mother named Aleisha Turner who wrestled with drug addiction as she strove to raise three children. It had been a few years ago, and the case had been... ...difficult... ...to say the least.

"Dr. Bargalony's a good man," Beverly finally remarked, not providing any particulars. "He seems sincerely interested in his patients."

"That's great to hear. Maybe he can do Pamela some good."

Brian stood.

"So, are you ready to talk to my niece?"

"Yes I am. I've been looking forward to rekindling our relationship."

Chapter Fourteen:

"**I'**M SORRY. I don't really remember you, Beverly."

"No, Pamela. Please don't apologize. You were only seven years old when you last saw me. I can't expect you to remember everything that was going on then. I'm sure there were so many people in and out of your life that it was hard to keep track of things."

The teenager merely nodded in response as Beverly continued.

"Let me explain why I'm here to see you."

Beverly repeated the spiel she had used with Brian, explaining the purpose of the CASA program and her part in the current investigation.

"So do you have any questions for me?" Beverly concluded.

"No. I'm okay."

"Well, I have plenty for you. I haven't spoken much with your parents yet. I just saw them for a few minutes at the Emergency Hearing. How are they doing?"

"OK, I suppose."

"No issues at home I should know about?"

"No. Things are good."

Beverly nearly said something. Obviously things weren't good with the teenager, considering the reason why she was involved with Children's Services. But Beverly decided to bide her time. She didn't want to come off as confrontational right at the start. She needed to earn Pamela's trust first.

"How about school, then? Everything all right with your classes?"

"Classes are fine," she admitted. "And boring."

"There must be something at school that interests you?"

"Not really."

"How about sports? Volleyball? Soccer? My grandson plays soccer. He's been doing it for years."

"I tried it once. It was too much running around."

Beverly decided to try another approach.

"Well, you don't need to participate in sports to enjoy them. Maybe you just like to watch sports? Basketball? Football?"

The last word seemed to strike a raw nerve with the teenager, who responded in a rushed torrent of words.

"Football is so dumb. A bunch of stupid boys rushing around and pushing each other down while they chase a stupid ball around the field. How stupid is that?"

The teenager's reaction surprised Beverly. Where before she had been uninterested in what they were talking about, nearly apathetic, she now seemed on the verge of outrage.

"Maybe you're right," Beverly continued, hoping to defuse Pamela's reaction to what looked to be a volatile subject. "I never cared much for football myself. Though my husband could spend a whole weekend watching his games. He preferred the college matches. He said they were more exciting than the professionals."

"They're all stupid."

Pamela turned aside after the comment, obviously reluctant to discuss the matter any further.

Beverly took time during the silence that followed by looking around the room. There were no personal items to be found; nothing in the bedroom to give an indication of the type of teenager Pamela Watkins had grown up to become.

A second perusal, however, took in something she had missed at first glance.

The Harry Potter book sat on a small folding table beside the bed. The pages were well-thumbed and wrinkled, as if it had been read on multiple occasions. It rested spine up, opened to a section of the book possibly two thirds of the way through.

"You must like to read?" Beverly asked.

Pamela followed the CASA volunteer's line of sight. "I like the Harry Potter books," the young girl admitted.

"I've never read them myself. But I hear they are really good."

A shrug was her answer.

"So what do you like about them?"

"I don't know. I guess because they're an escape."

"An escape from what?"

The teenager hesitated with her answer. "All the bad stuff in the world, I guess."

"Is there a lot of bad stuff in your world, Pamela?"

She managed a sarcastic tone with her answer. "You know there is. Or you wouldn't be here."

"You're right. That is why I'm here. I really do want to help you. In any way I can."

"It doesn't matter."

The response took Beverly by surprise.

"Why would you say something like that? I do want to help you, Pamela. Your family wants to help you."

"It doesn't matter," the teenager repeated. "Nothing you can do – nothing Tim and Angie can do – can help me now. It's too late for that."

"I won't accept that answer," Beverly continued, her voice taking on the most authoritative tone she could manage. "It's never too late to make amends for a wrong. It's never too late to correct a problem that needs to be addressed."

The teenager remained silent.

"You're running away again, Pamela. That's what this is all about, isn't it? You can't change things, so you do whatever you can to get away from it. Even if it means jumping off a bridge."

Pamela turned away then, shifting her whole body to face the wall, as though solace could be found there. Her body shook, as though gasping for air, but no tears accompanied the gesture.

Beverly, deciding it was best to change the topic, resumed in a quieter tone.

"There's something else you need to know about, Pamela. Regarding this case."

The teenager faced her again.

"You were still pretty little the last time I worked with you. But now that you're older, you can have more of a say in things."

"In what way?"

"You have the right to come to court if you want. To talk to the magistrate."

"What good would that do?"

"Well, if something's going on at home that's bothering you– ?"

"Everything's fine at home."

"Because if there's a problem, with Angela and Tim, you're entitled to talk to someone in authority about it."

"There's no problem with Tim and Angie. They've been great. I just needed this time, I guess. To get away from things. Clear my head. That's all."

"Has it helped?"

She took the time to consider the question. Her reply, when it came at last, was a meek response.

"I don't know yet."

Beverly wanted to say more. She wanted to draw the young girl further into the issues that were troubling her. But she knew she had to give it time.

So she decided it was best to just change the subject.

"You know, I don't usually get a chance to visit with the children I meet in my cases. I mean, after the cases are closed.

I get to know them for a while, but then when they don't need me anymore we go our separate ways.

"I'm sorry you're going through whatever it is you're going through. But it is nice to see you again. Ten years is a long time."

The bed groaned slightly as Pamela shifted position. "You knew my parents?" she asked.

"Yes. Angela and Tim– ."

"No. I mean my *real* parents."

Beverly hesitated.

It had been such a long time ago.

She had dug up some old notes on the case before coming over for the visit, to refresh herself on the circumstances of her first CASA experience. She even had some pictures of Pamela, as a child, that had been taken during the investigation. She remembered the little girl as quiet, a bit withdrawn, but quick to show affection once you got to know her.

The parents were a different story. She had met both of them several times during the case but never really got to know them. She remembered thinking they each loved their daughter, but neither quite knew how to properly express their feelings. The mother's reliance on alcohol impeded her judgment, while the belligerence exhibited by the father clouded his opinion on everything.

Many of the details were forgotten now, due to the passage of time, but she still had a general sense of what had gone down.

"Yes," she answered at last. "I knew your real parents."

"What were they like? There's so many things about them that I don't remember. What were they like?"

Beverly searched in her mind for the proper words.

"Troubled. Particularly your mother. She drank too much. And she knew it. But she couldn't stop. Even though I know she wanted to.

"She cared about you, Pamela. You meant a lot to her."

"Sure I did. That's why she gave me away to a couple of strangers."

Beverly released an exasperated sigh before continuing, frustrated with Pamela's view of what had occurred a decade earlier.

"It wasn't like that, Pamela. Believe me. That last day in court, on the day of the Custody Hearing, your mother got up on the stand, and by the time she was done there wasn't a dry eye in the room. Yes, she gave you away. But only because she knew it was the best thing for you. She knew she wasn't getting any better. With her drinking. And she knew she could never care for you the way she wanted to.

"The fact that she gave you away showed how much she loved you."

"That doesn't make sense."

"That's because you've never been a parent. It changes you, and the way you look at things. You put your child's needs ahead of your own. I truly believe that's what your mother did for you, when she gave you away. It hurt her, probably more than you can ever know. But she felt it was the best thing for her child. For you."

For several long moments nothing was said, as the teenage girl on the bed considered the information. Her voice, when she spoke again, showed no emotion. Rather it had a harder edge to it with the next question.

"And my father?"

Beverly searched in her mind for the right words to say, but there was no way to get around the truth of the matter.

"Your father had anger issues," she admitted at last. "He couldn't control his emotions properly. I don't know how much you recall of what was going on back then, but he even went to jail for a while, right before the adoption hearing. He just couldn't control his anger when he was around your mother."

Pamela turned away, to face the wall again.

"Right. Anger issues."

"But he wasn't all bad," Beverly added. "I think there was another side to him."

"I wish I could believe that."

"But it's true. I saw him with you a couple of times when you visited. At Children's Services. He was good with you. Patient. Attentive."

"He was attentive, all right." The words were tinted with sarcasm.

"You can't expect parents to be prefect, Pamela. They're only human. I think your parents tried."

"They should have tried harder."

That effectively put an end to the conversation.

Beverly sat in her car, pondering her interview with Pamela. She wanted so much to help the teenager. She wanted to help each and every child on each and every case she took on. But sometimes she wondered if anything she did even made a difference.

She knew about depression. She had been there herself. The accident that had taken Russell away had altered her life irrevocably. A part of herself had died with him. After his passing the days were empty, and the nights dragged by. Her life had changed forever, and she wondered every day how she was going to make it through to the next one.

She had never contemplated suicide. Things had never gotten that low for her. She understood how that could have been a temptation for some people, depending on the circumstances, but not for her.

Maybe it was because of her kids. Their support, their love, had pulled her through. Jennifer had been at the house constantly. Helping out with little chores. Preparing meals for her when Beverly forgot she needed to eat. Taking care of bills. They say the only things certain in life are death and taxes. Well, even after death the taxes were still there.

Somehow she had muddled through. But even as she recovered, even as she learned to accept her lot in life and the rotten hand she had been dealt with, she still felt empty. She still needed more.

Her work with CASA helped to fill the void in her life following Russell's death. It gave her a purpose. It gave her an opportunity to be constructive, and to be with other people. It allowed her to help children, and guide them to a better future.

She recalled her training – ten years ago now – and in particular something she remembered from an early class.

"You can be a stable force in a child's life."

Those were the words Malcolm McDougal, the Director of the CASA program, had used.

"You may not feel you're making a difference," he had said. "But consider what these kids are going through. Their lives have been disrupted. In many cases they are torn away from their families, placed with people they don't even know.

"They may be sent to different schools. Away from their friends and the teachers they know. And though we do our best to try to keep siblings together, that isn't always the case. Sad to say, brothers and sisters are often torn apart as a result of these tragedies in their lives.

"But you, as a CASA volunteer, can be a stable influence for them. By being there for them consistently, showing that you care and want to help, you can change the future of these children.

"They will never forget you. Believe me when I tell you, what you do as a CASA volunteer matters."

But was that really true?

Beverly had worked hard as a CASA. For ten years now she had investigated.

Reported.

Advocated.

But now she had found out her first case – her very first case – was with a young girl who didn't even remember her.

Had she really made a difference?

Were Pamela's current issues something new? Or were they a continuation of something else, something that started out when she was only seven years old, something Beverly and the caseworker and the magistrate should have seen then, instead of allowing things to fester for another decade? Issues that, had they been dealt with properly, might have prevented the teenager from contemplating suicide ten years later?

Beverly rode home in silence, barely paying attention to the streets she drove down. The nagging thoughts coursing through her head failed to give her any peace. When she arrived home she realized that the drive had been merely a blur to her, and she considered herself lucky that she had made it home okay.

She couldn't help wondering if it was the current case, and the circumstances surrounding it, that had made her so unobservant. Or was it an indication of something else?

She was getting older. She had to admit that. Maybe it was time to slow down.

Chapter Fifteen:

A NEW lady came to the house to visit with me. It wasn't Judy, the lady who took me in the car to Angie's house. This was a diff'rent lady.

Her name was Beverly. And boy was she old. I bet she must of been 'bout one hundred years old. She had gray hair. And wrinkles.

But I liked her.

She was really nice to me. She said she was gonna visit me every month, and that if there was something I wanted then I should tell her and she would get it for me.

I told her I wanted to go home.

She told me I couldn't do that right now.

She said maybe later, if Mommy stopped her drinking, and Daddy didn't get angry no more, then maybe I could go back home.

I missed Mommy. I knew she was sick a lot, and lots of time had a headache, but she was still fun to be with. Most of the time.

I missed Daddy too. I missed sitting on his lap when he read stories to me. I missed the way he used to brush my hair.

Daddy always made me feel special, when he called me Angel and we did fun things together. Sometimes he would be a horsey and I would ride on his back. He would even play dollies with me, with the big playhouse I got at Christmas.

Mommy would tell me it wasn't safe to be around Daddy. That when he got angry he could get nasty.

But Daddy never got angry with me.

And he never got nasty with me.

Beverly visited me every month. We would always talk for a while. She would ask me how school was. And whether I liked it at Angie and Tim's house.

Then after we was done talking for a while we would do something fun.

Sometimes she would bring a game with her, and we would play together. Or she would bring a puzzle, that we would make together. One time she brought a book with pictures we cut up and put together of diff'rent animals. It was a lot of fun.

I liked it when Beverly came to visit. She didn't tell me what to do, like Angie did. And she didn't cry and fuss over me, like Mommy and Daddy did. She was just fun to be with.

And she made me feel special, in a way I wasn't used to. When she visited it was like me and her were the only people in the whole wide world, and whatever I wanted to do, or whatever I wanted to talk about, was okay with her. Whenever we were together everything seemed good, and I didn't have to worry no more 'bout all the other things that were going on.

It was just me and her and our special time together.

Chapter Sixteen:

CONSULTATION TRANSCRIPT # 2210127 – EXCERPT

Dr. B:
Good morning, Pamela. It's a pleasure to see you again.
I realize our time together in the hospital was brief. And that you were not functioning at your best when last we spoke. In case you've forgotten, my name is Dr. Bargalony, and we'll be spending a lot of time together in the weeks to come. I hope you're agreeable to that arrangement.

Pa W:
Do I have a choice?

Dr. B:
Of course you have a choice. Life is full of choices. For you. For me.
You can walk out of here right now if you want. You can just tell me to mind my own business, and that you don't need me interfering with your life.
But I don't think you want to do that.

Pa W:
How do you know what I want?

Dr. B:
That's an appropriate question. I don't know you well enough to make that kind of an inference, do I? It is rather presumptuous of me, considering the circumstances, to assume anything about you.
So how about helping me out. Tell me something about yourself, so I can get to know you better.

Pa W:
Like what?

Dr. B:
Let's start with your home life. Your family. What are your parents like?

Pa W:
You mean Tim and Angie?
They're not really my parents, you know. My real parents, anyway. They adopted me when I was seven.

Dr. B:
Why would you say that? It strikes me as interesting that your initial response to my query is to inform me that you were adopted. Therefore, you don't consider the couple who raised you to be your real parents.
But you're wrong, Pamela. The fact that they adopted you testifies they are your real parents. They have taken on the legal and financial responsibilities of raising you. Of caring for you. Of looking out for your well-being. That's what parents do.

Pa W:
Yeah. They do all that. But they're not like.... You know. My *real* parents.

Dr. B:
So you mean they aren't your biological parents?

Pa W:
Yeah. That's what I meant.

Dr. B:
But they do take care of you? They do provide for you?

Pa W:
Sure. They do those things.

Dr. B:
What do you call them? Your adopted parents. Are they Mom and Dad? Mother or Father?

Pa W:
I never could do that. The whole Mom and Dad thing. I was seven when they adopted me. I already had a mother and a father. It just felt wrong to call somebody else.... You know. Mom and Dad.
I call them Tim and Angie.

Dr. B:
And how do all of you get along? Any friction? Any particular problems come up, issues that disturb you or things you wish they wouldn't do to you?

Pa W:
They're too stringent with their rules. Especially Angie. I guess they think they're looking out for me, and think they need to be telling me all the time what I can and can't be doing.
But I'm seventeen now. I'm not a little girl. I can look out for myself.

Dr. B:
You're never too old to have someone looking out for you. We all need assistance, from time to time. It's part of what makes us human. The social interaction we all require. The words of

assurance. The acceptance.

I'm sure you've heard the saying before, *it takes a village to raise a child*. That's more than just a clever catchphrase by Hillary Clinton. It refers to the concept that each of us, as an individual, is still part of a group, a community that teaches and nurtures and guides us along in life.

None of us can make it alone.

We all need other people in our lives.

Pa W:
Even you?

Dr. B:
Yes. Even me.

I want to help you, Pamela. Believe me.

But I can't start to help you until I know what you're going through.

And I can't begin to know what you're going through until you open up to me, and trust me enough to let me help you.

Pa W:
How do I know this will work?

Dr. B:
You don't.

But I assure you, it's a far better remedy than jumping off a bridge.

EXTENDED SILENCE

Dr. B:
I don't have any overnight remedies, Pamela. I can only assume that whatever issues are bothering you have been around for a long time. That the situations and circumstances in your life that disturbed you so much that you found yourself contemplating suicide.... Well, this was a long time coming.

It's going to take time to resolve things.

But I promise you this. If you trust me. If you open up to me, and honestly face whatever is bothering you. Then I can help you.

Can you accept that?

Pa W:
Yes. I suppose so.

Dr. B:
Good. Then we're off to a great start.

So let's get back to your family. What can you tell me about your parents, Tim and Angie?

Chapter Seventeen:

BEVERLY TOOK the seat offered to her, set her purse on the floor at her feet, then looked at the other three people in the room.

She had set up the visit earlier in the week, and was glad to be able to catch both Angela and Tim Watkins together. It was almost like visiting with old friends. Especially since so much of it felt comfortable to her.

Stepping into their house was like entering a time warp. Though it had been ten years since she had last visited, the place looked much the same as she remembered. She didn't recall the color on the walls – perhaps they had refreshed things in the interim – and some of the flooring looked new. But the basic living space and the arrangement of the furniture was familiar. She would have felt comfortable there, if not for the circumstances surrounding the visit.

The time Beverly had talked to the couple the day of the Emergency Hearing had been rushed, and they had still been reeling from the shock of what their daughter had attempted on the High Level bridge. It wasn't a good time to pry into their lives, even though Beverly knew that was something she had to do in order to fully understand the situation.

Which meant there were still things that needed to be discussed.

The early days of an investigation were important ones. Information gathered at the beginning often influenced so much of the rest of the case. Beverly needed to be certain she approached things accurately, and with all the pertinent facts she could assemble, before reaching any conclusions regarding what was going on.

Beverly was also interested to hear whether the two of them had been in contact with Pamela since the teenager had been released from the hospital.

Perhaps the only unexpected circumstance regarding the visit was the unfamiliar face of the third woman in the room. She had been introduced as Annie Klume, and she was a stranger to Beverly. She was the ongoing caseworker assigned to the case involving Pamela Watkins. She had replaced Patrick Zimmerly, who as an investigative caseworker routinely handed cases off following the Emergency Hearings. Beverly had seen Annie's name on the paperwork the CASA office had sent over, but the two of them had never met before.

Annie had a pleasant, but somehow weary voice. "It's nice to meet you, Beverly."

"You too, Annie. But I must admit. I didn't realize you would be here during my visit."

"I hope that's okay?"

"Of course. Just unexpected."

"Well, I talked to Angie the day after you scheduled your visit, so I figured we might as well come at the same time."

Tim spoke up once the introductions were concluded. "It is good to see you again, Beverly. I'm sorry we didn't get a chance to talk more the day of the hearing. We're glad you were able to step in again to help with Pamela. Angie and I appreciated everything you did when she was first placed with us."

"So you know each other?" Annie asked, surprised with this tidbit of information.

"Oh yes." Angie spoke up quickly, cutting off anything further her husband may have attempted to say. Her words came in a rush, like she could barely contain them. Gone was the belligerence she had exhibited during her initial visit with Children's Services, having been replaced with a nervousness that propelled her forward. A staccato rhythm drove her words.

"Beverly was the CASA when we adopted Pamela, ten years ago. She can tell you what good parents we are. And how good we were with Pamela. There were never any complaints, were there Beverly?"

"None at all," the CASA volunteer admitted. "Everything ran like clockwork."

"That's what we've been telling Annie. And why I still don't understand why they're taking Pamela away from us now. We didn't do anything wrong. At the hearing they kept using the word neglect, as if we let Pamela run wild or something.

"I can assure you, there was no neglect on our end. We did everything we could for Pamela."

"No one says you didn't," the caseworker was quick to point out. "But Children's Services would rather err on the side of caution where children are concerned. Until we understand why Pamela attempted suicide we want to tread carefully."

"It just seems so unfair, to keep us away from her like this."

Beverly entered the conversation to sooth the distraught mother. "I know you love Pamela. I saw it ten years ago, when the two of you took her in as foster parents. I know you had a few issues along the way, but it seemed like everything sorted itself out."

"We already talked about this, Beverly. There were no *issues*." Angela stressed the word issues, as an indication of the point she was making. "Everything was fine. Everything has been fine since the day she moved in with us."

Tim, his voice calm, continued. "There's no denying we had some adjustments to make, Angie. Everybody realizes that. Pamela went through a lot when she came to live with us. It was a confusing time for her."

"Of course it was," Annie remarked. "Moving into a foster home is tough for any child. No matter how rough they had it at home – and I've seen some pretty sad stories in my time at Children's Services – there's still a certain allegiance these children hold toward their parents. Life with them is the only type of life they're aware of.

"Then to be thrown into a strange environment, with people they don't know, it can cause all sorts of behavioral problems. Foster children misbehave. *ALL* foster children misbehave. I wouldn't believe you if you said otherwise."

Beverly picked up the conversation. "Nobody's holding anything against you, Angela. Believe me. We just want to help Pamela find her way through this."

Angela, her expression betraying her continued apprehensions, stammered out her next question. "And now we have another hearing to go to? What's that all about?"

"It's the Adjudication Hearing," the caseworker offered.

"Are they going to take her away from us? Will we still be able to see her?"

"We would like the Agency to assume Temporary Custody of your daughter," Annie explained. "This is just a formality. It allows us to help your brother with the financial burden of having an extra mouth to feed. It allows us as well to monitor her visits, to doctors and therapists and such. But we're not taking her away from you. Reunification is always the goal with Children's Services, and I see no reason not to push for Pamela coming back to you."

"And visits?"

"I have no problems with visits," Beverly announced.

Annie nodded in agreement. "Visits shouldn't be a problem. But since she is under your brother's care, the Agency will specify, for now at least, that all visits be supervised by him. You can visit there, or Pamela can come to your house. As long as Brian comes along."

"And if we agree to everything?" Tim asked. "At the hearing, I mean. Doesn't that as much as label us as being guilty of something? Admitting that we did something wrong?"

"Not at all," Annie pointed out. "I understand the situation. Your child's CASA understands the situation. This will all be brought up in court, so nothing goes against the two of you. But we still need to follow procedures, to assure that everything progresses properly."

Beverly leaned forward, as if to stress her next point. "It's what's best for Pamela. Right here and now. It's a long time before anything drastic would happen regarding custody. That gives Pamela time to recover, and us time to determine what's really going on here."

"And at this point," Annie continued, "Pamela is best where she's at. She told me herself that she wants to stay with her uncle."

"She said that?" Angela's tone betrayed her disbelief. It was like she felt her daughter was turning against her.

"She's going through a difficult time," the caseworker pointed out. "There are a lot of things she needs to sort out. It's no reflection on you. Or on the job you did raising her. But she needs some time to get through this."

"When's the last time you spoke to her?" Beverly asked.

Tim continued with their end of the conversation. "Last night. We call her every night."

"How did she seem?"

"She seemed fine. Not very talkative. But she is a teenager. It's not like when she was little, and she could talk your ear off."

"Has she given any indication of what's troubling her?"

"No. And we haven't pushed the issue. We wanted to give her the chance to get feeling better about things before we came down on her too hard. Brian says she pretty much keeps to her room. But she's back in school now, so that's a good thing."

"Yes it is," Annie agreed. "A return to normalcy is what she needs right now."

Beverly left the house with Annie Klume. She addressed the caseworker while they stood together at the curb.

"I feel so bad for what they're going through. The whole family. This has to be rough on all of them."

"Maybe the only good thing about it is, I don't see this case dragging out too long."

"Why do you say that?"

"Because Pamela is seventeen already. In less than a year she'll be emancipated out of the system."

"I hadn't thought about that."

A long sigh announced the caseworker's frustration before she continued.

"There isn't really a whole lot we can do to help her. If she doesn't come to grips with things in the next year then she'll turn eighteen and the case will close of its own accord. Once she becomes an adult we can't help her anymore."

"So she'll be abandoned by the system?"

"Not abandoned. Children's Services can no longer intervene on her behalf at that point. But there are other agencies, other social services that will become available to her.

"Which is good. Because no matter what else happens between now and then, once she turns eighteen it will be out of our hands."

Chapter Eighteen:

PAMELA MANAGED to avoid Bobby Beard for most of the first week back at school. It wasn't easy, considering they were in the same Political Science class together, as well as Mr. Behrend's American History. But by ducking out of the classrooms as quickly as possible she could lose herself in the hallways and make her getaway.

She didn't want to see Bobby. She didn't want to talk to Bobby. She didn't want anything to do with Bobby for the rest of her life.

It was all so different than it had been a few weeks ago.

She had never been one of the popular girls, which suited her fine. Pamela had her friends, even though she didn't move in a particularly large social circle. She was closer to Sally Murphy than any of the other girls at school, but there were others she hung out with from time to time.

She was involved in school activities, attending pep rallies and extra functions, so it wasn't that she was a loner. But she was comfortable with her small group of acquaintances. She felt no need to broaden her horizons.

It was a shock when Bobby asked her to his house after school to work on a history project together. They had never even talked before, except maybe a few words during class, and only then when it was absolutely necessary.

She didn't think he even knew who she was.

After all, he was a big shot at school, captain of the football team and all. And she was a nobody. So to think he was actually asking her over to his house came as a surprise.

She suspected of course that there was more to it than working on a school assignment.

Bobby had a bit of a reputation around school, a reputation envied by the rest of the boys. The other girls at school would talk about how he was. They said he had a *love 'em and leave 'em* sort of attitude. It seemed he had a new girlfriend every week.

Pamela was realistic enough to know there was nothing serious about any of his relationships, and accepted the fact that she wasn't making any long term commitments by agreeing to spend some time with him.

But she was curious.

She heard things.

From the other girls.

She had never been with a boy before. Not in that way. It was a new concept to her, but one she looked forward to exploring.

And to think her first time would be with the captain of the football team made things especially exciting.

She could have never imagined how horribly bad the experience would turn out.

That was all behind her now. She needed to move on with her life.

So she avoided Bobby. If she walked down a hallway and saw him coming her way then she would turn the other direction. While passing his locker she made certain to conceal her face with a book so she could pass without him seeing her. It all seemed a bit silly. Almost childish. But she was prepared to do whatever was necessary to avoid talking to him.

Not that he noticed. Bobby was one of those boys that assumed the whole world revolved around him. He didn't pay attention to others. He was too busy paying attention to himself.

As the week wore on Pamela felt more comfortable. It was obvious Bobby had no intention of approaching her. Of that she was grateful. Just one less thing she needed to worry about, while she pieced her life back together.

But as she left the school on Thursday afternoon, intent on reaching her bus, she became aware of someone beside her, matching her stride by stride as she walked along the sidewalk in front of the high school.

It was Bobby.

His voice was low, so as not to be overheard by the other kids in the area. "I need to talk to you."

Pamela snapped back her response. "I don't need to talk to you."

"Come on. You owe me that."

She stopped dead in her tracks to stare at him. "Owe you that? I don't owe you anything."

"Okay. Poor choice of words. I just need an explanation."

"For what?"

"They say you tried to kill yourself. Jump off a bridge or something. Is that true?"

Her anger evaporated immediately, replaced with a look of shame and embarrassment.

"It was stupid of me," she managed at last. "I know. I wasn't thinking clearly."

"Why'd you do it?" Bobby asked.

She didn't answer.

"Because of me?"

Her answer came immediately, in a louder tone.

"Of course because of you!" Then, as an afterthought, more to herself than to him, she added a disclaimer. "And other things."

"I didn't mean to hurt you, Pamela. Honest."

"Well, you did."

"I'm sorry."

"Sorry isn't good enough It doesn't make up for what happened."

"I know it doesn't. But I can't change that, can I? Especially since you refuse to tell me what I did wrong. All I can do is say I'm sorry."

"It's not enough."

"What, then? What do you want from me?"

"Just stay out of my life. Forever."

"Okay. You got it."

He turned and stormed away, looking for all the world like someone who had been wronged. The action struck Pamela as pretty ridiculous, considering the situation.

She didn't feel sorry for him. Bobby wasn't a good person. That's all there was to it. It had been a mistake to have anything to do with him.

And it was a relief to think that he was walking out of her life.

Chapter Nineteen:

THE DAY after Pamela's suicide attempt the Emergency Hearing had been held at the Juvenile Court. The decision had been rendered at that time to remove Pamela from her home. And while the order was legally binding, it was not intended as a permanent solution. The decision to intervene on Pamela's behalf was a temporary stopgap, just one station on the journey to the ultimate destination – rectifying the issues that were afflicting the young girl.

Further investigation was required, to be performed by the caseworker for Children's Services and the CASA volunteer assigned to Pamela's case. And within sixty days of the Emergency Hearing there would be held – as specified by law – an Adjudication Hearing.

This second hearing would listen to testimony and review the evidence pertaining to the case. In the unlikely event it was determined there was no need for additional intervention – meaning the juvenile was safe and well-cared for and required no further services from the county agency – then the case would be closed and the matter dropped.

This seldom occurred. In most instances further actions would be specified to monitor the safety of the child and the progress of the other participants named in the case.

So when it was time for court, it wasn't a surprise to Beverly that the Adjudication Hearing passed smoothly. Children's Services finalized the placement of seventeen-year-old Pamela Watkins in the home of her Paternal Uncle, Brian Watkins. Nobody contested the fact. No evidence needed to be presented. The court session was opened and closed in a matter of minutes.

It did seem a bit peculiar, though, in comparison to any of the other hearings Beverly had attended in the past.

Angela Watkins and Tim Watkins each sat at separate tables, each with their own attorney. Even though they were in agreement with one another, and determined to work together for whatever was best for Pamela, they were represented as individuals, and not as a couple.

While this seemed an unusual situation, the rationale behind the arrangement made sense. In most cases – previously to this one, it had been in all the cases Beverly had ever attended – the parents were at odds with one another. Bickering and contentions were common, with each party representing themselves in the most favorable light they could. Generally this was accomplished at the expense of their former partner. As such, each parent was entitled to their own legal counsel.

Angela and Tim were clearly in agreement now. They were determined to do what was best for their child. But there was no telling what the future would bring. Emotions were powerful things. As cases dragged on, and participants wearied of the legal hurdles they faced along the way, it wasn't uncommon for even the most agreeable of partners to drift apart in regards to their recommendations.

Tim had always been level-headed. Beverly recalled his patience in dealing with the young child the two of them had fostered a decade ago. Her visits during that time revealed him to be a devoted parent. By the close of the case, it was obvious Pamela had become attached to her new father figure.

With Angela it had been a different story.

Not that she had been a bad parent. She had stepped into a demanding position, and due to their home situation had accepted the predominant role in caring for Pamela.

An important aspect of parenting is discipline. Children need to learn the difference between right and wrong. With this in mind, Angela had been quick to criticize, often pointing out Pamela's faults to her as an encouragement to improve. Angela seemed to show little tolerance for mistakes, and no doubt lectured the youngster constantly. Though much of it was justified, it must have been a trying ordeal for a seven-year-old.

Beverly realized the woman meant the best. And while admitting her approach could have used some adjusting, there were as many parenting techniques out there as there were parents. Just because a parent handled a situation differently than someone else would didn't mean they were a bad parent.

So when it came time to award custody of the young child to her foster parents, Angela and Tim Watkins had won the CASA volunteer's approval and, more importantly, her recommendation to the court.

They were two different people, each of them welcoming Pamela into their hearts. They had demonstrated their affection for the child and showed her their love through acceptance and years of caring. They were united now for a common goal.

But sometimes things changed. Beverly had experienced this so many times in her CASA career that she accepted it as the norm. Situations are fluid, as are the thought-processes of the participants in a case.

Should Angela and Tim grow to disagree on what they considered the proper way to handle things as the case moved forward, it was best that they each have their say in the matter. That was why at the Adjudication Hearing, and at any future hearings, they each had their own counsel to represent them. It was the fairest, most equitable way of handling a situation that was starting out fine, but could deteriorate into something much different.

Annie Klume disappeared immediately after the hearing, citing her busy schedule and a visit she had to attend with another client. Tim and Angela caught up with Beverly just outside the courtroom door.

"So what happens now?" Angela asked. "Can we see our daughter?"

"Of course you can. The magistrate approved all our recommendations. As long as Brian is present then you can visit whenever – and wherever – you want."

"That's what we wanted to hear."

Tim, his voice ever calm, joined the conversation. "Thank you again, Beverly. I almost feel like it's ten years ago, and we're having to go through this process of proving ourselves all over again."

"Don't think that way. You certainly don't have anything to prove to me. Or to the courts, for that matter."

Angela resumed the couple's share of the discussion.

"It doesn't feel that way. Why are they putting us through so much? Can't they see that Pamela needs us more than ever right now?

"That's just it," Beverly offered. "Pamela is in a very vulnerable position. And yes, she needs your support. And encouragement. But be careful you don't overwhelm her."

"In what way?"

"We really don't know what she's going through, and why she even considered suicide as a way out. It could be something that started long before you even met her, when she was with her biological parents. Or it could be something more recent."

"Meaning because of us?" The accusatory tone of Angela's reply left no doubt she was feeling defensive.

Beverly chose her next words carefully.

"A recent complication isn't necessarily home related, Angela. It could have been something that developed at school. Or with her friends. I just think you need to be careful not to smother Pamela. She needs time to sort things out. Being in a

114

neutral environment, such as at her uncle's house, may help her to see things more clearly.

"She's also attending sessions with her therapist on a regular basis."

"And you think that will help?"

"Of course it will help. They're the experts. They deal with these situations all the time. They know the right questions to ask. As well as the ones to avoid. Pamela is in good hands.

"I will continue to visit with her once a month. If I notice anything disconcerting I will let you know. But you have to keep me informed as well. You know her background better than anyone. You know her moods. If anything is amiss, please let me know right away."

"We'll do that."

I certainly hope so, Beverly thought. Vigilance was the key to preventing another suicide attempt.

Pamela had been fortunate the first time, with the police intervening in time to prevent a tragedy. There was no guarantee her luck would hold out should there be another such attempt.

Chapter Twenty:

TIM TOOK me to visit Mommy and Daddy yesterday.

It wasn't at our 'partment. Tim says I'm not allowed to go to our 'partment right now.

So we went to a big building in the city, and we sat in a big room with a bunch of other kids and their families. Some of the families were sorta noisy. There was one little boy, that was littler than me, that cried a lot, and his Mommy would tell him to stop crying, but he wouldn't listen to her and he kept on crying anyway. I wished he would stop but he didn't.

There was a man at a desk that kept watching us to see what we were doing, but all we did was color and draw and play and stuff like that.

I didn't even get to visit with Mommy and Daddy together. Tim told me that wasn't allowed, either.

I visited with Daddy first. He brought some books to read to me, but they weren't my books from home. They were new ones. He said he bought them special so we would be able to look at them together. One of them had funny pictures of funny animals and we both laughed when he read it.

We had cookies together, and I drank a grape juice box. Grape is my fav'rite flavor, and Daddy knows that. That's why he brought me a grape juice box. Daddy said he wasn't thirsty so he didn't bring nothing to drink for himself.

Daddy seemed like he didn't want to be there. He kept looking at the man at the desk. Daddy looked kind of worried. I don't know what was bothering him, 'cause every time I asked him if he was okay he told me there was nothing wrong and he was glad he could visit with me.

It was nice to see Daddy. But we only got to spend an hour together. Daddy said that was all he was allowed to see me. But he promised me I would see him again in another week.

After Daddy left I had to wait in the room by myself for a couple of minutes. A nice lady came and sat down next to me and talked to me and told me they were waiting for Mommy to start her visit. I asked her why Mommy and Daddy couldn't visit together, and she told me that wasn't the way they did things.

Mommy fin'ly showed up. The lady told Mommy she was fifteen minutes late. Mommy said she had to take a bus to get there and the busses were running late and that's why she was late. I asked if I could take a bus with her someday, and she just smiled at me.

Mommy asked the lady if she could stay longer on her visit, since she was late, but the lady said it didn't work that way.

So I only got to visit with Mommy for 45 minutes instead of the hour we was 'posed to have.

Mommy didn't have much to say to me. It was like she didn't want to be there. She hardly smiled at me, either, even though she said she was happy to see me. It didn't feel like she was happy 'bout it.

I asked her if she had a headache, 'cause I figured that was what was bothering her. She said it was only a little headache, and that she would be okay.

Mommy didn't bring nothing with her, like Daddy did. She said she would do better next time, and bring something fun for us to do together,

But there was stuff in the big room that we were able to use. There was a puzzle of a puppy dog that we did together. And another one of a tiger, but that one was a little harder 'cause of all the stripes so I didn't like it as much.

It seemed like we didn't have much time together and then it was time for Mommy to leave.

She gave me a great big hug and told me how much she loved me. I told her I loved her too, and that's when she started to cry.

I started to cry too, but mostly 'cause I felt so bad for Mommy. She said it was lonely in the 'partment without me and Daddy there to keep her company. She said there was nothing to do but watch television and drink and it was making her sad.

Angie was waiting for me after the visit and took me back to her house.

She asked me if I had fun visiting my Mommy and Daddy. And I didn't know what to tell her.

It was nice to see Mommy and Daddy, but it would of been nicer to see them both at the same time. And it would of been nicer to spend more time together.

I told Angie the visits were okay, but I asked if I could go to my 'partment to visit with them next time. I didn't like the big room with all the other kids in it. It was too noisy.

Angie told me it wasn't safe at my 'partment with Mommy and Daddy. She told me that's why I was living with her and Tim now. 'Cause they were keeping me safe and making sure nothing happened to me.

I told her I was safe at my 'partment.

I told her I didn't understand why they wouldn't leave me and Mommy and Daddy alone.

I guess I must of sounded too loud, 'cause Angie told me it wasn't nice to yell at people. Even when you were mad about something. Angie tells me all the time what I should be doing and what I shouldn't be doing. She makes me feel like I don't do nothing the way I'm 'posed to.

I missed living with Mommy.

Mommy never yelled at me.

Except when she had a headache.

Then she would yell at me.

But she always told me later how much she loved me. And that I was her big little girl. And that made everything feel okay.

Chapter Twenty-One:

TERI STONE made it a practice to stop at her mother-in-law's house at least once a week. Her husband Joey was of course concerned about his mother as well. But his schedule wasn't as flexible as his wife's, so the opportunity didn't come up as often for him to check up on things.

Ever since COVID, Teri had started spending more time at home. When things first hit – that crazy time when people were panicking and afraid to leave their houses without wearing a mask, when the six foot rule was strictly followed instead of being ignored by one and all – Teri worked for a seven-month spell and only made it to the office on a dozen occasions. The rest of the time she worked from home.

It made her appreciate the versatility of the internet, which could serve a purpose other than shopping and social interactions.

And while she relished the changes in the work environment, and welcomed the way they effected her lifestyle, Teri couldn't help but feel bad for the shop personnel during that time. They had no option but to go to work every day. They grumbled about it, of course. And once in a while the company had provided lunch to the workers, as a sort of compensation for their efforts.

But somehow it didn't seem fair to her.

She heard so much talk during the COVID epidemic about nurses and the bonuses they were receiving. Teri gave people in the medical profession a lot of credit. They were on the front line of things, and were risking their health every day by going to work. They deserved to be recognized.

But were things really that much different for the shop personnel? For the people that couldn't stay home and do their job? After all, weren't they at risk every time they went to work?

Teri was certainly glad she was able to stay home during the worse of things. Even now, with the COVID fear having calmed down considerably and vaccinations an everyday occurrence, she only went to the office once or, at most, twice a week. This allowed her schedule to be more flexible. She could run an occasional errand during the day, and catch up on her work later in the evening as time allowed.

It helped that the kids were older now, and didn't require as much attention from her. Stephanie, after all, was sixteen, while Andrew was fourteen.

It made her feel old just thinking about it. Which had a great deal to do with why she felt so protective toward Beverly. Teri could feel herself slowing down. Activities that had seemed commonplace years ago were more of a chore now. Any amount of unaccustomed activity would leave her body aching in places she hadn't even been aware of.

She could only imagine what it would be like to be in your seventies.

Still, she was amazed at how much Beverly did accomplish. Her mother-in-law kept her house up. It was immaculate whenever Teri stopped by. She did her yard work, getting down on her hands and knees to weed her flower beds.

Teri wasn't sure she could do as much.

And the CASA duties Beverly performed were amazing. She had been a volunteer for years now and still maintained her enthusiasm. She loved kids and truly felt she was making a difference in the world.

She managed just fine on her own.

But, even so, Teri still felt obligated to conduct her weekly visits. It was her part in encouraging and supporting her mother-in-law.

"I don't know, Teri."

Beverly looked tired. She even sounded tired.

Teri was instantly alarmed.

"Are you okay, Mom? Is there anything I can do?"

"No. I'm fine. Really I am."

Beverly wandered into her living room and sat down on the flower-patterned sofa. Teri closed the front door behind them and followed the older woman into the daintily decorated room. Teri sat across from Beverly, but said nothing. She wanted to give her mother-in-law a chance to talk first.

"Maybe I'm just getting too old for this," Beverly stated at last.

"Too old for what?"

"This CASA work I do. Working on these cases. Seeing what these kids go through. I guess it's just starting to get to me. You know?"

"You have been doing it a long time now."

Her face relaxed slightly, as her thoughts wandered.

"Ten years ago. Ten years ago I got my first case."

Beverly leaned back, burying herself into the couch cushion, with a faraway look on her face.

"Her name was Pamela. She was the cutest little thing you ever saw."

"You say that about all the kids," Teri pointed out.

"I know. But this time it's the truth. She was such a sweet thing. And I was so enthusiastic. Ready to take on the world. Ready to save all the little angels out there, and protect them from all the bad things in their lives."

She paused, reflecting on the words just delivered, before continuing.

"I thought I had managed all that with Pamela. But now I just don't know."

"Why would you say that?"

"Because Pamela is back in the system again. She's seventeen now, and she tried to kill herself. She tried to commit suicide."

For a moment Teri didn't respond, as she took in the revelation from her mother-in-law. Her reply, when it came, was delivered in a stunned tone.

"What an awful thing to happen. It's no wonder you're upset. Do you know why she did it?"

"No idea. She refuses to talk about it. And I can't help but think that I failed her somehow."

Teri stood, crossed the room, and sat down on the couch beside the older woman. She gently placed her hand on Beverly's hand – which elicited a meek smile from her mother-in-law in return – before continuing.

"How did you fail her? You were there when she needed you. You offered love and support to a child going through a stressful time in her life."

"But was it enough? Did I miss something along the way? Something that's coming back now to haunt her and causing her so much pain that she can't even see a way out unless it's off the edge of a bridge?"

"I'm sure you did everything you should have done. Everything you *could* have done. In ten years things happen. Situations come up. I'm sure it has nothing to do with what she went through before."

"I keep telling myself that. But I don't believe it."

"Come on, Mom. This isn't like you. Where's that gung-ho spirit of yours? Where's Beverly Stone, CASA superhero?"

Beverly smiled at her daughter-in-law. Teri was joking around, trying to cheer her up, but she just wasn't having any of it.

"Beverly Stone. Yeah, right. Even the name doesn't mean anything. You know, when I go into court, to represent these children, my name isn't Beverly Stone. It's Beverly Johnson."

"What do you mean?"

"When I first started as a CASA, it was suggested I don't use my real name. Sometimes these cases go awry. Parents get angry. It's just better if they don't really know who you are."

Teri nodded in acceptance of the explanation before responding.

"Well, that makes sense."

"I guess it does. In a twisted sort of way. So I became Beverly Johnson."

"Where'd the Johnson come from?"

"It was my mother's maiden name. Easy to remember."

"That was smart."

"I was younger then," Beverly answered, with a smile on her face. "I could still think clearly enough for those kinds of decisions.

"But it all gets so confusing to me anymore. Sometimes I'll run into somebody I recognize. At the store or whatever. But I can't remember where I know them from. Is it somebody from CASA, so I should introduce myself as Beverly Johnson? Or maybe it was somebody from my school days. When I was still a teacher. So then I should introduce myself as Beverly Stone.

"I know it sounds silly, but it's getting harder for me to remember. I question so many things in my life anymore. And it just makes me feel…."

She paused, struggling with the proper word, and finally decided there was only one way to say what she was thinking.

"Old. It makes me feel old."

"You're not old, Mom."

"We both know that isn't true, Dear. I am slowing down. I can't deny it. Maybe I'm trying to do too much. Maybe it's time for me to stop doing my volunteer work and relax for the rest of my life."

"I don't think you mean that. You told me once how much you care for these children you advocate for. And how happy it made you feel when their cases were resolved and they could move on to a new, and better, phase of their life."

"That's true. And I still feel that. But anymore, I feel like I'm just seeing the negative. I dwell on the cases that have gone wrong, and wonder what I should have done differently. How I could have changed things."

Teri stood then, adding emphasis to her next words.

"Don't do that to yourself. You can't change the world. You know that. All you can do is try your best to make a difference for these kids. That's what you signed up for."

Teri allowed time for a reply, then continued when none came.

"These children are better off, thanks to the work you perform. I'm sure you *do* make a difference in their lives."

"I know I try. I honestly do."

"Nobody expects anymore from you, Mom. I'm sure of it."

"That may be true."

Now it was Beverly's turn to stand. She took several measured steps across the room, then turned to face Teri.

"But what about my expectations? What about the things I expect from myself? Have I truly accomplished what I set out to do? Or have I failed myself?"

Chapter Twenty-Two:

THINGS WERE getting easier at school now. The old routines, the familiar faces, helped to ease Pamela into a sense of normalcy. She managed to reconnect with some of her friends during this time, which went a long way toward improving her situation and her state of mind.

Sally Murphy was the first of her former acquaintances to approach her. Pamela was at her locker between classes when Sally stopped by. And though they only had a few minutes to spare, each of them bound for a different class with the ringing of the bell, it felt good to have someone talk to her that wasn't demanding explanations from her.

"How are you doing, Pam?"

"Okay."

Sally frowned, expressing her disbelief with her friend's remark.

"No. Really." Pamela continued. "I'm feeling much better now. I guess I was just confused about things for a while. That's all."

"And not anymore?"

"No. Not anymore."

"That's good to hear, girl. What would I do without you around to help me with my science homework?"

"So that's all I am to you?" Pamela laughed. "A tutor?"

"Of course not. You know that isn't true. I just want to see you smiling again."

"I try."

"Well, you keep right on trying. I'll catch up with you later. Okay."

"You got it."

It felt nice to have a normal conversation with someone.

After that it was like the dam had burst. More students approached her, even people she didn't really know, expressing their good wishes and telling her how nice it was to see her back at school and doing well. It felt good to be recognized and acknowledged, even though it had taken something as stupid as a suicide attempt to get noticed.

The attitude of the teachers started to change as well. At first it was as though they were uncertain how to handle her; like they were afraid of saying the wrong thing and causing further problems. So they steered clear, and allowed the teenager her alone time. And even though Pamela realized they may have meant well, it actually ended up making her feel more isolated and by herself.

It didn't take long for Pamela to come to the conclusion that her life wasn't about to change unless she took an active role in things. With that in mind, she readjusted her attitude. Never a model student, she started to participate more in class. She volunteered information, and was ready to answer when called upon. The instructors, recognizing the change, became more responsive to her, which made the adjustment that much easier.

Life became more bearable, then. Each day less of a burden.

She still struggled at night, fighting the nightmarish images that refused to relinquish their hold on her. She was restless, and woke up often. Each morning she dragged herself out of bed, even though she felt sleep had eluded her, and forced herself to move.

She remained quiet around her uncle, a situation he almost seemed to cultivate. He was so patient, and understanding, quick to reply to her occasional questions but not forcing her to open up until she was ready to. It had been good of him to give her a place to live, and Pamela realized she owed him some kind of consideration, or at least an explanation of sorts, to help him to understand what was bothering her.

But how could she talk to him about any of it?

How could she talk to anyone?

So their relationship remained unaltered. Brian gave her the space she needed, biding his time, while she worked things out on her own.

She had only seen Tim and Angie a couple of times since the incident.

That's how she thought of it now. As an incident; something from her past that was best not to dwell on.

She felt ashamed, with everything she had done and everything she was putting Tim and Angie through. She had let them down. They were no doubt hurting from the restrictions she had put on their lives, and the adjustments they now had to endure because of her actions. That was another hurdle she needed to face; another bridge that needed to be constructed, to close the gap that now lay between them. But Pamela wasn't certain how to accomplish the feat. She knew it was something that had to be done. But she couldn't imagine how.

Aaron made it a point to sit with Pamela at lunch a couple of times each week. On one occasion his brother Evan joined them. They were easy to talk to. They seemed comfortable with one another. She couldn't help but wonder if it was some sort of twin thing. They kept the conversation light, and – after their initial meeting – never mentioned the issues Pamela was facing.

She was still curious about something Aaron had said, during their first conversation together. It had been a flippant remark, delivered in jest, but she was certain there had to be a kernel of truth behind the comment. And it made her wonder.

She finally worked up the courage to broach the subject.

"You didn't really burn down your grandparents' house? Did you?"

Evan, with no hesitation, responded for his brother. "He sure did. You should have seen it. Flames shooting up everywhere. Firetrucks. The whole spiel."

"Why, that's horrible. Did anyone get hurt?"

"No. Nothing like that. We all recovered from it. Everything's good now."

"But why?" She stared at Aaron, is if seeing him for the first time. "Why would you do something like that?"

Evan continued the conversation. Considering what they were talking about, Pamela was surprised he kept a smile on his face during the discourse.

"He claims he hears voices. But I think that's something he's just making up."

Aaron, also smiling, turned away slightly, as if he could hear someone talking to him. He responded to the imaginary person beside him.

"What's that? My brother's a doofus? You can say that again!"

"Are you hearing voices now?" Pamela asked, a shocked expression on her face.

"He's just pulling your leg," Evan replied.

Both boys laughed but, a moment later, Aaron's attitude transformed into something more serious. Gone was the happy, carefree teenager of a moment ago. His voice contained an underlying sadness as he addressed her.

"I've been diagnosed with COS. Childhood-Onset Schizophrenia. And yes, I do hear voices talking to me. Or at least I used to. It hasn't happened for a long time now. But a few years ago they bothered me. A lot. They convinced me to do… …bad things. It was a tough time for all of us."

Evan joined the conversation. "It was pretty rough for my mother. Dealing with a child going though that, and all.

Things were better after Ted came back. And we were a family again. But still –."

"The thing is," Aaron interrupted, "we got through it. It was a bad time, and I try not to think about it. I can't forget what I did, or pretend it never happened, but it doesn't do any good to dwell on the past, either. So we can joke about it. Me and Evan. But believe me. It was rough."

"I'm sorry," Pamela said. "I had no idea. I didn't mean to pry."

"No. That's okay. It's part of who I am. But I was able to move on. And that's what you need to do. When things start looking dark again, just think about me. If I can get over what I went through, what you're going through should be a piece of cake."

Pamela wasn't certain if that was true, but she appreciated the encouragement.

"Thank you, Aaron. For sharing with me. I'm sure it wasn't easy."

Evan, a mischievous glint in his eye, leaned closer.

"Don't let him fool you. He likes to talk about himself. Enjoys the sympathy."

The young boy stood then, and punched his brother playfully on the arm.

"Come on, Aaron. We better head to class now. Catch you later, Pamela."

Chapter Twenty-Three:

CONSULTATION TRANSCRIPT # 2211025 – EXCERPT

Dr. B:
Tell me about your parents. Your biological parents.

Pa W:
Do I have to?

Dr. B:
We've been over this before, Pamela. We don't have to talk about anything you're uncomfortable with.
But I feel it would encourage your growth to come to grips with the complications that are bothering you. Unresolved issues have a way of festering. They never do go away. They only become more ingrained if we allow them to linger. They must be confronted to fully remove them from our psyche.

Pa W:
But I thought they had gone away. I thought I was over all that.

Dr. B:
But you were wrong?

Pa W:
Yeah. I was wrong.

Dr. B:
What happened?

EXTENDED SILENCE

Dr. B:
So tell me about your parents. Your biological parents. What were they like?

Pa W:
I think my mother was a lonely person. Whenever I think of her it saddens me. She was hurting inside. I'm sure of it. I guess a part of me understands that now.

Dr. B:
In what way?

Pa W:
When I tried to kill myself, I knew I was running away. Trying to get away from things that were hurting me.
I think my mother was running away, too. I guess I can even understand now why she drank so much, why she was so desperate to escape. But I don't know what from.
I think something bad must have happened to her. When she was young. I don't know what it was. But a couple of times she said things. And I could hear the hurt in her voice.
You know, I never met my grandparents. That is, my mother's parents.

Dr. B:
That's too bad. Familial ties can be important. They can impact our lives in substantial ways. Good or bad, they shape our thoughts and influence our perceptions of the world and

everything around us.

Pa W:
Well, they must have done a great job with her. She was pretty messed up.

Dr. B:
Did she drink a lot?

Pa W:
I don't think I can remember seeing my mother when she wasn't drunk. Or getting drunk. Or going to the store to get something to drink.
I remember walking to the corner with her one day. It was cold out. It must have been winter, because I can remember the snow on the trees. And how dirty the streets were, with all the slush and stuff.
Isn't it funny that I can still remember that?
She bundled me up real good. She always made sure I was warm. But she didn't put a coat on herself. It was like she was in so much of a hurry to get to the store that she couldn't be bothered to put a coat on.
She was going to the corner to get something to drink.
She was always drinking.

Dr. B:
That must have been difficult to understand. Especially for an impressionable young child.

Pa W:
I guess it didn't bother me. Not then, anyway. It just seemed normal to me. I suppose I figured that's what everyone did.
But she was never bad to me.
Sometimes she would yell at me. But that was only when she wasn't feeling good.
I think she tried. In her own way, I think she tried.

And I think her world fell apart even more when they took me away.

Dr. B:
What makes you say that?

Pa W:
Just in the way she acted. Like she lost interest in everything.
Even me.
Though, at the time, I felt abandoned by her. Like she didn't want me anymore.

Dr. B:
That would be difficult for anybody. And you were how old at the time?

Pa W:
I was six when it all started. By the time Tim and Angie adopted me I had turned seven.
You know, my mother never even said goodbye to me.
She just stopped coming to visits.
And after the adoption hearing she was supposed to visit one last time.
But she never did.
She never did.

EXTENDED SILENCE

Pa W:
And yet....
I still love her.
I don't know why.

Dr. B:
The maternal bond between mother and child is a tremendous connection. Babies will fixate on the first person they see.

Most often, and certainly in an ideal world this would be the case for every infant, that person is their mother. The attachment is immense, and can last a lifetime.

And consider as well, there's the chance that your mother was a different person altogether when you were born. Perhaps things weren't as hard on her then. Perhaps she hadn't started her drinking yet, and did provide the nourishment and enrichment a young child requires to thrive.

Pa W:

That's a nice way of looking at it. I only wish I could believe it was the truth.

I don't ever recall her being any different than I remember her. As a person that drunk too much.

But I still loved her. Even with all her faults. I still loved her.

Dr. B:

Why do you suppose that was?

Pa W:

I don't know. I guess I never really stopped to think about it.

Maybe it's 'cause I realize some things now that I didn't realize then.

Dr. B:

Such as?

Pa W:

Such as what life is really like. How hard it can be. It's not all pretend and playing with dolls, is it?

Dr. B:

That's all part of growing up, Pamela. We see the world under new, and more encompassing, horizons. We start to recognize that things aren't always right or wrong. The world is a multicolored spectrum that is often blind to us when we're

young.
Though, sad to say, many children get exposed to these harsh realities at a younger age than they should.

Pa W:
You mean me?

Dr. B:
What do you think?

Pa W:
I think the world can be pretty lousy at times. I found that out early and I'm still learning it.
But I did love my mother. I guess, in a way, I still do.
I wonder sometimes whatever happened to her.
I wonder if I should try to find her. To talk to her. Maybe ask her why all these bad things happened to me like they did.

Dr. B:
Many adopted children do seek out their birth parents. And for some it can be a good – even therapeutic – experience.
But for others the disappointment can be overwhelming.
From what you say, your mother was a troubled soul, searching for answers she never found. Do you really think she can answer any of your questions? When she couldn't answer any of her own?
That's a lot to expect from someone, Pamela.

EXTENDED SILENCE

Dr. B:
So what about your biological father?

Pa W:
I used to think I loved him. I used to think he actually cared about me.

Dr. B:
But now?

Pa W:
Can we talk about something else?

Chapter Twenty-Four:

IT WAS purely accidental that Brian Watkins even found the box. It was late November, and he had been getting the garbage together and inadvertently caught the edge of the bag on something in the garage. The resulting tear precipitated a cascade of junk onto the floor.

The empty box, which had been at the bottom of the bag, was one of the first objects to spill out.

Pamela was in her room. Brian tapped lightly on the door, and entered after her greeting.

His words were calm. Almost soothing. "Is there something you want to tell me about?"

She looked at the box in his hand – the words HOME PREGNANCY TEST emblazoned across the front – then turned away. The tears came instantly.

"I'm sorry, Uncle Brian. I wanted to tell you. I was going to tell you. But I didn't know how."

"I assume you took the test?"

She nodded.

"Was it positive?"

She nodded again, then turned to face him.

"Maybe it was wrong. Maybe the test didn't register properly. That could happen. Couldn't it?"

Brian looked at the box, reading the information it supplied. "I don't know anything about this sort of thing. Never thought I would have to. But it says 99% accurate. Those are tough odds to beat, Pamela."

"It was all a mistake. I never thought this would happen. I never expected this to happen."

"We have to let your parents know."

Pamela had been reclining on the bed. She swung her legs around, moving herself to a sitting position on the edge.

"Can't we wait? Until we know for sure?"

"I think this is pretty sure."

"I know. It's just…. It's just…."

The words caught in her throat, but after a few moments she managed to continue.

"What are they going to think of me?"

Brian knelt down on the floor in front of her. He reached his arms out and she fell against him, burying her head in his chest as the tears grew in intensity.

"They'll think their little girl made a mistake," her uncle responded. "You're not the first one this has ever happened to, you know. It's all part of growing up."

"Everybody keeps telling me my problems are all part of growing up," she remarked, the tears garbling her voice. "Isn't there anything good about growing up?"

"Of course there is. But we don't get to choose what comes our way. We have to take all the bad along with the good."

She made no response, though the tears abated slightly.

"But you know, maybe it's all this bad that makes the good seem even better. Did you ever think of that?"

She tried to smile as she made her response.

"If that's true, then somebody owes me a whole bunch of good. 'Cause I sure had my share of the bad stuff."

He gently pushed her away and looked into her eyes. She seemed so much like a little girl, frightened and uncertain and confused.

"Let's get hold of your doctor. See what she has to say about this. Okay?"

She nodded, sniffling back a tear.

"But then we go see your parents. They need to know what's going on."

She started to say something, but he wouldn't allow it.

"You won't be able to hide this for very long, you know. They're going to find out. Don't you think it would be better to let them know now?"

"If you say so."

"You know it's the right thing to do. And I'm sure they'll support you one hundred per cent. With whatever you decide to do."

The last words startled the teenager.

"What do you mean? Whatever I decide to do?"

"You have some tough choices ahead of you, Pamela. Do you even want to have this baby?"

"It's sort of late to ask that question now. Isn't it?"

His reply came in a more subdued tone.

"Not necessarily. There's always abortion."

For a moment they stared at one another, each afraid to speak, as though they had broached a forbidden subject.

"I never considered that," Pamela admitted. "Is that what you would do?"

"I never said that."

"But it is a possibility?"

"Of course it's a possibility. But is it the right one? For you?"

She made no response, pondering the question raised by her uncle's remarks.

"A baby does seem like a lot of work," she admitted at last. "Like it would really tie me down for a while."

"Not just a while. More like for eighteen years."

"I guess I never looked at it that way. Maybe I should get an abortion. It sounds easier, doesn't it?"

"Easier?"

He let the word hang in the air for a moment before continuing.

"It might be easier, Pamela. Right now. But consider this.

"If you are pregnant – and I'm assuming you are – that means you have a life growing inside of you. Right here. Right now. Can you really feel good about yourself if you take that life away? That's a decision that will live with you for the rest of *your* life. It shouldn't be made in haste. Or because it's more convenient."

A silence filled the room, the only sound the steady breathing of the two occupants, until the teenager spoke up.

"No."

She shook her head with a rapid back and forth motion that accented the word.

"No. I want to have this baby."

"Then consider this. Raising a child is never easy. Are you up to the task? Where will you live? Will you need to get a job? Who's going to watch the baby when you're at work?

"I'm sure there's hundreds of things to consider, and all of them are going to change your life."

The questions served to shake her resolve, as she struggled to compose herself.

"I don't know. This is all so sudden. I never thought something like this would happen to me."

"You can't change that now, Pamela. All you can do is make the best of it."

Brian stood, then looked down on his niece with a smile on his face.

"But you're not alone," he pointed out to her. "I'll help when I can. And I know your parents will, too. You'll be okay. I promise you."

Chapter Twenty-Five:

"WHAT WERE you thinking?"

The words hit Pamela like a physical blow. She had anticipated that Angela would take it hard. But she hadn't expected such a feeling of recrimination in her mother's reaction. She felt defensive on the instant and lashed back with the first words that came to mind.

"I guess I wasn't thinking, was I? I guess I'm still a stupid little kid who never learned to grow up."

"Now Pamela –"

Whatever else Tim meant to say was drowned out by his wife's reply.

"You're not stupid, Pamela. But I wonder sometimes if you have any common sense. Do you ever stop to think things through? Consider the consequences of the things you're doing? That's your problem. That's always been your problem. And now you've gotten yourself pregnant."

"That wasn't what I was trying to do. Believe me. If I could do it over again. –"

Angela held her hand out in a gesture of warning, a gesture which effectively put an end to the rest of the teenager's remark.

"Don't even go there, young lady. You did what you did. No amount of wishing is going to change that. Now you have to face up to it."

"It was a mistake. The whole thing was a mistake."

"I'll say it was. So what do you plan to do now about this little mistake of yours? Have you talked to the father about this?"

She turned away, embarrassed, before answering the question.

"No. He doesn't know about it. I don't want him to know about it."

"It's going to be tough to hide when you're walking around with a basketball under your shirt. Or didn't you think about that, either? What am I saying? Of course you didn't think about that. Of all the stupid things to do."

Pamela actually rolled her eyes.

"You said that already," the teenager pointed out.

Angela snapped back a response.

"Well, it's worth repeating. We've talked about these things before, Pamela. We've talked about what can happen if you're not careful. These boys, they're only after one thing. All they think about is sex."

Brian, hoping to make light of the situation, interjected. "Hey, leave us out of this. Not all boys are like that."

She glared at her brother-in-law. "Well, enough of them *are* like that. She should have known better."

A new thought occurred to Angela at that point, as she faced off against Brian.

"And you! She was living under your roof. How could you let this happen to her?"

Pamela was quick to leap to her uncle's defense.

"It wasn't like that. This wasn't Uncle Brian's fault. This happened before I moved in with Uncle Brian. This happened before I...."

Pamela stopped abruptly.

A stunned silence filled the room, as comprehension set in.

"Now I see what's happening," Angela remarked. "This whole thing. This you wanting to jump off a bridge. This whole thing was because of some boy?"

"No. That wasn't it."

"Then what was it?"

Pamela made no reply.

Angela's voice softened as she continued. "I'm just trying to understand what's going on here. You're tearing this family apart. Can't you see that? We can see something's bothering you, but you won't let us in. And now this. This accident with this boy."

"I told you it was a mistake."

"It was a mistake, all right. Maybe that's all you've been all along. One big mistake."

Tim jumped to his feet.

"Angie!"

The word exploded from his mouth.

"How can you say something like that?

"That's it. Stick up for her. Again. That's all you were ever good for, anyway."

It was her turn to stand then. She glared again at her daughter, then stormed into the kitchen.

Pamela was fighting back the tears before her mother even left the room.

"I'm sorry. I really am."

Tim moved closer, intent on comforting the teenager, then halted. He didn't want to undermine his wife's authority. He didn't agree with everything Angela had said. But he knew that, to help their daughter, he and Angela had to be consistent and agree with one another. It was a practice they had employed through Pamela's entire childhood, and he didn't see the point in changing things now.

"You have nothing to be sorry about, Pamela," he finally managed. "And you know your mother didn't mean all the things she said to you. She's hurting too, you know. We both are."

145

"But it's all true. All I do is cause trouble for you guys. That's all I ever do. Even when I was little –."

"Do not go there, Pamela," he interrupted. "Don't even think that. You brought so much happiness into our lives. You have to know that. And your mother knows that. She's just upset now. She's still trying to digest what's going on. That's quite a bombshell you dropped on us."

She smiled, meekly, but said nothing.

Brian awkwardly cleared his throat.

"Maybe we should just leave?"

"No. You two stay. I don't want to leave things like this. Give me a few minutes to talk to her."

Tim got up and followed his wife into the kitchen, uncertain what to say but aware he couldn't leave the situation in its present state.

Angela had a drink in her hand when Tim walked into the kitchen. He glanced at the glass, then gave his wife a questioning look.

"It's only ice tea," she reassured him. "Though maybe I should be drinking something stronger."

Her husband chose to ignore the comment.

"That was quite the scene you put on there, Angie."

"Don't go standing up for her. Of all the stupid things to do –."

"She knows what she did. She knows it was a mistake. She can't change that now. Do you want to make things worse by driving her away?"

"No. Of course not."

"And this on top of what she's been going through."

Angela stepped closer to him. Her expression was one, not exactly of joy, but rather of relief.

"But don't you see? This explains what she's been going through. This is the reason why she's been so upset lately. She found out she was pregnant, probably with a boy she doesn't even know that well, and she doesn't know how to handle it.

The whole thing makes sense now, doesn't it?"

He shook his head. "It doesn't work that way. You heard her. She just found out she was pregnant. She didn't know about it before...."

He stopped. It was still difficult to say the word.

He approached his wife, placing his hands on either side of her waist. She made no reaction to the touch, but he felt encouraged that at least she didn't shake off the gesture.

"Pamela is still our little girl. And her little girl problems have grown into big girl problems. We can't just kiss the hurt and make it go away, like it was a scraped elbow or something.

"She's hurting, Angie. She needs us."

"I know."

She fell forward, placing her head against his shoulder, surrendering herself to the myriad of emotions consuming her.

Her voice had lost its irritation when she continued.

"I just don't know how to handle this. When she was little, and something was wrong, I'd check the parenting books. They covered everything. Sleepless nights. Temper tantrums. It was all there. And it was... ...comforting, I guess, to know that I wasn't the only one going through it.

"But there's no parenting book to help us now. How do we know what to do?"

"We'll find a way. Somehow. We have to. For our daughter's sake."

"I know. And I'll try better. I really will."

"That's good. Because after all, whether you're ready or not, you're going to be a grandmother in less than nine months."

"Don't remind me. I'm not old enough to be a grandmother."

Suddenly a new thought occurred to her.

"What about our parents? Pamela's grandparents? What are we going to tell them?"

"We'll tell them how excited we are to have a new addition to the family on the way."

147

Chapter Twenty-Six:

T HE YOUNG girl that answered the door looked to be about eight years old. She exuded an outgoing, friendly manner; the precociousness of the young and the young at heart.

"Can I help you?"

Tim Watkins spoke up. "We're here to talk to Bobby Beard."

"My brother isn't home right now."

"How about your parents? Can we talk to them?"

"Dad's still at work. But I can get my Mom for you. Wait here."

She left them standing on the front porch and disappeared into the house.

Tim turned toward his wife, a trace of nostalgia in his next words.

"Seeing that little girl, it took me back for a minute. She reminded me so much of Pamela when she was young; the same curly hair, the same brown eyes. I guess I'd forgotten how much she's changed over the years."

Angela made no reply to the observation. Instead she grabbed her husband's hand, as though she needed the support his strength would bring her.

"This isn't going to be easy, is it?" she asked at last.

"No. But it has to be done."

Voices drifted to them from inside. Most of the words were indistinct, but a few comments, in a woman's raised voice, could be distinguished by the waiting couple.

"So who are they?" The reply was inaudible, but the "Then why didn't you ask them?" carried clearly to where they stood on the front porch.

Eventually a woman made an appearance, wiping her hands on a dishrag as she approached. She failed to disguise her annoyance, as though coming to the door was a major disruption of her schedule.

"What's this about?"

"Are you Bobby Beard's mother?"

"Yes I am. I'm Lisa."

She gave the information grudgingly, as though reluctant to divulge anything further than was necessary. It was the type of tone one would use on an unwanted salesperson. Or a new car salesman.

"I'm Tim Watkins. This is my wife Angela. We have something important to discuss with you. Regarding our daughter Pamela."

Recognition came instantly to Lisa. Her hand flew up to her mouth, stifling an exclamation.

"Oh! Pamela. We heard what happened. Or what almost happened. Thank God she was stopped in time. I'm so sorry for you. I just can't imagine what you must be going through."

Tim nodded. "Well, we were lucky. But now there are some other... ...complications. May we come in for a minute? There's some things we need to discuss with you regarding your son."

"What's my son got to do with anything?"

Tim glanced at his wife before continuing. Her face was set, resolved to complete the unpleasant chore they had set out to accomplish.

"I think it would be better if we talked inside," Tim informed her.

"Certainly," Lisa replied, her manner still hesitant. "We

can talk in the living room."

She led the way to a room furnished with family pictures. The smiling faces of Bobby and Hannah watched from every corner of the room, as though the area had been decorated as a shrine to the children. Pictures of her son in his football uniform dominated one wall. Several of the photos were posed, though many appeared to be action shots taken during various sporting events. Another wall showcased the young girl who had greeted them at the front door, posing in a ballerina outfit and various other dance costumes. One appeared to be a Christmas pageant of some sort, with the dancers decorated in flamboyant reds and greens.

"You're daughter's adorable," Tim began, hoping to alleviate the nervousness he felt.

Bobby's mother stole a glance at the collage of pictures surrounding them. A smile lit her face, the joy of a pleased mother shining through.

"We're very proud of her." She was quick to amend the declaration. "We're proud of both of them."

They were seated by now. Lisa resumed in a business-like manner, with an attitude that seemed somehow cold considering the subject. "We were all so sorry to hear about Pamela. I hope she's okay?"

"She's doing better now," Angela remarked. "Or at least, we think she's doing better now. She seems to be over the worse of it."

"That's good. Poor thing. But I still don't understand what any of this has to do with us?"

Tim managed to keep his voice calm. "It concerns your son. Your daughter said Bobby isn't home. Do you know when he'll be back?"

"Bobby?"

"Yes."

"I don't know."

She glanced around the room, as if noticing for the first time it was only the three of them.

She called out toward the back of the house. "Hannah? Do you know where Bobby is?"

The young girl shouted her reply. "Basketball practice."

"That's right. He's at basketball practice."

Lisa's words continued in a rush, the woman warming up to a subject she was interested in.

"Bobby is such an athlete. He just excels at everything he does. He's the captain of the football team, you know. He's such a good boy. Does well in school. There's talk he may even get a scholarship to the University of Toledo. We're very proud of him."

Tim managed somehow to find an opening when she stopped to take a breath.

"We need to talk to you about Bobby. This concerns him."

"But he's not here. Look, whatever this is about, it sounds like you're making too big of a deal about it."

"Our daughter Pamela. She's pregnant. She says Bobby is the father."

"What?"

Lisa shook her head in denial.

"No. There must be some mistake. It couldn't have been Bobby. It must have been some other boy."

"Pamela tells us it was Bobby."

"Then she's lying to you."

"Our daughter doesn't lie."

"Of course not. She's too well-adjusted to do that." The sarcasm dripped from her words. "What else would you expect from someone that tried to jump off a bridge?"

Angela was on her feet in a second, preceding her husband by moments only. Tim grabbed his wife in time to restrain her, certain that had he not done so Bobby's mother would have received a slap across the face.

Angela radiated anger. "How dare you talk like that about our daughter?"

"And how dare you accuse my son of such a shameful

thing? Bobby's a good boy. He's well liked, and well respected I might add, everywhere he goes. He doesn't need the likes of you two coming in here and slinging trash at him. And making these baseless accusations."

Angela gritted her teeth, holding back the words she wanted to say. Somehow she restrained herself enough to continue.

"Your... son... got... our... daughter... pregnant."

"So she says. I just think it's highly unlikely."

Tim held his hand up to his lips, cautioning his wife to silence, then faced Bobby's mother.

"I'm sure this is all totally unexpected, Lisa. I can understand your shock. Believe me, it hit us by surprise as well. But it doesn't change the facts. Our daughter is going to have a baby. Your son is the father. As such, I think we have a lot to talk about."

Anything further that might have been said was interrupted by the slamming of the front door and a flippant remark from the hallway.

"Mom? I'm home. Boy am I famished. What's for dinner?"

Bobby Beard walked in the room but froze instantly at sight of the visitors. He wore dirty sweat clothes. His hair, wet from an afternoon shower, was plastered to his forehead. He looked rough and wild, every bit the football player he was. But his expression, taking in the new arrivals, was that of a scared little boy caught with his hands in the cookie jar.

Angela took a step toward him.

"Is this Bobby?"

Bobby, bewildered, looked toward his mother for guidance.

"What's going on here?"

"These people. These...." Lisa stumbled for a word, then gave up on the attempt. "They're here to see you, Dear. They claim –."

"We don't *claim* anything," Angela remarked. "What

we're saying is the truth. Pamela is pregnant."

Bobby paused to consider the pronouncement before continuing.

"Pamela?"

It was all he could manage for the moment.

"Pamela Watkins," his mother supplied.

Lisa was on her feet by now. She had walked over to her son, and was standing now between him and the two visitors. It was as though she felt the need to protect him; like she was some kind of guard dog.

"You know," she continued, in the type of voice usually reserved for the very young. It was like she was talking to a six-year-old, rather than to the strapping teenager confronting them. "The girl from your school. These are her parents. They claim their daughter is going to have a baby, and they insist that you're the father. Can you believe this nonsense?

"Tell them Bobby. Tell them how wrong they are."

Three pairs of eyes focused on the young man.

For a moment he remained silent, collecting his thoughts. His chest swelled, as if he was going to give them a piece of his mind.

But then he exhaled. Like a slowly deflating balloon, all the energy escaped from him. He looked toward the floor, in an attempt to avoid their stares.

His answer was meek. Barely audible.

"It's true."

He took a deep breath and lifted his head. His voice was stronger now.

"If Pamela says I'm the father, then it must be true."

"No."

Lisa's hand moved toward her son, as though she could silence the words he had just said. Her face was a mixture of outrage and embarrassment. She looked at Tim and Angela, as though seeking help from them, but found no sympathy in that direction.

Chapter Twenty-Seven:

"**I** CAN'T understand how you could be so nice to that woman? She simply infuriated me. Someone needs to tell that boy's mother what she can do with that attitude of hers."

"It wouldn't have helped, Angie. I didn't see any reason to make a bad situation worse."

"Is that all this is? A bad situation?"

"Of course not."

Tim averted his eyes from the road long enough to look at his wife. He smiled, but she never noticed. She stared out the windshield into the darkness, seeing nothing, brooding over the recent conversation with Bobby Beard and his mother.

It had rained earlier, but by the time they were driving home from the confrontation the temperature had dropped. The precipitation had changed from sleet to snow, the white particles beginning now to cover the surroundings. It made driving more of a chore, but it also made the darkness of November a bit brighter. The whiteness reflecting the available light presented a sheen to the trees and bushes along the side of the road. Several houses they passed were already decorated for Christmas; the multi-colored lights added to the glow, sparkling as the fine flakes of snow swirled in the slight breeze of the evening.

It wasn't late but traffic was light. That was normal for the first snow of the season, Tim reflected. People were afraid of it. It was like every year the entire city of Toledo had to learn winter driving all over again.

Angela still fumed in the passenger seat beside him.

"You may as well get used to it," Tim continued. "They're part of the family now."

"No they aren't. They're not part of *my* family. Or Pamela's. You heard what Pamela told us. She doesn't want anything to do with that boy. Well, I don't blame her."

"It may not be that easy."

The traffic light changed to red ahead of them. Tim coasted to a stop, feeling a slight slippage beneath the wheels from the thin layer of ice that coated the street.

He stole a quick glance at his wife.

"It takes two to make a baby, Angie. We can't very well keep the boy away from his child. If he wants to be a part of the baby's life then, like it or not, we have to allow that."

"Well, I don't like it. And I don't see why I have to allow it. You saw their attitude. Like they didn't even care."

"They were surprised, Angie. Like we were. This isn't an easy situation for any of us. Especially Pamela."

"Don't remind me. I can't help but wonder how Pamela is going to get through all this. On top of everything else."

She shifted in her seat, to face her husband more directly.

"What happened to our little girl, Tim?"

"She grew up."

"When did that happen? It seems like only yesterday she was playing with her dolls. When her biggest concern was taking care of her artificial babies. And now she's going to have a real one of her own. Is she ready for that?"

"Are we ready for that?"

"We're going to have to be. She needs our help more than ever now."

"And she's got it. She knows that. But still…."

She stopped. A silence hung in the air, interrupted only by the intermittent swish of the windshield wipers. It felt stuffy in the car – a cocoon of warmth enveloped them.

Tim began anew.

"Remember when we decided to become foster parents? How excited we were?"

"It was a great opportunity," she admitted. "We could finally have a family. Something we'd been wanting for a long time."

"But it wasn't easy, was it? All the interviews. Attending parenting classes. Getting the house inspected, and then approved for children."

"I thought it would never end," she admitted. "There certainly were a lot of hoops to go though."

"And then when the day finally came. And we met Pamela for the first time…."

Angela, drawn into the conversation in spite of herself, took over the narrative. "I can still remember her standing on the sidewalk the day we first met her. Her clothes were wrinkled. One of her shoes was untied. Do you remember that? It's funny how vivid that memory is to me. I felt like she was something from one of those Charles Dickens stories. A lost waif of the streets.

"And she was so sad."

"It was a trying time for her, Angie."

"I'm sure it must have been. I guess in some ways I never considered what she was going through. I was so involved in our lives. And the changes *we* were going through. It must have been so hard for her."

"But we were there for her," Tim reminded.

He stole a quick glance at his wife. There was a trace of a smile on her face now. The bitterness of a few minutes ago had disappeared. Tim could only surmise that Angela was lost now in the remembrance of a happier time in their lives.

"*You* were there for her Angie."

"I didn't have a choice, did I? She was counting on us."

"She's still counting on us."

Chapter Twenty-Eight:

LISA SUTTER paced back and forth in the confines of her kitchen, like an animal trapped in a cage with nowhere to go. She was distraught; annoyed that nobody else could see the sense in what she had to say.

"This doesn't change anything," she announced.

"It sort of does, Mom."

Bobby sat at the table, across from his stepfather. Alec had arrived home shortly after Angela and Tim had departed. Lisa, still upset regarding the bombshell delivered by Pamela's parents, had related to her husband the news of the young girl's pregnancy. He had remained silent during the recitation, taking in her words and keeping his thoughts regarding the matter to himself, though he seemed particularly attentive to what his wife had to say.

Finally Lisa stopped her pacing, to take up a position by her son's side. She placed a hand on his shoulder, in a maternal show of support.

The teenager refused the affection by shrugging the gesture aside.

"But it doesn't have to change anything," she reiterated. "You have your whole life ahead of you, Bobby. Don't throw it away because of one foolish indiscretion with some girl you hardly even know."

157

"Indiscretion?" Alec uttered the single word, then fell silent following the glare he received from his wife.

Lisa resumed her pacing. "You know what I mean. Just because some crazy girl claims –."

"Pamela isn't crazy," her son interrupted.

"Don't stand up for her, Bobby. Who else but a crazy person would try to jump off a bridge? It's obvious the girl has some mental issues. She has her own problems. Do you really want to get involved with someone like that?"

She allowed him no opportunity to respond, as her words continued in a steady flow of emotion.

"And no matter how you feel about it, or how you feel about her, this doesn't have to change things. It doesn't have to screw up *your* life. You can still go to UT next fall. Get a degree. Make something of yourself. Don't let this mistake ruin your life for you."

"What about Pamela?"

Lisa made a motion with her hand, waving the idea away.

"She'll be okay. Her parents will take care of her."

Alec spoke up again. "That's a pretty cold attitude, isn't it, Lisa?"

"It's realistic, Alec. That's what it is. If the girl isn't responsible enough to keep herself out of trouble, then she'll just have to live with the consequences. It will be a good lesson to her."

"What about Bobby's consequences?"

"That's what I'm talking about!"

She threw her hands in the air, annoyed because her husband couldn't see the logic in what she was saying, before continuing.

"Is Bobby supposed to throw his whole life away because of this? I just want what's best for him. Can't you see that?"

She looked from Alec to Bobby and back again, searching for any sign of agreement from either one of them. But none was forthcoming.

"Come on, Lisa. You don't really mean that. What's best for him is to accept some responsibility and do what's right."

"What's right? How do we even know the baby is his? How do we know these people aren't just trying to take advantage of us? Looking for a free ride because they know Bobby's a good kid? Their daughter gets herself in trouble and they figure a good kid, a good kid like Bobby, is going to come to her rescue. It's not fair to him. And it's not fair to us. To put our family through something like this."

"The baby is mine, Mom. It must be. Pamela wouldn't say it if it wasn't the truth."

Her tone softened to a soothing lilt. "She's just trying to use you, Dear. That's all there is to it. Don't let them do it. Don't throw your life away –."

"It's my life!" Bobby stood. "I think I should have a say in it."

"Do you now? Well, you should have thought of that when you were fooling around with this girl. But you weren't thinking of that, were you? And now all of a sudden you think you have all the answers."

"Now, Lisa –."

"Don't say another word, Alec. This is between me and my son. Yes, my son. Bobby isn't your son."

"Then maybe you should ask Bobby's father what he thinks of this whole situation?"

"Don't think I won't. You can be certain I'll talk to Frank about this the first chance I get. I'm sure he'll agree with me. There's not a lot the two of us do agree on. But he's always wanted what's best for Bobby."

Bobby laughed at the thought.

"Sure he did," the teenager commented. "That's why he left us when I was only a baby. Left you to take care of the two of us while he went running off with his girlfriend."

"I won't be making any excuses for what your father did. What he did was wrong."

"But don't you see, Mom? You're asking me to do the same thing. You want me to run away from Pamela and her baby. Just like Dad did to us."

She was shaking her head no before Bobby even completed speaking. "It's not the same thing."

"Of *course* it's the same thing."

"Do you love her?"

The question startled Bobby. "What?"

"I asked if you loved her. Do you love this girl?"

"Oh come on, Mom. We hardly know each other."

"Sounds like you got to know her pretty well."

"You know what I mean."

"Yes. I know what you mean. This was only a physical attraction with you. That's what this was. Do you want to marry a girl you don't even care for?"

Alec voiced the next question.

"Marry? Who said anything about them getting married?"

Lisa smirked, as if she had exposed the fallacy in her husband's thinking and revealed how illogical he was being.

"Weren't you talking about consequences?" she reminded him. "And responsibilities? Well, if you want Bobby to do the right thing maybe he should marry the girl. They could move in with us together.

"Or maybe they'll get themselves a nice little apartment somewhere and live happily ever after."

"You know that's not going to happen."

Lisa's voice grew louder, adding emphasis to her words.

"Of *course* that's not going to happen. Because Bobby is NOT going to throw his life away because of some crazy girl. He's going to graduate from high school. He's going to go to college. He's going to get a degree, and a good job, and make me proud. Like he always has."

"Make you proud? Make you proud, Mom? Will you be proud of me if I turn my back on this girl when she needs me?"

"She doesn't need you. She has her parents to take care of her. She'll be all right."

"How do you know that?"

"I don't know that. Of course I don't. But I do know this. If you stay involved with this girl your life is going to change. And not for the good. It's not easy raising a child. You don't know what it's like –."

Bobby turned away, as though he had heard enough. "Not this again."

"Don't you turn away from me, young man. I'm talking to you."

He faced her once more, his expression an impassive mask. "Listen, Mom. You don't need to tell me again how tough things were when Dad left. You've told me a hundred times already."

"Well, maybe you should listen once in a while."

"I don't have to, Mom. I've heard it all before."

He sulked from the room.

His mother watched the departing figure, continued watching the vacant doorway for long moments after he left, then turned toward her husband.

"Do you believe that kid?"

"He's not completely wrong, you know."

"Now don't you get started. He's a teenager. What does he know about life? All he knows is football. He throws a ball and scores a touchdown and the crowd cheers while he soaks in the adoration. That's not real, Alec. That's a fantasy. He doesn't know how tough life can be."

"He's about to find out."

"But he doesn't have to."

Lisa sat down, reaching out for her husband. She grabbed his hands, caressing them as she looked into his eyes with a pleading that begged for his help.

"He's my little boy. I have to protect him."

"He has to grow up sometime."

"But not like this."

"He got a girl pregnant, Lisa. This isn't something you can just sweep under the rug and forget about. He needs to do the right thing."

"The right thing?"

She released her grip on his hands. Lisa sat back, staring across the table at her husband before continuing.

"The right thing is for Bobby to get on with his life. That's the right thing. I don't know why you think otherwise. What difference does it make to you what he does, anyway?"

"What if this happened to Hannah? What if it was our daughter that was in trouble right now?"

She shook her head back and forth, vehemently dismissing the suggestion.

"Hannah would never do anything this stupid. She's not a bad kid."

"So Pamela's crazy *and* bad?"

Lisa stood abruptly, as though she had something to say, then turned and stormed out the door.

She returned not twenty seconds later.

"Bobby is not your son," she reminded her husband. "He's my son. My baby. And I'll do whatever I have to, to keep him away from that girl.

"And if you don't like it, you can just...."

She stopped abruptly, flustered and embarrassed with herself at the same time.

As she left the room Alec could hear her mumble.

"Well, you know what you can do with it."

Chapter Twenty-Nine:

CONSULTATION TRANSCRIPT # 2212015 – EXCERPT

Dr. B:
You're more quiet than usual this morning, Pamela. I note a certain amount of reticence in your manner.

Pa W:
I don't know what that means.

Dr. B:
You're more reserved than normal, that's all. I feel you've begun to open up to me lately, and I would like to see that continue as we move along with our sessions.
Is there something disturbing you? Something you want to discuss?

Pa W:
I was stupid. That's all. And I did a stupid thing.

Dr. B:
We all do stupid things, from time to time. That doesn't mean you're stupid. It means you're human.

Pa W:
I'm pregnant.

Dr. B:
I see. How do you feel about that?

Pa W:
I'm scared, Dr. Bargalony. I never thought this would happen. We were only fooling around. That's all it was. I never expected it would lead to this.
I thought sex was supposed to be fun. The other girls.... I've heard them talking. About the things they've done. They always sounded so excited. So happy.

Dr. B:
Sex can be a wonderful experience, Pamela. If the circumstances are right. And if it's with the right person.
Was this the right person?

Pa W:
No.
I hate Bobby. I hate what he did to me. I never want to see him again.

Dr. B:
I'm confused, Pamela. If you hate the boy, why were you intimate with him?

Pa W:
I didn't hate him. At least, not when we did it. I was excited. I was excited when he asked to see me. And I was excited when we were together. It was something I never did before, and I was looking forward to it so much.
But it wasn't what I expected.

Dr. B:
Did he force himself on you?

Pa W:
No. It was nothing like that.
But I didn't enjoy it. Not like I thought I would. I was expecting this magical experience. This closeness. Like you see in the movies.

Dr. B:
Sex, as represented in the movies, is on many occasions far removed from reality.
It can be portrayed beautifully, and this is often the case when two people are in love. They can share an intimacy together that can be life changing.
But too often it's presented as a casual thing, merely for entertainment with no lasting value. An experience to be enjoyed and then forgotten, like anything else we do. You go out to a movie. You share a dinner together. Then you have sex and you each go your separate ways.
This is how it happens. Sometimes.
But it's not healthy. It's not the basis of a good relationship. It can leave a person feeling lonely and isolated and, instead of bringing people together, it can tear them apart.
Not to mention the consequences.

Pa W:
You don't have to tell me about that. I'm living the consequences right now.

Dr. B:
Becoming pregnant isn't the only consequence, though admittedly it is a significant one.
But there are other health factors involved. When you have sex with a man, it's like you're have sex with every woman he's ever been with. You expose yourself to a plethora of diseases

and complications.

Pa W:
I guess I wasn't thinking things through very well, was I?

Dr. B:
You're not the first one to make that mistake.
But these errors in judgment, these hasty decisions we make in our lives, can be true learning experiences. They can help us to grow in so many ways.

Pa W:
I don't know if I'm ready for it.

Dr. B:
I'm afraid, at this point, you don't have a choice in the matter.
What does the young man have to say about it?

Pa W:
I haven't talked to him. I don't want to talk to him.

Dr. B:
He needs to know.

Pa W:
Oh he knows, all right. My parents went over there last night and saw him.
But as far as I'm concerned he's not part of my life.

Dr. B:
But he is the baby's father. You can't exclude him. He's entitled to a say in the child's future.

Pa W:
Not as far as I'm concerned. I can do this by myself. I can take care of things alone.

Dr. B:
But you're not alone.
I'm sure your parents will be there to support you.   How do they feel about it?

Pa W:
They've been pretty good, all in all.
Angie went spastic at first. Telling me it was just another one of my stupid mistakes. She's always been quick to criticize me.

Dr. B:
That must be hurtful.

Pa W:
It is.
Or it was. At first.
I've sort of gotten used to it. It's just her way of dealing with things.
She's always been that way. Even when I first came to live with them.

Dr. B:
It must have been a disappointment to you. Considering what you were used to.

Pa W:
It was.
My mother…. My real mother…. She was always so distracted with things. With her drinking.
She never took the time to teach me anything.
So I guess there were a lot of things I didn't know about. I was pretty naive about so much.
There was so much I needed to learn.
I guess I'm still learning, aren't I?

Dr. B:
Life is the ultimate learning experience. Embrace it, Pamela. Learn from your mistakes and move forward, confidant that you can improve yourself and face adversity as it comes.

Pa W:
I don't believe that. It sounds like empty words to me.
I thought I had moved along. I thought, after ten years, all my problems were behind me. That all my shame was behind me. But it wasn't.
It all came back to me that afternoon with Bobby. It came crashing down in an instant. After ten years it was all still there. I couldn't keep it away. I couldn't hide from it.
And now this. On top of everything else. Seventeen and pregnant. What else can go wrong with my world?
What other stupid mistakes do I have to make?

Dr. B:
A mistake is only stupid if you don't learn from it. If a person continues to behave in a reckless manner then mistakes become habits, and bad ones at that.
Don't let negative thinking prevent you from moving on.
Because you must go on. There are people depending on you.

Pa W:
If you mean Tim and Angie, well, you're wrong. They don't depend on me for nothing. I could leave tomorrow and they wouldn't even notice.

Dr. B:
You know that isn't true. But that's not who I was talking about.

Pa W:
Who, then? Who in this world cares if I live or die?

Dr. B:

How about that spark of life growing in your belly? There's a new soul waiting to be born. Waiting to experience all of life's joys and pleasures.

Pa W:

What about the pain and sorrows? Who wants to experience that?

Dr. B:

We all have to, Pamela. But, more importantly, we all *get* to. It's life's adversities that make us who we are.

Pa W:

Well, it's sure done a great job on me.
Thanks a lot, life. Why don't you just leave me alone, and find someone else to screw around with for a change?

Chapter Thirty:

PAMELA APPROACHED Bobby Beard at his locker, between classes. She was aware of the other students passing by in the hallway, an occasional glance thrown her direction. But she didn't care.

She didn't know how many of them knew what was going on – what *had* gone on – between her and Bobby. She could only assume everybody was aware of it by now. Gossip tends to travel quickly around the school. And if they didn't know by now, they would certainly find out when her body started to change and she was showing the results of her indiscretion

As she looked at Bobby, and reflected on what had occurred, she found herself suddenly thinking about Hester Pryne.

Pamela had read "The Scarlet Letter" the previous year, in her American Literature class. It hadn't made much sense to her then, the whole idea of the shame that Hester would have experienced, and how the "A" on her breast exposed her indiscretion to the rest of the world. The book seemed to be making a big deal out of something that wasn't that important.

Pamela's opinion was different now. It *was* a big deal, this feeling of vulnerability, and being exposed to the crowd and risking ridicule for her behavior.

It made her angry, to think Bobby was the reason for what she was going through, and that anger manifested itself in her attitude as she set her determination to say what she had to say.

"I don't want you in my life, Bobby."

"You already told me that," he snapped back in reply.

"And I don't want you in my baby's life, either."

He reacted immediately.

"Who says I want to be?"

"Good. I'm glad that's settled then."

She started to turn away. He halted her with a single word.

"Wait."

She faced him once more.

"Listen. Pamela. I am sorry."

His voice sounded so apologetic, Pamela almost felt sorry for him. She was still angry, but no longer felt the need to lash out at him. Her tone moderated with her reply.

"We've been through this before, Bobby."

"I know. But I didn't know about…."

He paused, at a loss for words.

"The baby?" she prompted.

"Yes. The baby. I didn't know about the baby. The last time we talked. I guess I'm still sort of getting used to the idea. This changes things, doesn't it?"

"Not as far as I'm concerned. It certainly doesn't change the way I feel about you. Why should it?"

"Because we're going to have a baby. You and me."

She felt a return of the anger, exasperated that Bobby couldn't see the sense in what she was telling him.

"*We're* not going to have anything, Bobby. There is no we. There's only two stupid kids who made a stupid mistake and now I have to pay the stupid consequences. So just forget about we."

"Isn't there anything I can do? To help with things?"

"No. The only thing you can do is stay out of my life. Stay out of *our* life. I think it's better for all of us that way."

Chapter Thirty-One:

IT HAD snowed overnight, the first significant accumulation of the winter. The weather had been unseasonably warm until then. But considering Christmas was only a week away, the snow could hardly be considered as unusual. Especially in northern Ohio.

Beverly had neglected to pull her car into the garage the night before, intending to go out later and take care of it. So now she had to face the consequences for her procrastination.

She started the engine, turned the defroster to high, and stepped out of the car to tackle the unpleasant task of cleaning the windows. By the time the snow had been cleared away, and she sat down behind the wheel, the heater had cranked out enough warm air to the point where the temperature within the vehicle was bearable.

For a moment she considered canceling her visit with Pamela Watkins. She had scheduled it a month ago, but she could always make it later in the month. As long as she stopped by before the end of December she would still meet her CASA requirements.

She quickly dismissed the notion. People had holiday plans. She had holiday plans. To reschedule at this point was an unnecessary complication.

Winter driving didn't really bother her. She had grown accustomed to it years ago. It was the cold, more than anything else, that was an irritation. As she got older she found herself more affected by the extremes of winter.

Maybe she should head South after all.

Her brother Larry had done so six years ago, right after his retirement. Whenever they spoke he was quick to point out to her how nice the weather was in Florida.

"It's supposed to get up to 80 today, Sis," he announced on their last phone call, which had been barely a week ago. They were finalizing their holiday plans, and it had been nice to talk for a while. But as invariably happened, weather was a main topic of conversation.

"I'll be out in my shorts again," Larry continued, "soaking up the rays. What are you wearing this time of year?"

"You know it's cold up here. Quit rubbing it in."

"Just saying, that's all. Maybe you need to consider moving down here where the sensible people live? I don't know why you stay up in the cold north, anyway."

Of course he knew why.

Beverly's life was here. Her kids, and her grandkids, all lived within fifteen minutes of her. It was comforting to know they were all so close, and that at a moment's notice they could get together, and be there for one another. It wouldn't be the same, if she moved down to Florida. Just seeing her family a couple times a year, when they managed to make the trip down to visit her, wasn't enough. They were too much a part of her life to limit her time with them so much.

And her house; everything she and Russell had done over the years, all they had put into the place. Those memories couldn't be replaced. And though the memories would move with her, she knew it wouldn't be the same. Here she could feel his presence. It comforted her on the hard days. It got her through each night without him. The thought of leaving it all behind was more than she wanted to contemplate.

If that meant she had to brush off some snow once in a while, and brave some cold mornings when she'd rather be nestled in front of the fireplace with a hot cup of tea, then so be it.

She dismissed the thoughts of warmer climes and continued her drive, arriving shortly at her destination. She was greeted by Brian, who delivered a rather quixotic reply when she asked what was new.

"I better let Pamela answer that one."

The teenager was in the kitchen, working on some homework. Beverly sat down across from her. Brian excused himself so the two could talk in private.

"Your uncle said you had something to tell me," Beverly began. "Is there something going on I should know about, Pamela?"

"You could say that."

Pamela placed her hand on her stomach. It seemed to comfort her somehow. She smiled at the CASA volunteer, as though about to impart a secret.

"I'm pregnant," she announced.

"Oh my."

Beverly hesitated with her reply, and took a few seconds to attempt to read the young girl's expression. Considering the recent events, and what she was going through following her suicide attempt, Beverly wondered if this type of news was a good thing or a bad thing to a teenage girl still in high school. It certainly complicated the situation, and could be detrimental to the young girl's well-being.

But the smile remained on Pamela's face, encouraging Beverly's reaction.

"I'm happy for you. How are you feeling?"

"Good. Confused, about a lot of things. But good."

"And you're how far along?"

"Two and a half months. Can you tell?"

"I wouldn't have thought it by looking at you. You're

still such a skinny young thing. You barely show."

"It's in there. Believe me. And I have the morning sickness to prove it."

"Has it been bad?"

"Not really. Smells get to me, mostly. Certain odors that just make me want to…."

She finished the comment by wrinkling her face in disgust.

Brian, who had wandered into the kitchen just then to get a glass of water, broke into the conversation.

"She won't let me make bacon anymore. Haven't had a BLT in a month now. I may be going through withdrawals soon."

"Don't even say bacon, Uncle Brian. Just thinking about it makes my stomach turn."

"You know where the bathroom is," he flippantly replied. "I know you do, 'cause I hear you in there every morning when I'm trying to sleep, on your knees and worshiping at the altar of the porcelain goddess."

"So now I'm disturbing your mornings, am I?"

"Hey, a guy needs his rest."

He exited the kitchen, still laughing following the rapport with his niece.

Beverly smiled as she watched the interplay. It seemed so spontaneous. So relaxed. So….

Normal. That was the word she was looking for. After all Pamela had been through, it was pleasant to see her sharing a light moment with someone.

"So when's you're due date?" Beverly asked.

"June 15th. A week after my birthday."

"Then you'll be having a double celebration."

"I hadn't thought of that. It still seems such a long way away."

"It will be here before you know it."

"That's what everyone says."

She paused, as though her mind was somewhere else.

When she resumed, the joyful quality of her voice had evaporated.

"Beverly? Can I ask you something?"

"Certainly, Dear."

"Do you have kids?"

"Two of them. A boy and a girl. Plus three grandchildren, I'm happy to say."

"What's it like? Having a baby?"

It was such a simple question, but there were so many possible answers.

"It changes your world," Beverly admitted at last. "It's amazing that something in such a small package can have so much of an affect on you. On the things you do. On the way you look at life. You'll never be the same again."

"That's not what I meant. I mean…."

"What's it like actually *having* the baby? Giving birth. It scares me to think about it."

"Oh?"

"I mean, I can't talk to Uncle Brian about it. What would he know? And Angie never had one of her own.

"It's just you see women on TV and stuff. They're screaming like it's the most horrible thing in the world. Is it really that bad?"

"For some women, I suppose it is. I can't lie to you, it's painful. And childbirth can last a long time. I spent twenty-three hours in the delivery room with Joey.

"But it's a funny thing about pain. You remember that you had the pain. You remember that it was unpleasant. But the sensation itself goes away. And it's a good thing too, because otherwise no woman in her right mind would ever want to have a second child."

"That's what I was afraid of."

"Don't be afraid, Pamela. That will only make things worse. Just accept it and make the best of things. But it really is a miracle. You'll find that out for yourself, when that baby gets here."

Beverly paused a moment, lost in thought. Visions of Joey and Jennifer as infants returned to her. The recollection brought a smile to her face.

"But maybe I'm prejudiced," the CASA volunteer continued. "After all, I love kids. All of them, regardless of their age. I wouldn't be doing this CASA work if I didn't. Now Russell, he really loved babies."

"Who's Russell?"

"My husband. If there was a baby in the room he was drawn to it. Like it was some kind of magnet. He used to tell me, *Babies are clever packaging by God.* You can't help but love them. They're all wonderful, even though each is unique in their own way."

"That's a nice way of looking at things."

"That's the way Russell was. He was always optimistic. Always saw the good in people."

"He sounds like a wonderful person."

"He was."

Beverly was suddenly overcome with a sensation of melancholy. For long moments silence pervaded the room, with each of them reluctant to continue.

Beverly finally spoke up once more.

"So is it a boy or a girl? Or don't you know yet?"

"My doctor says I'll have a sonogram on the next visit. Then I'll find out."

"And do you want to find out?"

"Of course I do. That way I'll be ready for when she gets here."

"She?"

"I guess I'm hoping for a baby girl. For some reason I'm just thinking that's what it's going to be. Is that silly?"

"Well, you have a fifty-fifty chance anyway."

"Yeah. A daughter of my own would be nice."

"How about your parents? What do they have to say about all this?"

"They're on board. It was a bit of a shock to them, of

course. I mean, it was to me, too. But they seem to be excited about it."

"Where will you be staying? With the baby and all?"

"I don't know. It's been great being here. Uncle Brian is so easy to hang out with. He even plays video games with me. It was almost like a vacation. But I know it can't last forever."

"I'm sure your parents miss you."

"I know they do. And I miss them, too. It's just, with everything that's been going on, it was good to get out of there. For a while, anyway. But I think it will be good to get back, too."

"Is there anything else I need to know before I go? Any other bits of news you need to share?"

"No. I think there's enough going on for now."

"Then I'll see you next month."

Beverly rose from the table. But before she could leave Pamela spoke up again.

"There is one other thing."

"What's that?"

"The first time you visited. You asked me if I remembered you, from when you were my CASA back when I was adopted. Well, I lied."

"Oh? What do you mean?"

"I do remember you, Beverly. I remember you coming to the house every month. You always seemed so cheerful. So optimistic about things. It meant a lot to me. I enjoyed the time we spent together. I was glad when they told me you would be my CASA again.

"It's just that...."

She hesitated. The words came slowly when she finally found them.

"So much happened back then. So many memories. So many *bad* memories. It's hard to believe that was ten years ago. Some things I barely remember. Other things I'll never forget.

"But I tried. I've tried for ten years now. And I thought I was over things. You know? I thought I had left that life behind. Or that it belonged to some other person, and not me, and if I ignored it long enough it wouldn't be part of me anymore.

"And then something happened…."

She stopped abruptly, as though she had said too much.

"That's why I'm here, Pamela. To help you through things. So if there's anything you want to talk about –?"

"No."

She shook her head back and forth defiantly.

"No. I don't want to talk about it. I just want to forget it. And that's why, when you asked if I remembered you, I told I didn't. I couldn't face it. But I do remember how nice you always were to me. It helped then. And it helps now."

"It's been my pleasure getting to know you again, Pamela."

"But all those other things. I don't *want* to remember them. Why can't those things just leave me alone?"

"It takes a long time for the mind to heal. From bad experiences. From grief. And some things you'll never forget. But it does get easier. Believe me. Just take things one day at a time, and someday you'll notice that the sun is still shining. And the sky is still blue. And things aren't nearly as bad as you thought they were.

"You'll get there, Pamela. You'll get there."

Chapter Thirty-Two:

IMMEDIATELY UPON returning home Beverly logged onto her computer. She retrieved her CASA notes pertaining to Pamela Watkins and entered a few comments regarding the latest visit. The situation had changed, due to the young girl's pregnancy. Beverly couldn't help but wonder how this would effect the outcome of the case.

She then checked her list of contact information and dialed the number she was looking for.

She was pleasantly surprised to hear a woman's voice answering the phone, rather than the automated response system employed by most everybody anymore. The receptionist on the other end of the line was crisp and efficient sounding. "Dr. Antonio Bargalony's office. May I help you?"

"Yes. I'd like to speak to Dr. Bargalony, please."

"Are you a patient?"

"No. I'm a CASA volunteer for Lucas County. One of the children I represent is being treated by Dr. Bargalony. I was hoping to speak with him regarding how she's doing."

"What is the patient's name?"

"Pamela Watkins."

"One moment please."

The sound of muzak filled the background once Beverly was put on hold. The wait was longer than she had expected –

probably close to ten minutes – but she was reassured when she recognized the voice that came on the line.

"Dr. Bargalony."

"Good morning. This is Beverly Johnson. From the Lucas County CASA office. We actually met a few years ago, when you were working with Aleisha Turner. I was the CASA for her children."

"I remember, Beverly. How can I help you?"

"I'm advocating now for Pamela Watkins and I have a few questions for you."

"I don't know if I'll be able to answer them."

His reticence failed to surprise her. She was, after all, requesting patient/doctor information.

"If this is a HIPAA thing, I can send you proof of my court authorization, which allows me access to the child's medical issues."

"It's not that, Beverly. Though it would be a good idea for you to fax me that information once we're done talking. My receptionist will give you the number."

"That's fine. I can do that."

"But as far as answering any questions, we're still delving into Pamela's issues. I'm convinced that whatever is bothering her resulted from events that occurred earlier in her life, before she was adopted, and we've barely scratched the surface."

"Then maybe I can help you. I was her CASA ten years ago. Though I've been out of touch with Pamela for all that time, so I'm not current with everything that's been going on lately. I did, however, deal with her adopted parents, as well as her biological parents, at the time of her adoption."

"What were her biological parents like?"

She considered the question, and how to most accurately answer the doctor's query without interjecting any of her personal opinions into the discussion.

"They loved Pamela," she admitted at last. "I never doubted that. I think they just didn't know how to raise a young girl."

"I understand the mother was a heavy drinker."

"That's correct. I don't know how long she had been drinking. Or what her particular issues may have been. But in the time I knew her she was pretty unstable."

"Unstable? In what way?"

"Oh, I don't know."

She searched her mind for the proper word, finally selecting one that summed up her recollection of the woman.

"Inconsistent, I guess. One time she'd show up for a visit, all cleaned up and attentive and supportive of her daughter. Then she would miss two or three visits in a row. By the end of the case she stopped visiting altogether. She didn't even show up for her goodbye visit with Pamela, following the Adoption Hearing."

"Do you know what happened to her after that?"

"No idea. I don't even know if she's still around or not."

"How about the father?"

"Same thing. You have to understand, once the case closes I'm no longer involved. I lost touch with everyone."

"Of course. But how was the father with Pamela? What type of man was he?"

This time she didn't need to consider her reply. Instead, she voiced the first thing that came into her mind.

"He was violent. He was known to strike his wife. Domestic Violence is what got the whole thing started. He even spent more time in jail, during the course of the investigation, for confronting Stephanie – that was his wife – just before the adoption was finalized."

"Did he ever strike Pamela?"

"Not that I heard of."

She paused, to reach into her memories from a decade ago and retrieve what information remained regarding the family dynamics and the issues that had forced the young girl's removal.

"Pamela never said anything to me about it," Beverly informed him. "I think he loved Pamela. He seemed pretty concerned about her. Visited every week. I almost felt sorry for him.

"Of course I felt sorry for the mother, as well. But for different reasons."

"Thank you for the information, Beverly. It coincides with some of the things Pamela has recited to me."

His tone indicated the conversation was over, though Beverly was reluctant to let it end.

"But how is she doing, doctor? She seems better now. Not as moody. But she still hasn't said much to me. Has she given you any indication of what's been bothering her?"

He hesitated. Beverly felt certain he was reluctant to offer anything further, and she was prepared to remind him that as Pamela's guardian in the case she was entitled to all medical information pertaining to the teenager.

But before she could plead her case Dr. Bargalony resumed.

"She's opening up more. She's less reticent about discussing her issues. But as I said, it's early in the process. Therapy can take a long time."

"How about her pregnancy? You know about that, don't you?"

"Yes. Pamela informed me on her last visit."

"Does that change things?"

"It is an additional complication, for certain. But it could be a good thing. She has another life depending on her now. It may make her reconsider her actions differently in the future."

The concept hadn't occurred to Beverly.

"I never looked at it that way."

"It's a possibility, anyway," he acknowledged. "But I must be going now, Beverly. I have a patient coming. So if there's nothing else...?"

"Thank you doctor. Please keep me informed if you run across anything you think I should know about. And I'll fax my information to you as soon as I can."

Beverly's next phone call was to Whitmer High School, which resulted in further wait time on the phone. After speaking with three other people she was eventually connected to Delores Jarecki, who identified herself as Pamela's guidance counselor at the school.

"We're all very concerned about Pamela," the woman informed Beverly. "And we're keeping a close eye on things."

"Have there been any issues? Anything I need to be aware of?"

"No. Pamela appears to be adjusting well, considering what she's been through. Granted, I don't know the particulars behind Pamela's problems. But I'm sure something's going on at home or she wouldn't have even considered suicide."

The way the comment was phrased, Beverly got the definite impression the woman was on a fishing expedition, just trying to find out any detail she could about the teenager's life. And while the school needed to be informed, Beverly didn't feel they needed to be *that* involved with things.

"Pamela has had some issues," the CASA volunteer admitted, choosing to sidestep the issue as much as possible. "But she's working through them and things are looking much better. I just want to be sure she stays on track."

"Of course." There was a trace of disappointment in the woman's voice.

"Are her grades being maintained?" Beverly asked.

"I've spoken with some of her teachers. She's doing well, academically. She may even be applying herself a bit more since this all happened."

"That's good. How about her social interactions? With the other students?"

"I don't think she ever was one to hang out with a big crowd. When she first came back to school I would see her by herself a lot. But that seems to have changed in the last few weeks. No, I would say she's adjusting well, all things

185

considered."

"That's good to hear. Please keep me in mind, Mrs. Jarecki. If anything does change I would like to be informed as soon as possible. So I can stay on top of the situation."

Returning to her computer, Beverly entered the latest morsels of information she had obtained from her phone calls into her CASA notes regarding the case. It was encouraging to hear that Pamela was doing well. All indications were that the young girl was on the mend.

Maybe Dr. Bargalony was right. Maybe having a baby was a good thing for Pamela. As long as there were no further complications during the pregnancy, it may be what she needed to help with her recovery.

For now, Beverly could do nothing else but wait. Cases dragged on; sometimes for far longer than anticipated. She didn't expect that to happen in Pamela's case, but you never knew.

She was pleased with one thing she had learned today.

She apparently had made a difference, ten years ago, when she first advocated for a seven-year-old girl who was torn from her family and adopted by a loving couple. The fact that Pamela still remembered her, a decade after the events, proved it.

Chapter Thirty-Three:

IT JUST didn't feel like Christmas at Angie and Tim's house. It was nice. And there were presents and stuff. But it wasn't like being at the 'partment. It wasn't like being with Mommy and Daddy.

Angie and Tim had a pretty Christmas tree, a really tall one that reached all the way to the ceiling, with all white lights that made the whole room shiny. A really big star was at the top, so big it touched the ceiling of the living room, and it shined brighter than all the other lights. It was a lot bigger tree than we ever had at our 'partment. Tim had to stand on a chair to reach the top, it was so big, and it almost looked like he was gonna fall off, but he didn't.

There were stockings hung up on the fireplace, even a big one with my name on it. Angie told me Santa would fill it up on Christmas Eve when I was asleep, and that there would be candy in it and maybe an apple or some presents. She said Santa liked to leave stuff for good little girls, so I should be getting lots of presents.

I didn't tell them I don't believe in Santa no more. They seemed pretty 'cited 'bout it. And it was fun to pretend with them. Even though I was getting too old for that kind of stuff.

We made cookies together after decorating the tree, me and Angie and Tim, and that was fun. Angie let me help a lot. I got to pick up pieces of cookie dough with my hands, and even got to use the rolling pin to make the cookies flat. But Angie had to help me with some of it, and it was awful messy. I had to change my clothes when we were all done 'cause I was covered with flour and sugar and cookie stuff.

They had lots of cookie cutters with lots of diff'rent shapes. We made cookies that looked like a snowman. And cookies that looked like a Christmas tree. They even had one that looked like a sled, but that cookie kept breaking so we didn't make too many of them.

When the cookies were all done Angie made some icing. There was green icing and red icing and blue icing, and some of the icing was white. The cookies looked nicer with the icing on them, and they let me have a couple of them with a big glass of chocolate milk.

They told me it would be a lot of fun on Christmas, because there would be some kids visiting that were my age and we could all play together. But I told them I would rather be at my own 'partment, and with my own toys, and play with Mommy and Daddy on

Christmas.

I didn't even get to see Mommy and Daddy on Christmas.

Daddy visited with me three days before Christmas. He brought me a new game. I don't remember the name of the game, but you had to pick cards that had numbers on them and you moved 'round a board and sometimes the other person would get to move your piece. We played the game a couple of times and then it was time for Daddy to go.

It always went too quick when I spent time with Daddy. Seems like we hardly had time to do nothing and then he had to go.

Daddy gave me a big hug, and told me I was still his angel. He told me next Christmas we would all be together, me and Daddy and Mommy, and we would have our own tree and our own house and nobody would tell us what we could do.

Mommy didn't show up for her visit.

I guess she must of forgot.

She told me she was gonna be there.

She said she had a special Christmas present for me.

But she must of forgot. And when I saw her again, after Christmas, she didn't have a special present for me after all. She didn't have no present for me.

But that was okay. I had enough presents already. Angie and Tim got me some nice stuff.

But all I really wanted was to see Mommy and Daddy on Christmas.

Chapter Thirty-Four:

THE LIGHTS from the artificial tree in the corner blinked with a steady, almost mesmerizing, regularity. They colored the walls with a spirited ambiance that fit appropriately considering the season. The reds and golds were particularly brilliant, while the more muted tones of the blues and greens were practically concealed within the needles and artificial pine cones of the display. The star at the top was white, and nearly touched the ceiling.

It was Christmas Eve morning, and the Watkins household was preparing for a family get together.

Brian and Pamela arrived to find Angela in the kitchen, in the process of removing a tray of homemade cinnamon rolls from the oven. Heat radiated from the room, infusing the entire house with a comfortable warmth. It satisfied as well the requirements of a traditional Christmas, lending a Norman Rockwell ambiance to the setting.

"Something smells good," Brian announced, as he removed his boots and took off his coat.

Angela called out in reply. "They're fresh from the oven. Come and get them while they're hot. I hope the smell doesn't bother you, Pamela."

"No. It's okay. I seem to be over the worse of the morning sickness now."

"Where's Tim?" Brian asked. "I didn't see his car in the garage."

"Oh, they called him from work. You know how that place is. It's like they can't do a thing unless he's there to hold their hands."

Still holding the tray of fresh baked goods, she managed to close the oven door with a sideward motion of her hip. It slammed shut, chattering metallically as it closed.

"Some kind of issue with a delivery," Angela continued. "He shouldn't be too long."

Tim was the manager of a local tire store. He had planned on taking the entire day off, but the sudden emergency had cut into his home time. It was one of those inconveniences in life that had to be contended with due to his position at the company.

Brian grabbed one of the muffins, blowing on it to cool things down before taking a substantial bite. "Well, if he doesn't get here quick, I can't guarantee any of these will be around for him to come home to. They taste great, Angie."

"Thank you."

As she set down the cooking sheet a twinge seemed to shoot through her. She moved her hand to her stomach, exclaiming as she did so. "Oh, my."

"Are you okay?"

"Yeah. It comes and goes," she informed him, caressing the spot. "Been having some tummy issues all morning. Just a slight pain, that's all. Must have been something I ate last night that didn't agree with me."

"Probably too much egg nog," Brian suggested. "I told you to lay off that stuff."

Angela ignored the remark.

Pamela, joining the pair in the kitchen, managed somehow to squirm past the table to get to the refrigerator.

"Can I have a glass of milk, Angie?"

"Certainly, Pamela. Help yourself."

It was a major ordeal, avoiding one another and navigating the cramped confines of the little room. But the two women seemed accustomed to it, performing the maneuver like a well-rehearsed dance routine, while Brian stood and watched it all from his position in the doorway.

"Well?" Angela stared at her daughter. "How did the sonogram go?"

"Fine." Pamela stroked her stomach, an unconscious habit she had developed lately. "Everything was fine."

"That's not what I want to hear and you know it. Is it a boy or a girl?"

"I can't tell you."

"What do you mean, you can't tell me?"

"I want to wait until Tim's here. And tell all of you at once."

"Do you believe this girl?" She faced her brother-in-law with the question. "I bet she told you."

"Wrong," Brian announced. "Won't say a word. Told me I just have to wait."

"Well, your father will be home soon. And I know he's dying to find out."

Angela grabbed another tray of rolls from the counter and popped them in the oven. "That's the last of them. Maybe I can relax now."

Contrary to her words, Angela approached the sink and began rinsing off some dishes before placing them into the dishwasher.

"We're supposed to get more snow again tonight," Brian announced, to no one in particular.

"That's what I heard," Angela responded. "But I don't mind. As long as it's going to be cold, we may as well have some snow."

"Especially on Christmas," Pamela added.

Finished with the dishes, Angela moved away from the sink. She took one step then stopped abruptly. She moaned again, then reached for a chair to steady herself.

"Don't know what's going on here. Maybe I better sit down for a bit." Her motion was shaky, unsteady, as she took a seat.

Pamela moved closer, placing a hand on her mother's shoulder. "Can I get you anything?"

"No. I'm fine. Really. I just need to…."

She started to rise from the chair when an exclamation of pain escaped her lips.

Brian, concern on his face, didn't even bother to finish his breakfast roll. "That doesn't look good. Where does it hurt?"

"It started in the center of my stomach. But now it feels more like it's on the right side." She rubbed the area in question, leaning forward at the same time. "I'm sure it will go away. I'm sure…."

She clutched both hands to her stomach as she grunted in pain, then jerked from the action.

"Is it sore?" Pamela asked.

"Tender. That's all."

By now Brian was on his feet. Concern was obvious in his voice.

"Come on. We're getting you to the hospital."

He made a motion toward her, a motion she quickly dismissed. "Don't be silly, I'm okay. I'm sure it's nothing."

"It doesn't look like nothing."

He grabbed her arm.

"Come on. Let me help you to stand up."

She resisted for a moment, then closed her eyes in pain. She held her breath, gritting her teeth in agony, doubled over now.

"Maybe you're right."

"Of course I'm right."

"What should we do?" Pamela was beginning to panic. "Tim's not here yet. Shouldn't we call him?"

"You can call him from the car. Grab your mother's purse. It should have all her insurance information."

Angela nodded in agreement, fighting back the tears. "My purse is in the living room Everything's in there. But the breakfast –?"

"Don't worry about the breakfast. Pamela, make sure the stove's turned off. And grab a blanket or something. It's cold out there."

With Brian's assistance Angela made it out to the car. He placed her in the back seat, strapping the restraining belt around her then helping her to lay down. Pamela carefully placed a blanket over the moaning woman, tucking it around her for the warmth it provided. She then took the shotgun seat across from her uncle.

The teenager had her cellphone out, Tim's number on the display.

"Which hospital?"

"Tell him Flower." He glanced in the rearview mirror at his sister-in-law. Her eyes were clenched, her jaw set to fight back the pain. "It's the closest," he continued.

Pamela punched her phone and waited for the call to go through. It instantly went to voicemail.

"He's not picking up. Should I leave a message?"

"No. Call the shop. They'll be able to get hold of him."

"I don't know the number."

"Google it."

Pamela entered the information and, once prompted by the online service, punched the store's number. Moments later a voice came on the line, a voice she instantly recognized. Before he was even through naming the tire store she cut him off.

"Tim! It's Pamela. Something's wrong with Angie!"

"What?!"

"She's got some kind of pain. In her stomach. We're taking her to Flower Hospital right now."

"Okay. I'll meet you there."

Brian abandoned his typically cautious style of driving and arrived at the emergency room in record time. It was quiet at the hospital, nearly deserted, as if emergencies had taken a holiday along with everyone else. Brian jumped from his car, approached the entrance, and waited impatiently as the sliding glass in the doorway opened. He then sprinted to the front desk.

"Can we get some help here? I've got a woman who's in a lot of pain."

The lack of activity at the site may have accounted for the rapid response they received. Or it could have been the normal routine at the facility. Regardless of the reason, a nearby orderly instantly sprang into action, grabbing a wheelchair and following Brian outside. Pamela was still attempting to extricate Angela from the back seat, struggling with the pain-wracked woman. With the orderly's help they managed to get her onto the chair and through the doors into the emergency room.

The two departed down a hallway, further into the compex of rooms. A nurse had materialized, seemingly from nowhere, and joined the duo, asking a bevy of questions which Angela attempted to answer as best she could.

Another nurse blocked Brian and Pamela from advancing any further. "Relationship to the patient?"

"I'm her daughter," Pamela announced.

Brian's reply overlapped the teenager's. "She's my sister-in-law."

"We'll need some information before we can process her," the nurse informed them.

"I can take care of that," Brian replied. "Can't Pamela go back there with her?"

"Okay. Go ahead."

Pamela handed Angela's purse to her uncle and sprinted down the hallway, the same direction taken by the stricken woman and her escort.

Tim showed up less than ten minutes later. He ran to the front desk, where he was greeted moments later by his brother.

"I'm Tim Watkins," he informed the receptionist at the

desk. "I understand my wife was brought here."

"They took her right back," Brian told him. "Pamela's with her now."

"What's going on?"

"I don't know. Haven't heard yet. She started having some kind of stomach pain. We got her here right away."

"Thanks. I appreciate you taking care of things the way you did."

Tim turned toward the clerk at the desk.

"Can I see my wife?"

"Let me find out where they put her and we'll have somebody take you back there."

It only took a few minutes, but for Tim it seemed much longer. He paced in front of the desk until a young woman approached him. "Mr. Watkins? I can take you back to see your wife."

"Thank you."

"You'll have to wait out here," she informed Brian.

They left him there. Brian slouched back to one of the waiting chairs.

"And a Merry Christmas to you, too," he mumbled under his breath, feeling suddenly useless following his recent bout of activity.

Chapter Thirty-Five:

T HE THREE of them sat and waited.

Time dragged by, with the tedious slowness experienced by anyone who awaits news of a loved one's condition during moments of stress.

The hospital had assumed appendicitis, a diagnosis that had been readily verified, and emergency surgery was dictated. A doctor had been out to speak to the family while the surgery was being prepared.

"I'm Dr Faulkner," he began. "I will be assisting during the surgery. Angela is being prepped right now."

"And you're certain it's appendicitis?" Tim had asked.

"Yes we are. The CT confirmed it, though considering her symptoms – the elevated temperature and low blood pressure, both of which are textbook indications of appendicitis – we were pretty confident of the diagnosis from the outset. Considering where the pain was localized, it didn't leave room for much of anything else.

"The appendix has already burst, which means we need to operate immediately to remove it."

Tim considered the information for a moment, along with the meager knowledge he had regarding the condition.

"A burst appendix? That's a bad thing? Isn't it?"

"It can be," the physician admitted. "There's always the chance of infection of the inner lining of the abdomen, or peritonitis. When this happens it becomes necessary to remove the appendix as well as all signs of the infection. In your wife's case, she got to the hospital pretty quickly. So there hasn't been much opportunity for the infection to spread. We're confident surgery will take care of everything just fine."

The explanation did little to set Tim's mind at ease.

"What's involved with the surgery? What will she be going through?"

"To begin, we'll be putting your wife under general anesthesia, so she'll be out for the entire procedure. She won't feel a thing. This is common for any appendectomy."

He recited the words as though he was lecturing a class, rather than discussing the process with a family member. It almost sounded like a rehearsed response; like a spiel he had used in the past, an explanation he relied on whenever the occasion arose.

"We prefer to perform laparoscopic surgery," he continued, "where 3 or 4 small incisions in the stomach allow us to insert the instruments necessary for the procedure. This would include a tube, to inflate the stomach to allow more room within the cavity, as well as a laparoscopic camera and light so we can monitor the progress.

"In your wife's case, however, we will most likely need to perform an open surgery, which calls for a more substantial incision. This is always our second choice in these cases. The primary physician hasn't made the final call yet."

"So what are the concerns with this open surgery?"

"As with any surgery where you're going under general anesthesia there are concerns."

The doctor's inflection moderated after that, becoming more lifelike and almost conversational.

"But these are all common procedures, Mr. Watkins, performed countless times each day. Over 200,000 cases of appendicitis occur each year in the U.S. alone. Rest assured, these are tried and true procedures. And you have a fine doctor. Your wife is in good hands."

"How long is the surgery?"

"Typically an hour for the procedure itself; possibly an hour or two to recover from the anesthesia. Has your wife been put under before?"

"I believe so." Tim stumbled over the answer. "Yes, I'm sure of it. I'm sorry. I guess I'm just not thinking very clearly."

"Understandable. If your wife never had any issues in the past, there's no reason today should be any different."

Pamela, having remained silent throughout the discourse, voiced the question uppermost on her mind.

"How about the recovery? When will she be going home? I know she'd hate to miss the holidays."

"I'm afraid she'll be celebrating Christmas in the hospital this year. She'll have to stay for a day or two, at least, but it shouldn't be any longer than that. And of course she'll have some discomfort after she gets home. She'll need to avoid heavy lifting until she's fully recovered."

Tim felt his mind swirling, taking in all the information as he processed what was happening and considered the possible complications. He knew Angie would be okay. He failed to consider anything otherwise. But he still couldn't help but be concerned.

Dr. Faulkner concluded the discussion with an air of confidence, as though the situation had already been resolved.

"Your wife is in good hands, Mr. Watkins. I can't stress that enough. You have absolutely nothing to worry about. Someone will be out to notify you as soon as the procedure has been completed."

All Tim could manage by then was a meek "Thank you."

As the doctor walked away Pamela questioned her father further.

"I don't understand. What is an appendix, anyway? How can they just get rid of something that's part of your body?"

Brian supplied the answer. During the doctor's recital he had Googled information regarding the appendix. He referred now to the statistics uncovered by his search.

"Sounds like it doesn't do much of anything. *Its exact function is unclear*, according to one site. *It's an evolutionary holdover that serves no purpose.*

"Another site says it *may store certain healthy types of bacteria*, whatever that means. Either way, if it starts to act up it has to go. Sure gives you a lot of confidence in the medical profession, doesn't it?"

As soon as the flippant remark left his mouth Brian reconsidered his words.

"I'm sorry, Tim. I didn't mean it like that. I'm sure the doctors know what they're doing."

"It's okay. I'm not worried. Besides, Angie's a fighter. She won't let something like this get her down."

"It's too bad she won't be home for Christmas," Pamela remarked. "I know she always looks forward to it so much. All the decorating she does. And the cooking –."

"Don't get me started." Tim laughed, warming to the subject. "Every January first I have to start a diet all over again."

"You'd never guess it by looking at you," Brian joked, as he tapped his brother playfully on the stomach.

"I wonder when I'll get to tell her my news?" the teenager asked.

Tim stared at his daughter, a questioning look on his face. "What news?"

"My sonogram. I had it yesterday."

"That's right. I'm sorry, Pamela. I had forgotten all about it. With everything going on and all."

"That's okay, Tim. I understand. It's just I've been wanting to tell someone –."

"Don't say a word," her father interrupted. "We'll wait until your mother's out of surgery. So we all hear together. She wouldn't want to be left out."

Tim reached out, cautiously grabbing Pamela's hand.

"You know, with everything that's been going on lately, with what you've been going through and all, it seems like we haven't had the chance to slow down and take a look at things properly. And now this with your mother. It helps to put things in perspective.

"You're very special to us, Pamela. I hope you realize that."

"I do."

"No. I mean it. We love you, Pamela. You know that. Or, at least, you should know that. Maybe we don't always say it enough. But it's true. And whatever it is that's bothering you, we want to help. We want to be there for you."

She smiled. Her voice was quiet as she spoke, as though reflecting on what had just been said. "You are there for me. I know that. You and Angie have always been so good to me. Sometimes I feel I don't deserve it."

"Don't ever say that. Everyone deserves good things. Everyone deserves to be happy. Especially you."

He leaned over, gave her a quick kiss on the cheek, then released her hand and turned away, resuming his vigil, secure in the knowledge that his wife was all right and would pull through the surgery just fine.

Chapter Thirty-Six:

HANNAH WASN'T the first one awake on Christmas morning, which was a bit unusual.

Lisa Sutter had fought the urge to get out of bed, but eventually her bladder had decided the issue for her and she forced herself from the protective warmth of the covers. Disengaging herself from the blankets disturbed Alec, who stared at his wife as she threw on her bathrobe and stepped toward the doorway.

"Is it time to get up already?" he asked. Drowsiness slurred his words.

She shrugged. "Somebody's awake. I can see the Christmas lights are on. That daughter of yours. I swear, she gets up earlier and earlier every year."

"She's your daughter too, you know."

"Yeah. Don't remind me. It's too early to even think about it."

Lisa headed toward the front of the house, guided by the illumination from the Christmas decorations, prepared to greet Christmas with her daughter.

But it wasn't Hannah sitting and staring at the lights. It was Bobby.

She sat down beside her son.

"Merry Christmas, sport."

He didn't say anything to acknowledge her presence.

She reached over to playfully pat his knee.

"So what's up?"

"Just thinking."

"About what?"

"Pamela. And the baby."

Lisa let loose an exasperated sigh. "Not this again."

"It just doesn't seem fair, Mom. This baby thing. It changes Pamela's life. I mean…. *Everything* in her life. And yet I'm supposed to pretend that nothing happened?"

"Well, of course you can't pretend nothing happened. But there's no reason it should ruin your life, either."

"I just feel there's something I should be doing."

She tried to disguise her frustration, but failed at the attempt. "Like what? What are you going to do? Didn't you say she told you to stay out of her life? That she didn't want you to have anything to do with the baby?"

"Yeah, but –."

"So it's decided. There's nothing you can do about it."

At this point Alec entered the room, a cup of coffee in his hand. He sat, took a sip of the brew, and asked of no one in particular "What's happening?"

"My son," Lisa exclaimed, "is feeling guilty about getting that girl pregnant."

"That girl has a name, Mom."

"I know she has a name."

"And she deserves better than this."

"You're not doing anything wrong, Bobby. The girl doesn't want you in her life. Case closed."

"And you're okay with that?"

He became aware suddenly that his mother's hand still rested on his knee. He pushed it away and stood up, towering over her as he continued.

"You're okay knowing there's a little boy out there that's your grandson? Or a little girl that's your granddaughter? And you may never get to see them?"

She stood, to meet his eyes more directly, thinking she might intimidate him with her stare. But Bobby had grown over the years, filled out from all his physical activity. He was no longer the little boy she had regarded him as for so many years. Lisa found herself looking up to her son, which made her immediately feel small.

So she walked away, approaching the bay window overlooking the front yard, and stared outside for a moment to collect her thoughts. The darkness of the winter morning was relieved by the Christmas lights from the neighbor's house. The morning glowed with promise; the blue lights on the roof-line and the green lights draping the trees beckoned with a feeling of tranquility.

The scene failed to soothe her emotions.

Finally she turned, facing her son once again.

"Of course I'm not okay with this. And I wasn't okay with you and *that girl* having sex in the upstairs of my house, either. But I guess things don't always go the way we want them to, do they? And we can't change that. So the best we can do is get on with our lives. Just make the best of a lousy situation and get on with our lives."

"But it's not fair."

"Of course it's not fair!" Her voice had risen in anger. She took a moment to compose herself, and began again in a more subdued tone.

"All your life I've tried to protect you from things. I thought that was my job, as your mother. Maybe I shouldn't have smothered you the way I did. Maybe I overreacted in my desire to be there for you. But you were my responsibility, Bobby. Mine alone. Who else did I have to rely on?"

If she had expected an answer none came. Not that she noticed, as the words continued to rush forth in a torrent of pent up feelings.

"When your father left us it tore me apart. But I had to be strong. For your sake. I had to pretend that everything was okay. Even when it wasn't."

She stepped closer.

"But I don't want to go through something like that again. All the drama. The yelling. The fighting. I can't go through that again. And if you keep up these foolish ideas, thinking you're going to help this girl, you're only setting yourself up for the same kind of situation. The same kind of disappointment. I don't want that to happen to you."

Lisa continued to stare at her son. Bobby had turned away, as though he didn't want to listen to what was being said. She found herself addressing his back.

"I'm only thinking of you, Bobby."

"No."

He turned to face her, a sad look on his face.

"You're only thinking of yourself."

He left the room without another word.

Lisa sat down again, waiting for her husband's response. But he remained silent, drinking his coffee, absorbed in his own thoughts. She tried to read his face, to discern what was on his mind. But his blank expression provided no clue to what he was thinking.

"Aren't you going to say something?" she asked at last.

"If you want me to agree with you, it's not going to happen."

"I didn't expect it to."

"I just don't understand how you can be so cold to that poor girl."

"That poor girl?"

She repeated the words slowly, as though she needed to absorb them into her system; to fully understand the meaning of the phrase. Her voice was calm – almost relaxed – when she continued.

"I *was* that poor girl, Alec. Eighteen years ago. When I had Bobby."

"Then you know how hard it's going to be for Pamela."

She shook her head slowly back and forth, denying the truth in his words.

"Bobby was a mistake too, you know. Me and Frank, we didn't know each other that well. We were never in love. We never should have had a baby together."

"But Frank did the right thing. He married me."

Alec smirked. "Maybe he's not as much of a jerk as I thought he was."

"But that's just it. He thought he was doing the right thing. But he wasn't. He wasn't doing the right thing.

"Those were the most miserable five years of my life. I hated my life. I hated Frank, for putting me through all that. I hated Bobby, for tying me down and forcing me to put up with the miserable existence I had. Every time he cried, every sleepless night I spent because of him, I hated him for. Do you know what that's like, Alec? Can you imagine hating your own child?"

He turned away momentarily, to avoid her stare, but said nothing.

"I hated myself," Lisa continued. "Everyday I looked in the mirror, and I hated myself. I can't put someone else through that. I *won't* put someone else through that. They'll be better off if they don't even try."

"Maybe things will be different with them, Lisa. Maybe they can work through all this."

"I don't see how."

"Don't you think we should at least give them a chance to find out for themselves? See what happens?"

For long moments there was no reply. Lisa had worked herself up during her recitation, her breaths coming in heaving gulps of air. She slowed now. Relaxed. Composed herself. When she resumed her voice was quiet and calm, almost eerily so.

"I think we should move."

"What?"

"I spoke to my manager. You know my office has a branch in Nashville. She says I could start there whenever I want. With no loss of pay. No loss of seniority."

"Just like that? Pack up everything and take off?"

"Why not? Maybe it would be good for us? You've been hating the winters up here lately. This is the chance to get somewhere warmer. Get away from the snow."

"What about me? It would be like starting all over again. I'd have to find a new job."

She waved aside the contention.

"You're in construction. You can go anywhere. You can slap up a piece of drywall in Tennessee the same as you do here in Ohio."

"Then what about the kids? They won't be happy with the idea of moving."

"Hannah's easy going. She'll make new friends. It won't be a problem."

"And Bobby? It's his senior year, Lisa. It won't be an easy time for him to leave school."

"He doesn't have to."

Her voice became more excited as she warmed up to the idea.

"I've been giving this some thought. Bobby can finish up right here," she reasoned. "I can move down to Nashville ahead of you, get a house, get our life back on track. Then you and the kids can come join me at the end of the school year."

He paused, considering the logic of her words.

"Bobby will be eighteen by then," he reminded her. "He can make his own decisions. And he may not want to move."

"That's a choice he'll have to make."

"And you think this is the solution? To run away from everything?"

"It's a chance to leave all this mess behind us. It will be good for all of us. Especially Bobby. And he'll see it someday. He'll understand why we're doing this."

Alec took a long drink from his coffee. Then he stood, taking several steps to leave the room. He paused in the doorway to look back at his wife.

"And you're determined to do this?"

"I think it's the right thing."

"Then I'll back you up. We'll do it as a family. But don't tell them today. Wait a week or so, anyway."

He took another step. But this time, when he spoke, he didn't face his wife.

"Don't ruin Christmas for them. At least give them that."

Chapter Thirty-Seven:

T HE HOUSE was nothing less than chaotic.

Wrapping paper was everywhere, torn and wrinkled vestiges of the presents that had been neatly stacked beneath the tree just a few short hours ago. White snowmen and red Santas and green Christmas trees adorned the discarded parchment with a colorful arrangement that brought even the litter of the season to life. A tower of empty boxes leaned in a corner, threatening to topple over at the least provocation. Their recent contents were strewn now about the room, temporarily forgotten, abandoned in the pursuit of other activities.

A half-dozen folding chairs were arranged haphazardly amidst the chaos, anticipating the arrival of assorted family members. Holiday greetings emanated from a Bluetooth speaker perched on the bookcase. The music, immortalized by the likes of Nat King Cole, Andy Williams, and other ghosts of Christmas past, was lost in the cacophony of voices mingling throughout the house.

Beverly entered the living room and instantly felt at home.

"I love it," she commented.

Her daughter Jennifer, still clutching Beverly's coat after greeting her mother at the door, displayed her embarrassment.

"I'm sorry, Mom." She glanced around, searching for a clean spot, and decided at last to place the coat on the back of a rocking chair in the corner. "It's just hard to keep things cleaned up around here."

"Christmas isn't for cleaning. It's for sharing time with family."

"Well, we're doing that, all right."

Thomas, Jennifer's husband, entered the room, a cup of hot chocolate in his hand. "Merry Christmas, Beverly."

"Merry Christmas, Thomas," Beverly responded. "Am I the first one here?"

"Heavens no. Joey and Teri are in the kitchen. Emily's downstairs, with Stephanie and Andrew."

"It will be nice to visit with all three of my grandkids. Maybe I'll just pop in and say hello."

"Don't expect much of a greeting from them," Thomas warned. "I'm sure they're captivated with their video games."

"Is Larry here yet?" Beverly asked.

By now Jennifer had returned to the room, in the interim having retrieved her mother's coat and stashed it in the front closet. She grabbed a bunch of wrapping paper from off the floor, scrunching it all together into a smaller ball in anticipation of throwing it in the garbage.

"Uncle Larry hasn't gotten here yet," she offered, in answer to her mother's earlier query.

"Well, they had a long drive up from Florida. It sounds like they got in pretty late last night."

"Where are they staying?"

Beverly sat down on one of the folding chairs before continuing. She seemed to have forgotten about visiting the kids in the basement, wrapped up as she was with the ongoing conversation..

"They're at Lucy and Ken's."

"In that small house of theirs?"

"There's always room for family. Speaking of which, where's everyone sitting today for dinner?"

"I don't know."

Jennifer still held her wadded up bunch of wrapping paper clutched in her hands. She looked around for a few moments, searching for a place to put it, then abandoned the attempt. It ended up back on the floor where it had started.

"I didn't think it would be so crazy here today," Jennifer admitted.

"You're the one that wanted to do Christmas dinner," her mother reminded.

"I know. And I'm looking forward to it. It's just that I wasn't expecting it to be so much work."

Beverly smiled. "Welcome to my world. I've been doing these celebrations for years now. It's nice to get a break from it."

A new voice entered the conversation.

"And you deserve it, Mom."

Joey walked over, planting a kiss on Beverly's cheek.

"Merry Christmas, Mom."

"Thanks, Dear. You're looking fit as ever."

"Only because my wife keeps after me."

"Not today." Beverly's daughter-in-law, Teri, announced from the doorway behind her husband. "You get a pass today, but only because it's Christmas. But tomorrow it's back to the diet."

Joey shook his head, a feigned look of sorrow on his face. "More stale bread and water."

Teri delivered a friendly jab to her husband's arm. "It's not that bad. You'll have them believing I'm a tyrant."

"Nobody could believe that," Beverly assured her.

"Thanks, Mom, for the vote of confidence. You're looking mighty chipper today. Must be over the doldrums."

Jennifer, taking an interest in the conversation, accosted her mother. "What's that? Is there something I should know about?"

"It's nothing. I was just feeling a bit down a while ago when Teri stopped by."

"And it's over now?" Teri prompted.

Beverly thought back to her last conversation with Pamela Watkins. The teenager's words, from their visit a week ago, came back to her.

I do remember you, Beverly. I remember you coming to the house every month. You always seemed so cheerful. So optimistic about things. It meant a lot to me. I enjoyed the time we spent together. I was glad when they told me you would be my CASA again.

It had felt so good to hear the words. It was like a vindication of everything she had worked for; everything she had done for the last ten years. It really had been worthwhile.

Beverly smiled at the others in the room.

"I'm feeling much better now. I guess sometimes you need to stop and appreciate what's good about life, and forget about all the bad stuff."

"Hear hear to that," Thomas announced, raising his mug of hot chocolate in salute.

Just then the sound of running feet reached them, followed by Jennifer's daughter Emily entering the room. At eleven, she was the youngest of Beverly's grandchildren.

She was also the least inhibited of them, a trait she most likely picked up from her mother. The little girl had yet to enter that reserved state when children try to hide their emotions. Instead she was content to enjoy her childhood with all the enthusiasm she could muster.

"Grandma!" She approached Beverly and delivered a hug. "Merry Christmas, Grandma."

"Merry Christmas to you too, Dear."

"Do you want to see what I got for Christmas?"

"You bet I do."

At that moment Beverly couldn't have been any happier.

Chapter Thirty-Eight:

PAMELA AND Brian arrived at the hospital with a box of Russell Stover chocolates. Pamela knew it was Angela's favorite, which seemed appropriate for the occasion. They had bought the candies at the last minute – at the only convenience store they had found open on their ride to the hospital – having discovered Christmas morning wasn't the best time to go shopping. It was unwrapped, though Angela didn't seem to notice.

"We come bearing gifts," Brian announced, as they entered the room.

Angela, still tired from the surgery, managed a smile. Her stomach felt tender. And it was beginning to itch at the incision. She wasn't really sore. The doctor saw that she was adequately medicated, so pain hadn't been an issue. But things certainly weren't back to normal.

She had yet to eat anything as well. Just the thought of food repulsed her, even if it was her favorite candy. But she kept these thoughts to herself.

"Thank you so much," she managed.

Pamela placed the candies on the tray at the foot of the bed, then leaned over to give her mother a hug. She did so gently, afraid of bruising anything. She delivered one quick squeeze and then she pulled away.

"How are you feeling, Angie?" the teenager asked.

Tim answered for his wife.

"She's still pretty tired. Not much of an appetite yet. But the nurses say that's pretty normal following the surgery."

"We're just glad you're over it," Pamela announced, voicing the sentiment shared by all in the room. "You had us worried there, you know."

Angela managed a smile before replying.

"I had myself worried, too. When something like that happens you can't help but wonder what's going on."

She paused a moment, considering her words.

"I think that was the most frightening aspect of the whole incident. The not knowing. It's hard not to think the worst. I guess I should consider myself lucky that it wasn't anything more than it was."

She smiled then, an apologetic expression presented to the entire family.

"I just feel bad," she continued. "That I ruined everyone's Christmas."

Her husband answered, the affection in his voice obvious. "Are you kidding?"

Tim reached out toward his wife, gently caressing up and down her forearm where it lay exposed by the flimsy hospital gown she wore. It was a gentle touch; a loving touch. It was a moment shared between a loving couple, oblivious to those around them.

Tim, aware at last of the others in the room, drew his hand away and continued.

"I can't think of a better gift than to know that you're feeling better and all this crazy business is behind you."

They exchanged a smile.

The moment was a quick one, interrupted by Pamela clearing her throat to draw everyone's attention to her.

"Well?" the teenager asked.

Brian responded. "Well what?"

"Isn't anyone going to ask me?"

Puzzled looks answered her.

"The sonogram?"

"Of course." Tim actually slapped his open palm against his forehead, as though knocking some sense into himself with the mock show of stupidity. "How could we forget? What's the big news?"

"I'm going to have…."

She paused for effect.

"…a baby…"

Brian interrupted. "We all know you're having a baby, kiddo. Just spit it out."

"Boy," she announced. "I'm going to have a baby boy."

"How wonderful." Angela was beaming. "Did the doctor have anything else to say? How are you progressing?"

"Everything's looking fine. I'm right on target with the pregnancy. No complications."

"Do you have any names picked out?" Brian asked.

"Not yet. Oh, I've got a few floating around in my head . But I'll have plenty of time to sort that out later."

"You know," her uncle continued, "you can't go wrong with a name like Brian."

Angela held back a laugh, fearing it would cause too much discomfort, but managed a light chuckle as she responded. "Honestly, Brian. Have you no shame?"

He held his hands out, in mock indignation. "What? Brian's a good solid name. There's plenty of famous people named Brian."

"Name one," Tim prompted.

"I'll name three. Brian Wilson. Brian Adams. Brian May."

Pamela just stared in confusion. "Who *are* those people? I never heard of them."

"Come on. You've heard of Brian Wilson."

No reply.

"From the Beach Boys?"

She continued to stare at him in wonder.

"Good Vibrations? California Girls?"

"I think you're talking to the wrong generation," Tim informed him.

"Doesn't anyone listen to classic rock anymore?"

"Besides," said Pamela. "I don't want to name him after anybody in the family. No offense."

Tim and Brian answered simultaneously. "None taken."

"I just want him to be able to start life with his own name. As a unique person. I don't want anybody thinking he was named after so and so, and like he's got some sort of reputation to live up to."

"Nothing wrong with that," her father admitted.

At that moment a nurse popped her head into the room. "Everything okay in here, Angie?"

"Just fine, Thelma."

Angela turned toward her husband. "Thelma's been taking care of me all morning."

"My pleasure," the nurse announced. "And she's been a model patient. Hardly a peep out of her all night."

"I must admit," Angela informed them, "I slept good last night. I don't know what they gave me, but it sure knocked me out."

"Well, we appreciate the attention," Tim informed the nurse. "But it's too bad you have to spend Christmas here, instead of with your family."

"It's no problem," Thelma answered. "I didn't have nothing going on today, anyway. My kids aren't flying into town until tomorrow morning. That's when I'll be celebrating my Christmas."

"Well, I hope it's a Merry one."

"It's gonna be a fat one, that's what it's gonna be. I told my husband to pick up a ham, and I can't believe what he came home from the store with. We could feed an army with that thing."

"There's always leftovers," Brian remarked.

"I don't know about leftovers, with that bunch of mine. But I'm sure we'll have plenty for a meal or two, at least.

Anyway, I'll check in later and see how you're doing."

After the nurse's departure Tim turned to say something else to Angela, only to discover she had fallen back to sleep. For a moment he was lost in reflection as he studied the curves of her cheeks, and the set of her chin, and the way her eyelids fluttered slightly as she slept.

I could have lost her, he thought.

"Let's give her some rest, guys. She's earned it after what she's been through."

Pamela and Brian walked into the hallway first. Tim lingered a moment longer, gazing at the woman in the hospital bed and thinking how lucky he was to have her in his life.

He left the room, quietly, to join the others.

Chapter Thirty-Nine:

CONSULTATION TRANSCRIPT # 2301024 – EXCERPT

Dr. B:
Good morning, Pamela. I trust you had a pleasant holiday?

Pa W:
Not exactly. I spent a lot of it in the hospital.

Dr. B:
Was there an issue with the baby?

Pa W:
No. It was nothing like that. I'm having a boy, by the way. I had my sonogram, and they say everything is looking good.

Dr. B:
That's good.
But you mentioned the hospital?

Pa W:
It was Angie. My mother. We had to take her there on Christmas Eve. Her appendix burst.

Dr. B:
I'm sorry to hear that. There can be a great deal of complications following an incident like that.

Pa W:
I guess. Angie seems to be doing okay with it. She's home now, but it did mess up her Christmas.

Dr. B:
And she is recuperating well, I assume?

Pa W:
Yes she is. But the whole thing, with her being in the hospital and all, kind of makes me look at things different.

Dr. B:
In what way?

Pa W:
To begin with, I started to miss her.
She's always been around the house. If I needed anything I could always go to her, and she was there for me.
Even since I've been staying at Uncle Brian's she's been there for me. For visits. Or phone calls. I could always count on that.
But when she was in the hospital, and during the surgery, I couldn't help thinking, what if something happens to her? Something really bad? And I never get to see her again? It just seems hard to imagine that one day a person can be here, and the next day they can be gone.

Dr. B:
It's always hard to deal with the loss of a loved one. It's a literal point of no return. After we lose someone, you can't help but consider all the things you could have said, but never found the words for. Or all the things you could have done; the

opportunities that are gone forever. It's too late for any of that once someone passes away.

Pa W:
I guess I never stopped to think how final that would be. I've been lucky, I guess, to not have to go through that before.
And when I think of what I almost did – what I tried to do – back in September, I can't help but wonder what people would have thought about me. After I was gone. How it would affect them.

Dr. B:
Our lives touch countless others, Pamela, sometimes in ways we don't even realize. The loss of any soul is a burden to those they leave behind.
But you have been through this before. In a manner of speaking. When you were removed from your parents, even though it wasn't due to their passing, it may as well have been. The ties you had to your mother and father were severed. Once you were adopted they were out of your life.
That can be a life-changing experience, especially to a seven-year-old. An experience such as you went through can have immense consequences for a developing child.

Pa W:
And it did.
But not like this.
This was different somehow.
Death just seems so final. I can't imagine going on in a world where I didn't have Angie to turn to.
It made me look at our relationship another way.
I guess there was always a lot of friction between me and Angie. Right from the start. It was like I could never please her. She was constantly picking on me. I didn't put my clothes away right. Or I left my toys in the way. Anything I did, she found a way to criticize me.

I could never understand that.

Dr. B:
But now you do?

Pa W:
I guess. In a way.
My mother – my *real* mother – was never like that. I guess she loved me. Everyone said that she loved me. I know she was never mean to me.
But she never really spent time with me, either. I don't ever remember her reading a book to me. Or watching something on TV with me. It's like I was just sort of there. You know?
But Angie isn't like that. I think the things she does – the stuff she says to me – is because she does care for me. And she's trying to help me. In her own way.
Does that make sense?

Dr. B:
I think you're absolutely correct in your assessment of things, Pamela.
It would be the easiest thing in the world for a parent to always let their child have their own way. The child would be contented, which would make things less difficult for the parent. On a certain level, anyway.
But, in the long run, it's not the right way to raise a child.
Good or bad, children learn from the people around them. The decisions their parents make, the morals and values they live by, influence a child profoundly.
A good parent understands this, and knows that it's up to them to mold their child into the best person they can be.

Pa W:
That's what I want to do.
I want to love my little boy, and do everything I can for him.

But I don't want to make the mistakes my parents did. I don't want him to have to go through the things I had to go through. It even makes me reconsider Bobby's role in my child's life.

Dr. B:
Bobby? The father, correct?

Pa W:
Yeah.
Bobby treated me badly. What he did was wrong. Though, when I look back on it, I realize he may not have been as much at fault as I thought at first.
But I need to think about this some more before I talk to him about it. I don't want to do the wrong thing. For me. Or for my baby.

Dr. B:
It's always good for a child to have their father be part of their life.

Pa W:
Not always.

Chapter Forty:

PAMELA WAS talking to Aaron at the lunch table when Bobby Beard showed up. It was noisy in the cafeteria, the mingling of students' voices and shuffling of teenagers' feet, trays and dishes and silverware being moved and rearranged, all combining into a background clatter of confusion that permeated the room. Pamela wasn't even aware of Bobby's presence until after he started talking.

"You'll be glad to hear you're getting your way, Pamela."

There was defiance in his manner. His eyes were focused on the young girl, as if she was the only thing in the room to see. It was a mesmerizing, almost intimidating look, and failed to conceal the underlying anger he obviously was feeling.

It instantly made Pamela uncomfortable.

Aaron, noticing his friend's reaction, spoke up.

"If you want me to leave –?"

"No."

Bobby's exclamation cut short anything further Aaron may have wanted to say.

"This won't take long. I just want Pamela to know. I won't be around to get in the way. That's what you want, isn't it? You want me out of your life? Well, you've got it."

Pamela, still somewhat bewildered by the explosive nature of Bobby's declaration, managed a reply.

"What do you mean? What's going on, Bobby?"

"My parents decided to move to Tennessee. My mother got a transfer with the company she works for. Looks like I'll be moving down there with my stepfather and sister, right after I graduate."

"I heard you were planning on going to the University of Toledo after graduation?"

"Well, my plans sort of got sidetracked when my parents heard your big announcement. They think it's best that we just leave town. They don't want to be around when…. You know.

"So, I'll just have to make other plans, I guess. Kiss my football scholarship good-bye."

Pamela, having recovered from her initial surprise, found her voice.

"I hope you're not expecting me to feel sorry for you, Bobby. This sort of changes my life too, you know. Do you think I wanted any of this?"

"Then I guess neither one of us is happy about the way things turned out."

"I didn't say that."

Bobby paused, considering what she had just said.

"What's that supposed to mean?"

"It means I'm having a baby, Bobby. Our baby. I didn't plan it to happen like this. But I wouldn't change it. Not now.

"I know I've had a lot of doubts lately. But not with this. I'm going to be the best mother any baby ever had. Just wait. You'll see."

"But that's just it, isn't it? I won't see, will I? Everyone keeps telling me that I should just stay out of this whole mess. That I don't belong here. Apparently I'm not fit to be a father."

"Nobody's saying that."

"It doesn't matter what they're saying, does it? I'm finished with this crap. Have the baby, don't have the baby, I don't care. All I know is I won't get in your way, no matter what you decide to do."

He turned and stormed away, not giving her the opportunity to respond.

For several seconds she watched him, as he weaved his way through the crowded cafeteria. She was still looking after his departure when Aaron interrupted her thoughts.

"Are you okay?"

"Yeah."

She looked down at the food on her plate, pushing it around abstractedly with her fork. Throwing the utensil down, she leaned back in her chair and sighed.

"Yeah. I'm just fine."

"You don't look fine."

"Well I am."

"This is what you want, isn't it? To have Bobby Beard out of your life?"

"Of course it is."

"Then why do you sound so upset?"

"I don't know. I guess...."

She leaned forward, placing her hands on the table for support.

"I know I don't want him in my life. I barely even like Bobby. I wish I had never had anything to do with him. The whole thing was just a stupid mistake, a stupid mistake that's going to affect me for the rest of my life."

"I know what you mean. Things never quite happen the way you expect them to, do they?"

"That's for sure."

"But this is a good thing. Right? Didn't you want Bobby to leave you alone?"

"I suppose." She hesitated with the words, uncertainty tainting her reply.

"So what's the problem?" Aaron asked.

"I guess it just doesn't seem fair to him. Like he has no choice in these decisions that are affecting his life. I mean, how would I feel if everyone was telling me what I could or couldn't do? I don't think I would like it very much."

"So what's the alternative?"

"I don't know. I guess part of me thinks, maybe I was wrong for being so mad at Bobby. I mean, it's his baby too. Doesn't he have a right to be part of his son's life?"

Aaron considered the question.

"That's a tough one. I guess you need to ask, what's better for the baby?"

"What do you mean?"

"Is it better for the baby to have Bobby around? Can he be a good influence?"

"I don't know. I really don't know what kind of influence he can be. I don't know him that well."

She paused abruptly, as though a new thought had just occurred to her.

"And then there's his parents," she remarked.

There was no uncertainty in her voice as she continued.

"I don't want them anywhere near my baby."

Chapter Forty-One:

CHANGE IS a strange commodity.

Some people embrace it, relishing the opportunity to explore new experiences and discover new sensations. They are drawn to the excitement of expanding their horizons. This type of individual looks forward to change as an advancement, increasing their participation in life, moving away from the mundane and toward previously unknown possibilities.

These people are most likely the exception.

For most, change can be intimidating. Once a routine has been established it's often difficult to even consider changing it. Change means the struggle of learning something different, with the prospect of failure a risk that looms large over each new endeavor. It may encompass making decisions and choices that can remove a person from their normal comfort zone, placing them into situations they don't feel equipped to handle. Change can mean interactions involving new people, unfamiliar people, with views and ideas that may not coincide with your own view of the world.

So, for most, the path to change is a difficult one, burdened with pitfalls and unexpected stumbling blocks.

Yet, even with all its difficulties, change eventually becomes the norm. New procedures become accustomed routines. Hurdles that once blocked us become stepping stones to new achievements.

Everyone must face change in their lives and, for the majority of us, we learn to adapt. So everything changes.

Even change.

Pamela Watkins had changed a lot since early September, since that fateful day on the High Level bridge when she had contemplated throwing it all away. She had been forced to reevaluate her view of life and her place in it. She had been introduced to the daunting task of reassessing priorities and responsibilities. And now, due to the interactions with the people around her – and prodded by the required self-examinations undertaken through her therapy – she had grown to accept many of the issues she had previously struggled against.

The news of her pregnancy, on top of everything else, was a tremendous change, perhaps one of the largest any woman can experience. Such a circumstance could have driven her further into despair; back to that dark time when she had contemplated suicide.

But Pamela had survived it all.

And Pamela had grown.

She had become more comfortable with herself. She was more aware of the intricacies of everyday living and how to deal with the stresses in her life.

As such, her case with the judicial court system had reached the point where it moved along at a steady pace.

The winter months, those harsh days of darkness that drag on for most people, somehow passed by as a blur for Pamela. As they did for those concerned with her progress.

Brian Watkins was adjusted now to his niece's presence. Not only had he adjusted, but he had grown to relish the time they spent together. Having another person in the house, even when they were in separate rooms and not interacting with one another, relieved a loneliness he hadn't even been aware of. For the first time since he had been on his own he felt like part of a family. He spent more time with his brother than he had for years, reestablishing shared interests and activities they had long ago forgotten

Angela and Tim had grown closer as a couple, in a manner they couldn't have contemplated earlier. For ten years they had been mother and father, occupations they cherished and enjoyed. But they had also grown apart as husband and wife. With more time together they rekindled their love, which had never disappeared but had lain strangely dormant, hidden by the burdens of life. Their renewed affection for one another was intensified following Angela's surgery, when both came to realize how important they were to one another.

They too had changes in their lives, which they anticipated with eagerness. They looked forward to their daughter's return to their household. And they found the concept of becoming grandparents appealing, even though it wasn't under the best of circumstances.

Perhaps the only one who hadn't experienced any changes was Beverly. For her the case had come to a standstill. The CASA volunteer still fulfilled her obligations; she visited with Pamela each month, she kept in contact with the parents, and she communicated with Annie Klume, the caseworker, regarding the progress of the case. At this point, there wasn't anything further to be done except to monitor the situation.

In late March Children's Services held a review meeting regarding Pamela and her case. Annie was of course there, along with Shantel Monaghan, the supervisor from the agency. Angela attended on the family's behalf, along with her brother-in-law Brian. Tim was unable to attend due to obligations at work, while it had been decided it was best to allow Pamela her time at school rather than to interrupt her schedule further.

Beverly was the last to arrive for the meeting, which started once everyone was present.

"The baby will be here in a couple more months," Angela announced to the assembly, "so we need to focus on that. It's time for Pamela to get some normalcy back into her life. It's time for her to come home."

Shantel reacted to the comment by addressing Brian. "How do you feel about that, Mr. Watkins? Would Pamela be in agreement with that?"

"I think it's what she wants," he responded. "We have talked about it, and I think she's ready. Besides, Tim and Angie have a lot more space at their place than I do. Pamela and I are practically tripping over each other as it is. I can't imagine what it would be like with a baby at my house."

"This can't just be a matter of convenience," the social worker pointed out. "Is it the right thing to do?"

"I think so," Brian replied, with no hesitation. "And more importantly, it's what Pamela wants."

Beverly spoke up. "She does seem a lot better than when I first talked to her, after the incident. But I still worry."

"About what?"

"What was it that was disturbing her so much six months ago? I talked to Dr. Bargalony again, just last week. And while he seems pleased with Pamela's progress, I get the impression he feels there are still issues Pamela hasn't resolved."

"That may be a moot point," Annie Klume offered.

"Why would you say that?"

"Because she turns 18 in another six weeks," the caseworker pointed out. "She won't be a minor anymore. So at that point, any decisions in her life are entirely up to her, as long as she doesn't put the baby at risk."

"But has anything changed?" Beverly asked. "Like Shantel pointed out, this can't just be a matter of convenience. Don't we owe it to Pamela to do what's best for her? And isn't what's best for her getting to the root of her problems, so things can be resolved and she can move on with her life?"

"It doesn't always work that way," Annie pointed out. "The kind of solution you're looking for isn't an overnight remedy. I do think it would be good for Pamela to continue her therapy, even after the baby is born. It can only do her good."

"Besides that," Angela added, "Pamela has improved so much already. She's not the same person she was six months ago. I think having a baby has really changed her. It's given her something to focus on. Something outside of herself."

Beverly considered a moment. "It won't be easy for her."

"But she won't be on her own. Tim and I will be there for her."

"I'm not going anywhere either," Brian said. "She's got lots of support, Beverly. I think she'll be okay."

"Then I think it's decided," Shantel announced. "The next hearing is only weeks away. Lucas County will file a motion to terminate the case, citing a resolution to the circumstances that instigated the proceedings to begin with, and testifying that all parties are in agreement with the decision. "

"And then our daughter can come back home?"

"Yes, Angie. She'll be coming home."

After the parties separated, following the conclusion of the meeting, Annie Klume stopped to have a word with Beverly.

"You don't seem convinced about this."

"I just have my doubts. That's all."

"What is it about Pamela's situation that's disturbing you?"

"I just feel like I failed her once before. I don't want to make the same mistake a second time."

"How did you fail her?"

"I was her CASA ten years ago. I was supposed to be looking out for her. And doing what was best for her. If I had done my job properly then, maybe none of this would have happened."

"You don't know that, Beverly. From everything I've heard, her home life with the biological parents was a toxic situation. Who knows what might have happened to her if she had stayed in that environment? Instead she was with a loving couple that cared for her and nourished her.

"You did the right thing ten years ago, Beverly. You're doing the right thing now."

Chapter Forty-Two:

I COULDN'T understand why we left Angie and Tim's house so late. We had to get downtown so I could Visit with Mommy and Daddy. I only got to see them once a week. I didn't want to be late. Daddy would be waiting for me.

I asked Tim when we would be leaving, and he looked kind of sad. Then he told me Daddy wouldn't be visiting with me that day.

When I asked him why, he told me Daddy did something he wasn't 'posed to do. Daddy went to see Mommy at the 'partment, he said, and Daddy wasn't allowed to do that. And he says Mommy and Daddy got in a big fight.

I asked him if Mommy had to call the police again. Like she did last time, when they took me away. And he said yes. The police came and they put Daddy in jail.

When I asked him when I could see Daddy again he said he didn't know. He said the adoption hearing was only a month away, and he didn't know when Daddy would get out of jail.

It made me sad to think of Daddy in jail, all alone and by himself. It just sounded like such a scary place to be. like it was dark and dirty with bars everywhere. Or at least that's what it always looked like on television.

So Daddy was in jail, and I couldn't see him.

But Tim told me Mommy was 'posed to be there, and that I would be able to visit with her. But I wondered if that was true. Mommy didn't visit very much anymore. I think sometimes she just forgot 'bout me.

Mommy did make it to the visit, but she looked real sad. And her cheek looked real sore. I asked her what happened, and at first she wouldn't tell me. Then later after we visited a while she did tell me.

She told me Daddy hit her. She said Daddy had come to the 'partment, and they argued again. And he hit her because he was angry with her.

I asked her why Daddy was angry with her.

She said Daddy blamed her for me being taken away. Daddy told her that if she didn't drink so much none of this would of happened. That if she didn't drink so much we could still be a family and I would still be with them.

Then Mommy got an angry look on her face. Mommy said none of it was her fault. She said everything was Daddy's fault. And she called him a bad name again.

She said she called the police, because she didn't want Daddy to hurt me.

She said she was always afraid that Daddy would hurt me.

I told her that would never happen. My Daddy loves me. I know he loves me. Daddy would never do nothing to hurt me.

She told me I just didn't understand.

She said some people were just bad. That bad people can't be trusted.

I told her she was wrong. That Daddy wasn't a bad person. That she was the bad person. That if she didn't drink so much, then Daddy wouldn't push her, and she wouldn't have to call the police, and everything would be okay.

So it wasn't Daddy's fault that they took me away.

It was her fault.

Maybe I shouldn't of said that. But I was angry with Mommy, and it made me mad that she kept saying everything was Daddy's fault. When it was really her fault.

Then Mommy started to cry.

That was the last time I ever saw my Mommy.

Chapter Forty-Three:

IT WAS a perfect summer morning, the type of morning that convinces you springtime has indeed passed. The temperature, even in the early morning hours, was warm enough for short sleeves, though the breeze still brought a lingering coolness that testified the sweltering days of summer had yet to arrive on the scene. Along with the chill, the breeze also brought a hint of perfume from the profusion of purple, pink, and white lilacs that had bloomed weeks earlier and had yet to relinquish their color. Or their fragrance.

The fact that it was a Saturday was an extra bonus. The school year had not yet ended, and students everywhere were aching for their freedom from the forced enslavement of education, and anxious to make the most of the day they had been given.

Several of the neighborhood children took advantage of the day off by getting out their bicycles. A hastily thrown together basketball game at the park filled the morning with excited cheering from the participants. One enterprising young girl had even set up a lemonade stand in her yard, hopeful of attracting some thirsty customers.

But it wasn't just the children enjoying the warmth. The local dogs were out in surprising numbers as well, allowing their owners the opportunity to get some exercise as the animals explored the sidewalks, noses to the ground, sniffing out morsels of knowledge.

Beverly arrived to find Pamela sitting in a lawn chair on the front porch of her Uncle's house, a book in her hand. This time it was HARRY POTTER AND THE DEATHLY HALLOWS. The book rested on the bulge of the young girl's belly, which had swelled considerably since the previous month's visit. The teenager seemed captivated with the writing, and failed to notice Beverly's arrival until the CASA volunteer greeted her.

"Good morning, Pamela."

"Good morning, Beverly." She set the book down on the table beside her. "I wasn't expecting to see you until next week."

"I was in the neighborhood, visiting my son, and I thought I'd stop by. I hope that's not a problem?"

"Of course not."

The teenager looked around, as if suddenly noticing her surroundings.

"Isn't it a lovely morning?" Pamela asked.

"It certainly is." There was another chair on the porch, which Beverly claimed as her own. "You're looking good today, Dear."

"I feel good. It's nice to get out of the house for a change."

"I know what you mean. My garden needs lots of attention. I'm looking forward to tackling it, and getting rid of some of the weeds."

Pamela, lost in a personal reverie, continued, as though the older woman hadn't said anything.

"When I sat down this morning, before I picked up my book, I found myself just staring at the sky. Noticing the deep blue color, and the puffiness of the clouds. And the trees, looking so green and vibrant. It's like I'm noticing colors for the first time in my life."

She focused again on her visitor.

"I used to always love fall," Pamela continued. "With the changing leaves, the reds and the golds. But last year it all seemed so drab to me. I guess my whole life was drab to me then."

"You were going through a difficult time. I think it's a good sign. That you're seeing things differently now. It means you're moving on."

"I hope so. I don't want to go back there. To where I was. When I felt so alone."

"You were never alone, Pamela. Your family was always there for you."

"I know that. I knew that last year, too. I guess I was just too involved in my own problems to see it. It's easy to look at what's bad in your life, and not stop to think of the good things. I don't ever want to go back there again."

Beverly was pleased to hear the determination in the teenager's voice.

"It does seem like you're moving on with your life. I'm so glad to see that."

The young girl smiled, a secret little smile, as though she knew something no one else was aware of. She ran her hand gently over her belly in a circular motion.

"He's kicking a lot now," she informed Beverly. "I'm feeling him every day. Sometimes he even wakes me up in the morning, he's moving around in there so much."

"Well, you only have a couple weeks to go. He's doing a lot of growing. Do you have everything ready for when he gets here?"

"Not everything," Pamela admitted. "But a lot. Tim fixed up the spare room, turned it into a nursery. They got me a crib and a changing table. A lot of the big stuff, anyway."

"So when are you moving back?"

"I hope it's any day now. Annie suggested I should wait until the court date, just to be sure nothing else comes up."

"Then you haven't heard yet?" Beverly asked.

"Heard what?"

"It's part of why I decided to stop by this morning. The magistrate accepted the recommendation from Children's Services. The court date has been vacated."

"What's that mean?"

"It means there won't be another hearing. It's all over now."

"That's a relief. These last few months…."

She paused, considering her words.

"I feel like I haven't been able to move on with my life lately. Like I'm stuck in some kind of holding pattern and just getting through each day. It will be nice to have things like they used to be."

"Well, not quite like they used to be," Beverly pointed out. "You've got some big changes coming, Pamela. What with the baby and all. Plus the end of the school year isn't too far away. I assume graduation won't be a problem?"

"It's hard to say. A lot depends on when this little guy decides to make his appearance. The school's been real good about things. Working around my schedule with doctor visits and all. Mrs. Jarecki says if I can't make it to the ceremony they'll work something out, to make sure I get my diploma."

"That's good to hear."

Beverly paused, considering whether to continue with her thoughts. She finally decided it was best to just say what was on her mind.

"But I have to tell you, Pamela. I still have my concerns. About how you're feeling. After all you've been through."

"I'm doing great, Beverly. Really I am.

"I'm going to keep on seeing Dr. Bargalony," the expectant mother continued. "It's getting easier to talk to him about things. He's never judgmental about what I've gone through. He always seems to say just the right thing to me."

"That's good to hear."

"And I promise you, Beverly. I will NEVER consider something like suicide again." She patted her tummy and smiled. "I have too much to live for."

Beverly stood, an uncomfortable look on her face.

"Then my work here is done. I most likely won't be seeing you anymore. This must be one of the hardest parts of my job. Saying goodbye."

"I do want to thank you, Beverly. This is twice you've been here for me. I do appreciate all you've done."

Pamela stood. The maneuver seemed a bit awkward, as though she was still unaccustomed to the added weight in her belly.

"One thing I do remember, Beverly. From when you used to visit me, ten years ago."

"What's that."

"You used to give me the biggest hugs. You know, I'm still not too old for that."

Beverly fought back a tear. She approached the teenager and they embraced.

Pamela whispered in the CASA volunteer's ear.

"Thanks for everything."

"It was my pleasure, Pamela. You just take real good care of that baby."

"You don't have to worry about that. He's in good hands."

Beverly made it to the car and drove slowly away. She didn't turn around, or wave goodbye. She just kept her eyes on the road. She didn't want Pamela to see her crying.

I'm such an old woman, Beverly thought. *I knew this day was coming. Just like it does in all my cases. You'd think I'd be used to it by now.*

Chapter Forty-Four:

T HE WALLS were painted a pastel blue. It was a light and airy color that managed to impart a delightful sense of whimsy to the room. Yellow curtains hung at the windows, blowing ever-so-slightly from the breeze that penetrated the chambers. Some of the late afternoon sunlight managed to sneak past the material, highlighting a rectangle of carpet at the center of the room. The effect was cheerful and bright – suitable for a baby's room – and, at the same time, nearly magical, as dust motes danced in the air like a cluster of minuscule fairies from Never-land.

Pamela stood in the doorway, admiring the job her parents had done with the decorating. Everything seemed perfect. The crib was positioned in one corner, with a mobile of hanging animals fastened to the headboard. Beside the crib sat a dresser and changing table, the drawers partially opened to reveal the diapers and outfits that awaited the new arrival. Blues and yellows seemed to cover every available surface, leaving no doubt that the room was a nursery.

Angela and Tim stood behind Pamela, breathless, waiting for the young woman's reaction.

"Well?" Angela prompted. "What do you think?"

"It's perfect."

She turned around, throwing an arm around each of them and managing, even with her bulging belly, a group hug. "Thank you so much. This is a room any baby would be glad to grow up in."

"We're glad you like it."

"Like it? I love it! I just feel like it's too much."

"What do you mean?" Tim asked.

"It's just that...."

Pamela stumbled for the words. A rocking chair was positioned across from the changing table, with a fluffy unicorn pillow on the seat. Pamela picked up the pillow and held it close to her chest, eyes closed for a moment, then sat in the rocker. The chair made a slight creaking sound as she began a steady back-and-forth motion. She failed to look at Angela and Tim as she began talking, her attention devoted to the floor.

"I don't deserve this."

Angela crossed the room and sat on the floor at Pamela's feet, positioning herself to more directly face her daughter. She held Pamela's hand and looked up into eyes that were beginning to moisten with tears.

"That's nonsense, Pamela. Why would you even consider such a notion?"

"Because of everything I've put you through these last eight months. The suicide attempt. Going to live with Uncle Brian all this time. And the baby.

"I'm sure this isn't what you had planned for your little girl. I can't imagine what you must think of me. How much I've let you down."

"You didn't let us down," her mother assured her. "You could never do that."

"That's nice to hear, but we all know that isn't true."

"Don't talk like that. Don't even think like that. We realize you're going through a rough time. That's all. Everybody goes through spells where the bad seems to outweigh the good. When, no matter how hard they try, things just don't go their way."

"But not like this," Pamela insisted, her voice rising in pitch. "I've caused so much trouble for both of you. You must hate me."

Tim stepped into the room. His voice was firm as he spoke up.

"Don't even go there, young lady. We could never hate you. You should know that by now. And as far as the mistakes you made, feeling sorry for yourself isn't going to change anything that's already happened. You need to get those kinds of thoughts out of your head and move forward with your life."

Pamela smiled. It was a weak little smile, as though she was trying to convince herself of the truth in what Tim was saying.

"Dr. Bargalony says the same thing. He tells me I can't keep blaming myself for things that have already happened. Especially things that were out of my control. I couldn't do anything about them then, and I certainly can't change them now. All I can change is the way I look at things. And the way I deal with things."

"He's absolutely right," Angela remarked. "You have too much going for you, Pamela. Too much to look forward to. Your baby will be here any day now. My gosh, your birthday's next week already. It's time to celebrate these things. Enjoy them."

Angela faced her husband.

"Can you believe it? Our little girl is going to be eighteen?"

"And she's grown so much," Tim added in agreement.

Pamela laughed, rubbing her belly as she did so.

"Growing is right! If this baby gets much bigger I'll need a wheelbarrow to get around."

"That's not what I meant," Tim assured her, adding his laughter to hers.

"But it's true. I never thought I'd put on this much weight."

"But that's a good thing," Angela remarked. "You want the baby to be healthy. These women that starve themselves during pregnancy, like they're afraid of putting on too much weight, aren't thinking of the baby. They're only thinking of themselves."

"I don't know how they do it. Even if I don't eat I still put on the pounds. This guy's gonna be a real bruiser, that's for sure."

Tim smiled at the thought. "Probably be a football player when he grows up."

Pamela sobered up instantly, turning away from her father.

"I don't want to talk about it."

She raised herself to a standing position, balancing herself on the arm of the rocker as she did so.

"I'm sorry," Tim told her. "I didn't mean to –."

"It's okay, Tim. Forget about it."

She walked to the doorway and paused. Turning to face them, she forced a smile on her lips.

"Thank you for everything. For the room. For accepting me, even after everything I've done. Everything."

She left them there and walked to her bedroom, closing the door behind her and effectively putting an end to any further conversation.

Chapter Forty-Five:

THE KNOCK on the door was quiet. Nearly unobtrusive. Bobby Beard looked up from his video game, but otherwise gave no indication that he was even aware of the interruption.

Alec Sutter's voice sounded from the other side of the panel.

"Bobby? Can I come in?"

Bobby continued with his game, making no effort to even acknowledge his stepfather's presence.

The door opened. Alec cautiously peeked his head around the corner and peered into the boy's bedroom.

"Bobby? Can I talk to you?"

"It's a free world. I can't stop you from talking."

Alec entered the room then stood a moment, saying nothing. It was obvious from his demeanor that he was uncomfortable with the situation.

"Can you turn that off for a minute? This is important."

Bobby hesitated, obviously reluctant to comply, then paused the game. He placed the controller on the computer stand, his movements slow and deliberate, and rotated his chair to face his stepfather.

"I'm listening."

"It's about us moving to Nashville."

Bobby spun back around, picked up the controller, and resumed playing his game again.

"Bobby!"

"There's nothing to talk about, Alec."

"Yes there is."

"Like what?"

Bobby faced him again.

"You and Mom decided what we were gonna do. You decided you know what's best for me and Hannah. You never even gave us the chance to discuss it."

"Your mother's looking out for you, Bobby. That's all."

"Don't give me that, Alec. My mother cares about herself, and that's all there is to it. She's embarrassed that her son got a girl pregnant, and she's running away from it. That's all she's doing. She can't face the truth about what's going on."

Bobby turned away once again.

"And you, Alec. You're no better than she is. You're both a couple of cowards. This whole thing is unfair, and you know it."

"Now you're the one who's not being fair. Your mother has always put your needs first. Even above her own. The things she's done for you over the years –."

"Yeah. She's a regular saint."

Though Bobby's words expressed his anger his manner failed to show any emotion. It was like he was purposely provoking his stepfather, deliberately antagonizing him, doing his best to accelerate the conflict between them.

Alec stayed calm. He walked further into the room, then sat on the edge of the bed.

"I understand what you're going through here."

Bobby faced the older man again, a look of disbelief on his face.

"Do you, Alec? Somehow I find that hard to believe."

"But it's true. This wasn't my idea, you know. There are other ways to deal with this... ...problem."

"So that's all this is to you? A *problem*?"

"That's not what I meant."

"Then what did you mean?"

"I'm saying, there are other ways this situation could have been handled. Moving to Nashville doesn't do anything toward resolving the situation."

"Then why are you going along with it?"

"Because that's what married people do. They stand by each other. They support one another in their decisions."

"How about their children?"

Bobby stood, turning and taking two steps away. He faced the wall as he continued.

"Don't parents support their children, too? It would be nice to have a mother that stood beside me on this, instead of ducking her head in the sand and pretending like it never happened."

"That's not what's going on here, Bobby. Parents need to make choices – hard choices – all the time, when it comes to their children."

"But look at the choice you're asking me to make. You're asking me to desert my son. You're asking me to leave Pamela all alone, facing the consequences of our mistake. Of *my* mistake. Is that right?"

"No it isn't."

Bobby turned, surprise evident on his face.

"There's a lot of things you don't know about me, Bobby. There's a lot of things your mother doesn't know about me. About my life. Before the two of us got together."

"So you're keeping secrets from her?"

"It's not like that. Some things she doesn't need to know about. There's just nothing to be gained by telling her everything. It doesn't change our relationship. Besides, what I'm about to tell you doesn't concern her. It happened a long time ago. Before the two of us even met.

"But it does concern you."

"What's that supposed to mean?"

Alec hesitated, as though deliberating whether to continue or not.

"Hannah isn't my only child," Alec admitted at last. "I had another little girl. A long time ago. It's been years since I've even thought about her. But lately, she's been on my mind a lot."

"Because of this thing with Pamela?"

"Yes. Because of this thing with Pamela. I see what you're going through. I see what your mother is asking of you. She's asking you to forget about the baby. Like a child is something you can just walk away from and get on with your life, as though nothing happened.

"But it's not that easy. Believe me."

Bobby considered a moment. He sat down once more, stared at the walls of his room while he collected his thoughts, then faced his stepfather directly.

"So what happened? To your daughter?"

"It's hard to explain. Maybe I was too young to know any better."

Now it was his turn to stand, as he began to slowly pace back and forth in the cramped confines of the bedroom.

"But no. That's just an excuse. I was stupid. *We* were stupid. Plain and simple. Her mother and I tried to make it work. We fought and argued and butted heads over so many things, but we still tried to make it work.

"You know, part of what your mother says does make sense. We weren't right for each other. So we tried to make it work. Because of our little girl. But it wasn't good for us. And it wasn't good for her."

He paused a moment, and Bobby allowed the silence to linger until his stepfather was ready to resume.

"We lost her, Bobby. We messed up big time and they took our little girl away from us."

For several minutes nothing was said. Alec remained locked in remembrance, while Bobby considered his stepfather's words.

"I don't get it," the young boy admitted at last. "What's all this got to do with me?"

"Because that loss was something I'll never forget. Because that failure, as a parent, is something I'll never forget. I don't want to see you do something you'll live to regret."

"So what are you telling me here, Alec? What's all this advice you're trying to give me? What are the words of wisdom you're sending my way?"

By this point Bobby had become more agitated. His voice, as he spoke, increased in crescendo with each interrogation he delivered.

"It's this, Bobby. I don't know what's going on with you and Pamela. And maybe you're the same as I was. Just too hard-headed and stupid to ever make this work out. Maybe there isn't a future for you in Pamela's life.

"But she's having a baby. She's having *your* baby. Can you walk away from that and feel good about yourself?"

"What choice do I have? Pamela made it pretty clear that she doesn't want me in her life."

"But she can't stop you from being in your *baby's* life. You have the right, as the father, to have a say in all this."

"And how's that going to work? With me in Nashville?"

Alec cut him off, his tone steady and deliberate.

"You don't have to go to Nashville."

For a long moment there was no response. When it came at last Bobby spoke slowly.

"What are you saying?"

"You're eighteen now, Bobby. You're an adult, and you're capable of making your own decisions. Just because we're moving, that doesn't mean you have to come with us. If you want to stay here you can."

Bobby laughed, with a short chuckle of derision.

"Sure. I can stay here. But where would I live, Alec? How would I support myself?"

"Get an apartment. Get a job. Other people have done it."

"You make it sound easy."

"I never said it would be easy. It will be hard. I can't deny it. But you have to ask yourself, what's the best thing to do?"

"You mean, because of the baby?"

"No. I mean because of you. What do *you* want? Are you content to just walk away from this whole thing? Knowing there's a child out there that belongs to you? A child out there that you are responsible for?

"Or are you willing to fight for that?"

For a moment not a word was said, as the two of them looked at one another and the import of Alec's words hung in the air.

"I just don't know what to do," Bobby finally admitted, his voice having lost its earlier anger.

"Well, you better decide pretty quick. Because this much I know. Once you leave Toledo – once you head down to Nashville to start a new life – it will be even harder to change your mind.

"Some things in life there's no returning back from."

Chapter Forty-Six:

C ONSULTATION TRANSCRIPT # 2306097 – EXCERPT

Pa W:
I guess I've always been uncomfortable with my body.
No.
That isn't exactly true. I think Angela had a lot to do with the way I feel about these things. Always telling me *Good girls don't do that sort of thing* or asking me *Do you think that's really appropriate for a girl your age?*
I guess, until I went to live with Tim and Angie, I just didn't know any better. I didn't understand what could happen. What would happen.
But I found out, didn't I?

Dr. B:
You're not the first one to make that kind of mistake, Pamela. But consider this. Many girls are unprepared for the reality of the sexual experience when first exposed to it. Your initiation may not be as unique as you think it was.

Pa W:
How can you say that?
How can you *know* that?

You weren't there. It was my experience. Mine alone. And that day really messed things up for me.

Dr. B:
Which day are you referring to here?

Pa W:
The day Bobby and I had sex. The day we made this little wonder that's growing inside of me, right now.
The day my life came crashing down on me.

Dr. B:
I'm afraid you'll need to enlighten me further. You're obviously extremely upset. What don't I know that will help me to understand the way you're feeling?

Pa W:
I don't even know where to start.
You have to understand, my time with Bobby was my first experience with sex. It was the only time I had ever been with a boy.
It wasn't what I expected.
You hear things. The girls at school talking about it. And of course it's everywhere, on TV and the movies and all. So I've wondered about it. How could I not wonder about it?
But I don't think I was prepared for the reality.
I was nervous – and excited – at the same time. So many questions in my mind. So many doubts.
It wasn't that way with Bobby. He just seemed comfortable with it. I don't know whether that's some kind of guy thing, or just a reflection on the type of person he is. It was like, for him anyway, it was the most natural thing in the world for us to be together.
Me, I was afraid the whole time.
Afraid someone would walk in on us, which Bobby said wouldn't happen.

Afraid he wouldn't be happy with me, and that I'd disappoint him.

Afraid I would do something wrong, and prove to him how totally inexperienced I actually was.

It wasn't easy, taking my clothes off, and pretending I was okay with things. I managed to do it somehow. I don't think he even noticed how hard it was for me. How uncomfortable I was.

It wasn't what I was expecting. You know? It all went so quick. I don't even know if I really enjoyed it or not.

I guess, for a few minutes, I did feel special. Like I was getting all this attention. And like, for a few minutes anyway, I was the only thing on Bobby's mind.

But then, when it was over, things changed.

EXTENDED SILENCE

Dr. B:
It's okay to talk about it, Pamela.
What you experienced – the feelings you had – aren't out of the ordinary. It's part of growing up.

Pa W:
Maybe. But what happened next.....
That can't be normal.

Dr. B:
What happened, Pamela?

Pa W:
I was still on the bed. I was....
Naked.
And I felt naked. You know? Vulnerable.
I don't know what I was expecting, but it certainly wasn't what happened next.
Bobby grabbed his cellphone. And he had this big smile on his face. He seemed even more excited then he had been before....

Before....

EXTENDED SILENCE

Pa W:
He said he wanted to take pictures. Of me. Laying there. Naked.
I couldn't believe what he was saying.
It just felt so wrong.
So demeaning.
So....

Dr B:
Dehumanizing?

Pa W:
Yes.
Dehumanizing.
Like I wasn't a person anymore. Like I was just this... ...thing.
This thing he could just use.
He didn't care about me.
He never cared about me.
I guess I knew that, all along. When I agreed to have sex with him. I realized I wasn't anything special to him. I knew he'd been with other girls before.
But I was still expecting something more.
And the way he talked about it. Like it was no big deal.
He even laughed about it.
He said he had lots of pictures. Of lots of different girls. And that I should feel special.
But how could I feel special? Especially like that?
And then he said something else. Words I'll never forget.
I guess he was sort of joking around. Trying to get me in the mood, I suppose.
But when he said that....

Dr. B:
What was it he said to you, Pamela?

Pa W:
Come on, Angel. Show me what you've got.
Just like that.
Like everything was okay.
But as soon as he said that it hit me.
So many memories.
So many things I had tried to forget.
So many things I thought I *had* forgotten.
And, I guess, maybe I did.
Until I heard those words.
Come on, Angel. Show me what you've got.

Dr. B:
What was it about those words that disturbed you so?

Pa W:
They were the same words I'd heard before.
From my father.
When he used to….

EXTENDED SILENCE

Pa W:
He used to take pictures of me.
When I was little.
And then he would make me do things.
Things I didn't want to do.
Things a little girl should never have to do.
The same words.
Come on, Angel. Show me what you've got.
The same words.

Chapter Forty-Seven:

ANGIE AND Tim seemed so happy, the day they came home from the court hearing. They said the adoption had gone through, and I would be living with them for good now. They asked me if I was excited about that.

How could I be excited?

Angie and Tim were nice. And they paid attention to me. And did things with me. And all those things were okay.

But it wasn't like being with Mommy and Daddy.

They weren't my Mommy and Daddy.

The next day they took me to the place where I used to visit with Mommy and Daddy. They said I would have to say goodbye. That I would never see Mommy and Daddy again after that, but at least I could see them one last time.

It almost made things worse.

It didn't seem fair to me.

Why would they take me from Mommy and Daddy?

Why couldn't things just be like they were before? Before Mommy and Daddy had their fight? Before the people took me away?

I guess I must of cried a lot. Angie and Tim, they kept telling me things were gonna be okay. That I would feel better in a little while.

How did they know that? How did they know what I was feeling?

They told me Mommy and Daddy weren't bad people, but they just didn't know how to take care of a little girl like me. And that's why I had to go away from them.

When we got to the place for our visit Mommy wasn't there. But at least Daddy was there. I guess he must of been out of jail by then.

Daddy told me he was sorry, that Mommy prob'bly wasn't feeling good and wouldn't be saying goodbye, but that he knew Mommy missed me.

Then he gave me a big hug. And he called me Angel. He always said I was his Angel, and that I was the prettiest girl in the world.

And when he hugged me, he whispered something to me. I guess he didn't want nobody else to hear what he was saying, 'cause his voice was real quiet.

He told me to remember our secret. That the things we did together, just me and him, that was our secret, and nobody else needed to know about it, because that was just our secret between me and him.

He said I should never tell nobody else 'bout the games we played. And the special things we did together.

He said he loved me.

And he said he would never forget me.

I never seen my Daddy cry before, but he cried that day. And he said he was sorry 'bout the way things turned out.

He told me he tried. He said him and Mommy had tried. But they just couldn't do it.

And then he said I was better off with Angie and Tim.

I don't know why people keep telling me I'm better off with Angie and Tim.

Why don't they ask me what I want?

Why don't they listen to what I have to say?

So I said goodbye to Daddy.

And we both cried. And hugged some more.

And then they took me home. Home to Angie and Tim's house.

But it didn't feel like home.

It wasn't my home.

Chapter Forty-Eight:

CONSULTATION TRANSCRIPT # 2306097 – EXCERPT

Pa W:
You have to understand.
I loved my father.
Yes, I loved my mother. But that was different. She was always there, but we were never close. I don't think she knew how to be close to anyone. It was like....
It was like she felt she didn't deserve to be happy. Like she wasn't worthy of it, or something. I don't know.
Maybe that's why she drank so much. To try to stop feeling so sorry for herself.
She cut herself off from the rest of the world. Including me.
So, in many respects, my father was all I had.
He would read to me at night. I loved to sit on his lap, and listen to the funny voices he made, and just share that time together with him. It was all mine, and nobody could take that away from me.
We would go places together, him and me. Sometimes to the store. Or even just to the gas station. Any little trip seemed like an adventure to a young girl that didn't have much else in her life.

A lot of times he was the one that made my dinner, because my mother was sleeping off her latest hangover. And we would sit at the table, and we would talk, and I felt like he was actually interested in me.

Dr. B:
That must have been reassuring for you.

Pa W:
It was. It made me feel special.
And, in my eyes, he was special as well.
So I loved my father.
I would do anything for him.
I did… …do anything for him.

EXTENDED SILENCE

Pa W:
I didn't realize the things he was asking me to do were wrong.
How would I know?
How *could* I know?
It was the only life I knew.
He took pictures of me. Like it was a game with him. But they were the types of pictures no father should ever take of their little girl.
And the things we did….
I knew they were wrong. Or, at least, I felt they were wrong. It just didn't feel right, somehow, to do those kinds of things.
But my father, he told me that if I loved him I would do what he wanted.
And he was all I had.
Can you understand that?
I didn't want to lose him.
I was afraid to refuse him. I was afraid, if I stopped doing those things he wanted me to do, then maybe he would stop doing the other things. The things I enjoyed so much, like spending time

together and all the good stuff.
I didn't want to lose the good times.
So somehow I made it through the... ...other times.
And I did whatever he told me to do.
Because I was his little girl.
Because I loved him.

Dr. B:
What your father did was despicable, Pamela. You do realize that, don't you?

Pa W:
Of course I do. Now I realize it. But not then. Not when it was all happening.
Back then I loved him.
When they took me away, and sent me to live with Tim and Angie, I loved him.
And after the adoption, when I had already lost my mother, I still clung to the hope that I wouldn't lose my father. I couldn't bear the thought of it. That's how much I *still* loved him.

Dr W:
It's not uncommon for an abused child to love their abuser. Any attention – even when it takes the wrong form – can be gratifying to a child who has nothing else.
When did you start to recognize the truth? That what your father was asking you to do was inappropriate?

Pa W:
I guess it wasn't until later, when I was living with Tim and Angie, that I began to realize how wrong it was. It wasn't until somebody started paying attention to me, started to care enough about me to tell me what was right and wrong, that I realized what my father had done to me was not normal.
That's when I started to feel the shame.

Dr. B:
It wasn't your shame, Pamela. It was your father's. What he did to you....

Pa W:
It doesn't matter, does it?
It doesn't matter why I did those things.
Yes, I was young.
Yes, I was naive.
Yes, I didn't realize what he was asking of me.
But I still did them.
And for a long time.... A *very* long time..... I had to live with those memories.
I guess eventually I moved on. And started to forget what had happened. Or maybe I just started to pretend that it was all some kind of nightmare. Or that it had happened to someone else.

Dr. B:
The mind tries to protect us, Pamela. By suppressing those kinds of memories. When horrific things happen to us we need to move on with our lives. We need to forget those things.

Pa W:
And I did.
At least, I thought I had gotten over it.
But that day with Bobby made everything feel so real again.
I guess maybe I was vulnerable. After what we had just done, maybe those kinds of thoughts were on my mind.
But when he said those words.
And all the memories came back to me.
I couldn't stand it.
I didn't know what to do.
I remember running from his room. And leaving his house.
I remember wanting to get somewhere, anywhere, where I could escape from those memories. Where I could get away from

them.

Dr. B:
And you thought suicide was the answer?

Pa W:
I know I wasn't thinking clearly. I know it wasn't the right thing to do.
But I was so desperate.
So anxious to get away from things.
What else could I do?

Dr. B:
You could have done what you're doing now, Pamela; seeking help from a professional, and opening up during these sessions. These are the tools that will serve you best. By examining your past and understanding how to properly deal with that past, you will find the answers to what's bothering you. This is what will get you through these trying times.

Pa W:
But it's not working, Dr. Bargalony. The memories are still there. The shame is still there.

Dr. B:
I told you once before there are no miracle cures. I can't give you anything to help you to forget. It's part of your life, Pamela. Part of who you are. Part of what made you the strong young woman you now are.
You may never forget what happened.
But you need to accept the fact that none of this is your fault. The fault lies with your father, not you.

Pa W:
I hate him.

Dr. B:

Your anger is certainly understandable. And justified. But don't let the hate consume you. This can be a new beginning for you. You will soon be welcoming a new life into this world. Don't make the mistakes your parents made.

Because you are *not* your parents.

You are your own person. You can make of this world whatever you want to.

For you.

And for your baby.

Chapter Forty-Nine:

"SO HOW does it feel to be an adult?"

Pamela merely shrugged.

"Come on," Tim persisted. "Today's your birthday. You're eighteen now."

"It's just another day," she replied matter-of-factly. "I guess it doesn't feel any different than yesterday."

"That's not how you used to feel. Used to be you were excited about your birthday. You could hardly wait for it."

The two of them sat at the kitchen table. Tim was enjoying his morning coffee, savoring the sweet aroma of the brew and sipping from his cup in a leisurely fashion. He really wasn't much of a coffee drinker. By the time he added the sugar and creamer he might as well have been drinking a hot chocolate. But there was something about the smell of coffee in the early morning that appealed to him.

It was nostalgic. It reminded him of mornings when he was growing up; how he would lay in bed, listening to his mother busy downstairs making breakfast and preparing his school lunch, and that sweet fragrance would waft up to his room to greet him.

More than anything else, he enjoyed the reminiscences conjured up by his morning drink.

Pamela sat across from him, picking at her bowl of cereal. She looked uncomfortable, reaching over her belly as she took another spoonful. Anymore she always looked uncomfortable. Everyday activities had become a chore for her. She seemed to tire quickly, now, lacking the energy to do even the most simple of tasks.

Angela stood at the stove, stirring the oatmeal she had prepared for herself. "Don't mind your father," she suggested. "He's just having fun with you."

Tim persisted, ignoring his wife's remark. "But it *is* a big deal. You only turn eighteen once in your life. You're an adult now, with a world of possibilities ahead of you."

"It doesn't feel that way."

Pamela set her spoon on the table and looked down at her belly.

"I think my possibilities have narrowed some, thanks to this little guy."

"They haven't narrowed, Pamela. They've just readjusted to *new* possibilities. So you better get used to it."

"Oh, I'm used to it. It's hard not to accept what's happening, when you carry a load like this around with you all day. I only wish it wasn't so uncomfortable. I feel like I hardly sleep anymore. If it's not the back pains, then it's this little critter kicking up a storm. Why does he have to be so active at nighttime, anyway?

"I can hardly wait to get this over with and get things back to normal."

"Normal?" Angela stole a quick glance at her daughter. "If you're waiting for normal, then you're in for a disappointment. Things are hardly going to be normal once that little guy shows up. Changing diapers. Five o'clock feedings. Girl, you're life is going to be *anything* but normal."

"You know what I mean."

Tim, seeing an opportunity for some friendly harassment, couldn't resist the urge to speak up to his wife.

"What would you know about five o'clock feedings, Angie? We never experienced any of that."

"That's true. But we will now. And don't think you're going to sleep through it every night, buster. Pamela's going to need our help through all this."

"No. You guys won't have to worry about that," Pamela reassured them. "I'll take care of everything. This is my baby. My responsibility."

"But we want to help. You know that, don't you?"

"Of course I do, Angie. But you and Tim have helped so much already."

"Listen here, young lady." Tim's voice was stern. Commanding. But the smirk on his face betrayed that his comments were made in jest. "Just because you're eighteen now doesn't mean you aren't still our little girl."

"I know that."

The young woman stood, an awkward procedure that involved gripping the arms of her chair, sliding it away from the table, and leaning back to counteract the weight from her stomach. She paused a moment, to ensure she was balanced correctly, then grabbed her empty cereal bowl from the table as she moved away.

"It will be SO nice to be able to walk like a normal person again."

"It won't be long now," Angela reminded. "Your due date is only a week away."

"It feels like forever."

She waddled to the sink and rinsed away the residue at the bottom of the cereal bowl before placing it in the dishwasher. After wiping her hands on a dishrag she approached her father, placing her hand on his shoulder. He grasped her hand with his, smiling up at her but saying nothing.

Pamela returned his smile before speaking.

"I appreciate everything you guys have done for me. I can't imagine going through this alone."

She left the kitchen. Both parents watched her retreat. For a moment nothing was said, until Angela spoke.

"She's grown up so much."

"Yes she has."

"Do you think she's okay?"

"What do you mean?"

Angela turned off the stove and sat at the table, across from her husband.

"She's been through so much lately, Tim. This last year, with the suicide attempt and all –."

"That's all behind her, Angie."

"How can we be sure of that?"

"I guess we can't be. But she seems better. More like her old self."

"But that's just it." She wrung her hands together in nervousness. "She seemed okay before. Before she tried to jump off that bridge. I had no idea anything was bothering her. Did you?"

"No."

"Then maybe it's not over yet. What if she tries something else?"

"We'll keep an eye on her."

"But what if –?"

"We'll keep an eye on her, Angie." His voice was firm, demanding no contradiction. "We know to be on the lookout now. She surprised us before. We weren't expecting it. We know better now."

"I suppose that's true. But it just worries me so much."

"And it should. But we need to keep on as if everything is okay. For Pamela's sake. For the baby's sake."

"I know. It's just that –."

Anything further she was about to say was halted by the sound of approaching footsteps. Pamela shuffled through the doorway. Her face held an odd mixture of emotions. Embarrassment, perhaps, but behind that the glow of happiness and excitement.

"Guys? Guess what?"

She motioned with her hands, indicating a wet spot on the front of her bathrobe.

"I think something's happening."

Tim was on his feet in an instant, rushing to her side.

"Maybe you better sit down."

"I'm okay, Tim. Really."

As she said the words she allowed herself to be led to a chair. Her father held it out for her, holding her hand as she took her seat.

Pamela looked at Angela, their eyes finding one another.

Both women smiled.

Angela's voice contained a slight tremor as she spoke.

"You're going to have a baby!"

"Yes I am!"

Chapter Fifty:

BOBBY BEARD pulled his history book from his locker, slammed the door, and gave the combination a quick spin to reset the lock. As he turned to walk away he noticed Garry Debrue approaching.

"Hey, B-B. Have you heard?" Garry asked.

"Heard what?"

Garry moved closer, in conspiratorial fashion.

"Sally says she just got a text. From Pamela."

"So?"

"She's in the hospital."

Garry paused, waiting for the information to register with his friend. He allowed Bobby several seconds to answer, but when nothing was said Garry continued.

"They took her to the hospital, dude. She's having the baby."

"Now?"

"Yeah. Right now."

Garry was excited, and no doubt expected a similar reaction to the news.

Bobby, maintaining a blank expression on his face, turned to walk away. He muttered a half-hearted reply to his friend as he took a step.

"That's nice."

Garry grabbed Bobby's arm, physically arresting any forward motion.

"That's all you have to say?"

"What do you expect me to say?"

"That maybe you're excited?"

"What's to be excited about?"

"Come on, B-B. You can't kid me. I know you've been looking forward to this."

"Looking forward to what?"

Bobby's voice was beginning to rise, his growing frustration obvious. A few students, detecting the outburst, turned to face the duo. Then, perhaps even more quickly, turned away to avoid the scene.

Bobby moderated his tone.

"Pamela's having my baby. My baby, Garry. And I'm not a part of that. So what is there for me to be excited about? She wanted to do this on her own, didn't she? Well, that's what she's got."

Garry, not content with the reaction, decided to press the matter further.

"Don't you think you should at least go down there? To the hospital?

"Why? Like I said, she doesn't want me there."

"It doesn't matter. You should still go down there. I know if it was my baby –."

"But it's not your baby, Garry. Is it?"

He didn't allow his friend the opportunity to respond.

"You're not the one going through this, so why don't you just leave me alone? This isn't any of your business."

"Come on, dude. You don't mean that."

"How do you know what I mean?"

"Look, B-B. I'm talking to you as a friend. Don't you see that?"

Bobby said nothing. Instead he looked down at the floor, as if seeking an answer. Or maybe it was just an escape; a way to avoid looking at things directly.

Garry, glancing around, noticed that the halls had emptied since the start of their conversation. A few students still lingered, but most had made their way to classes. The bell was no doubt about to ring, announcing the start of the next period, and of necessity it was time to cut the conversation short.

"I guess we should get to class," Garry observed, resignation in his voice.

Bobby failed to respond, and Garry took a step away. Then he stopped. Moving closer to his friend, he leaned forward in a show of confidence.

"I know how you feel about this, Bobby. I know this isn't easy for you. But nothing is going to change if you don't make it happen."

"I'm not sure I want things to change."

"What do you mean?"

Bobby hesitated before answering.

"I'm scared, Garry."

As he spoke the words a metamorphosis seemed to occur, with an alteration sweeping over the young man. Gone was the high school football star, the confident young man who was sure of himself and ready to conquer anything. Gone was the happy-go-lucky teenager without a care in the world, whose only ambition in life was to throw a football and score a touchdown.

In his place was a frightened child, faced with overwhelming responsibilities and decisions he was not equipped to handle.

"I didn't want any of this, Garry. I'm not ready for it."

"Do you think Pamela was ready for it?"

"Of course not."

"Do you think you're better than her?"

"I didn't say that."

"Well, you sure act like it."

Having found another reason to push the matter further, Garry approached his words with gusto.

"I've been listening to you for months now. You talk big about responsibility. How it's not fair that your parents expect you to move away and forget about all this. Can you really do that? Or was it all talk?"

"I don't know," Bobby admitted.

"Well you better decide."

Garry walked away, taking several steps from his friend, then turned back for one last look. He never said a word, just shook his head slowly back and forth in wonder.

Chapter Fifty-One:

B RIAN GLANCED at his watch yet again, noting with frustration that it had only been thirty minutes since Tim had left the waiting room. It seemed a lot longer than that. He couldn't help wondering if his brother's extended absence was a good sign or a bad sign.

He pulled out his cellphone to check his text messages. He scrolled through again, on the off chance that somebody had contacted him since last he looked, but the newest message he had received was from Tim. It had showed up that morning, informing him they were at the hospital with Pamela and things were progressing.

From what little Brian knew about pregnancies, he realized labor often took a long time. Especially with first babies. No sense in panicking and rushing down to the hospital. There was nothing he could do to help at this point, anyway.

He had been at work when the message came through, so he took his time and finished up several of the projects on his desktop. As it was they took longer than he had anticipated.

Still, he wasn't concerned. He knew his brother would let him know how things were going.

By the time he got to the hospital it was early afternoon.

And still no baby.

Tim was gone now, to check on the status of things, and Brian thought back to a conversation the two had shared shortly after his arrival that afternoon.

"I can't believe I'm back in this place again," Tim had commented, in a melancholy sort of voice that wasn't in keeping with his brother's typical positive attitude. "It doesn't seem that long ago since you brought Angie here. On Christmas Eve, of all days. Talk about a Christmas to remember! I still recall how scared I was on the drive over by myself, wondering what was going on and whether she would be okay."

"Well, you don't have to wonder about things now," Brian pointed out. "We know why Pamela's back there, don't we?"

The words had been delivered in an attempt to lighten the mood, but they failed to serve the purpose. Tim had continued with his brooding.

"It's just been a crazy nine months, that's all. Beginning with that stunt of Pamela's."

He glanced at the walls around them, as if noticing where he was for the first time.

"That was another trip to a hospital. The one that started this whole mess. It wasn't this hospital, but after a while they all start to look alike, don't they?"

Tim buried his face in his hands and sighed.

"I don't know how many more hospital visits I can take."

"That doesn't sound like you, Tim."

"Maybe it isn't me," he admitted. "Maybe I'm not the same guy I was nine months ago, before Pamela tried to jump off that bridge. Maybe it changed me, everything that's been going on."

He looked up at his brother.

"I'm sure you've felt it too, Brian. The way things have changed. For all of us. Admit it. The last thing you wanted was to have your niece living with you this past year."

"I admit it threw off my routine a bit. And it took some getting used to. I never realized how much having another person around, a person you're responsible for, could cut into your free time. Just knowing that you have to be there for them.

275

I guess, when you and Angie were going through it, I never noticed how involved it all was.

"But I was glad to do it. It felt good, being there to help you guys out. You know that, don't you Tim?"

"Of course I do."

"And I'd do it again if I had to."

"Let's just hope you never have to. Let's hope all this crazy business is behind us."

Tim sighed, as though releasing his pent up frustrations.

"It's all good days ahead," he announced. "I'm sure of it."

Brian checked his watch one more time. His brother had been gone now for forty minutes, which seemed to indicate that things were progressing at a faster pace. Maybe the waiting was almost over?

Brian returned to his phone, calling up a jigsaw puzzle app he had recently installed, and whiled away the time until, eventually, Tim returned to the waiting room.

"Well?" Brian asked. "What's the verdict?"

"She's fully dilated, and the contractions are about two minutes apart now."

"So what does that mean? In non-medical terms. Any minute now?"

Tim shrugged. "Could be. Or it might be an hour. I guess whenever the kid's ready he'll let us know."

"Man. He's not even here yet and he's already calling all the shots."

So they sat down again to continue their vigil.

It wasn't long before a nurse appeared, but not with the news they had been anticipating. Instead she brought a visitor.

"Mr. Watkins?" the nurse began, addressing Tim. "This young man says he belongs here."

Bobby Beard, from several steps behind, gave a meek "Hello" as the nurse continued.

"He claims he's the father of the baby."

"He is."

"Then I should get him prepped –."

"No." Tim stood, to reinforce the importance of his words. "He won't be going into the delivery room. Leave him here with me. I'll take care of things."

The nurse hesitated, considering what course of action she should take. Bobby Beard gave no indication that he was annoyed, or even surprised, by Tim's remark. She took this as an indication that she was no longer needed there and took her leave.

"Can I join you guys?" Bobby asked at last.

Tim hesitated with his answer. He finally gave in with a sigh.

"I can't stop you, so you may as well. This is my brother, Brian. Brian, this is Bobby."

"So you're the father?" Brian asked, the directness of his query tempered with coldness.

"Yes I am."

Tim continued. "So what do you want, Bobby?"

"I want to see Pamela."

"I'm not sure this is a good time."

"I realize that, Sir. And I don't want to intrude on your family. But I think…."

He cleared his throat, hesitant to say any more. His voice was more confident as he continued, as though he had summoned forth a hidden reservoir of courage.

"I have a right to be here. Don't I?"

"Yes. You do."

"Then I want to see Pamela. And I want to see my son."

"Pamela's still in delivery, Bobby. And your son isn't here yet. We're still waiting for him."

"Oh." The young man suddenly looked bewildered; like he was unsure what he should do next. His bravado of a few minutes ago had disappeared.

"I thought you didn't want to get involved with any of this?" Tim asked. "When we spoke at your mother's house –."

"Those were my mother's words," he interrupted. "Not mine."

"Then how *do* you feel about it?"

"I'm sorry, Sir."

"Sorry?" It wasn't the response Tim had expected. "Sorry for what?"

"For what I put your family through. What I put Pamela through. I should have behaved differently. I should have owned up to my responsibilities, and not left it all on Pamela. I only hope it's not too late to make amends."

"You don't owe me an apology. But it would be decent if you gave one to Pamela."

"I would if I could. That is, if she's willing to talk to me. Last time we spoke, she seemed convinced she didn't want to see me again. So I've been keeping my distance."

"Too bad you didn't think of that sooner," Brian put in, his words dripping with sarcasm.

"Now's not the time for blame, Brian."

There was no reply, and Tim turned to face the teenager once again.

"There's something I don't understand here, Bobby. Why is Pamela so angry with you? Maybe it's none of my business, but since this concerns my daughter I feel I have the right to at least ask the question. What happened between the two of you?"

"I don't know."

Tim and Brian both expressed their doubts, their faces a clear indication of their disbelief.

"It's the truth, Mr. Watkins. When Pamela and I…. You know."

"You can spare me the details. I know what happened between you two." He took a cursory glance around the waiting room. "I think it's pretty obvious why we're all here."

"But I didn't do nothing wrong. I swear. I didn't force her into nothing. She wanted to do it."

"That's good to know. Not necessarily what a father wants to hear about his daughter, but I appreciate your candor."

Bobby took a few steps further into the waiting area, head bowed, lost in thought. Approaching one of the chairs he sat down, composing himself before continuing.

"I don't know why Pamela got so upset. She actually ran out of my house that day. She wouldn't even speak to me about what was bothering her."

"Something must have happened."

He shook his head in denial.

"I don't know what it would have been. That's the honest truth. Maybe I wasn't the most affectionate. Maybe she was expecting more. But I didn't do nothing wrong."

"She tried to kill herself, Bobby. She nearly committed suicide. Is that on you? Because of something you did to her? Or said to her? Was that your fault?"

The young man raised his head. Anger flared in his eyes, as though he was about to speak out, but the sensation evaporated. When he did reply his voice was calm.

"I hope not. I never wanted to hurt her. I didn't want any of this to happen. Believe me. Now it's screwed up Pamela's life. It's screwed up my life. If I could change things I would. But I can't. It's too late for that, isn't it?"

Tim felt no answer was necessary. He walked over to sit down next to the boy. His voice was calm – nearly relaxing – as he continued.

"I think you both had to do a lot of growing up. Real fast. That's never an easy thing. For any of us."

"So what should I do now?"

"I'm not the one you should be asking that."

"Then who? I can't talk to my mother. She wants to just forget the whole thing."

"What do *you* want to do?"

He glanced toward the hallway, as if looking for the delivery room, hoping to see Pamela.

"I'm responsible for that baby in there. I want to be here. I want to see my son."

"Then you should stay. I won't ask you to leave. But there are a few conditions.

"You will remain here, in this room, until I have a chance to see how Pamela is doing. She's going through a lot in there. She doesn't need any extra anxiety right now."

"That's not what –"

Tim held up his hand, motioning the young man into silence.

"This isn't a debate, Bobby. I will come get you when, and if, I feel Pamela is ready to talk to you. I don't want you saying anything to disturb her. This is a special day for her. Don't ruin it."

"I won't."

"She needs this special moment to call her own, especially after everything she's been through this past year. Not everyone gets this, you know. Childbirth is something Angie and I never experienced together. We never had the opportunity to welcome a new life into the world."

A puzzled expression crossed Bobby's face.

"But Pamela –?"

"Was adopted," Tim supplied, in explanation. "But that doesn't mean we cherish her any less. She's been a big part of our life, maybe the biggest part of our life, for over ten years now."

"I didn't realize that. She never said anything about being adopted."

"I sort of got the feeling that you two didn't get the chance to know each other that well."

"That's true. I guess that's my fault, too."

"You have to stop blaming yourself for everything, Bobby. It doesn't do any good to wallow in self-pity. You need to move on as best you can."

Bobby nodded, reflecting on the information just delivered.

"I just hope Pamela finds a way to forgive me. For whatever pain I've caused her."

No reply came, due to an interruption from a uniformed nurse. Her face was beaming with joy as she approached Tim.

"Congratulations, Mr. Watkins. You now have an eight pound three ounce grandson. If you'll follow me, your daughter would like to show him off to you."

Tim was on his feet in seconds, passing the nurse and heading down the hallway before she could even complete her announcement. The nurse paused to address Brian and Bobby, who had both risen to their feet.

"Someone will be out shortly to let you know when you can come in to see the baby."

Keith Julius

Chapter Fifty-Two:

PAMELA LOOKED like she had just completed a marathon.

Her hair was wet with sweat. The strands draped over her face, clinging to her forehead and cheeks. The perspiration had soaked into the hospital gown she wore, which hung limp and damp against her, a testimony to her recent ordeal. Her skin was red, flushed from the hours of exertion she had recently endured. Her lips were chapped; she licked them often.

She was the picture of total exhaustion, save for the smile on her face and the glow of happiness in her eyes.

The first thing Tim thought, when seeing his daughter propped up in the hospital bed, was that she had never looked so beautiful.

The second notion that crossed his mind was in regards to the bundle she held in her arms. He was quite certain he had never seen a baby this little before. It rested comfortably, breathing in a sure and steady manner, its tiny chest moving in and out. His features were delicate and fragile. It was hard to believe Pamela had created something so precious.

So frail.

So perfect.

He entered slowly, afraid to disturb the moment. He wanted it to last forever – this feeling of bliss and contentment that overwhelmed him at sight of the three of them together.

Angie. Pamela. And the baby. They were his world, and he couldn't have felt more satisfied than he was at that moment.

Pamela spoke out in a quiet, motherly tone, as though she'd been accustomed to using the lilt all her life.

"Come on in, Grandpa. Somebody wants to meet you."

Angela sat in a chair on one side of the bed, her eyes drawn to the baby. Tim moved to the unoccupied side of the room, then hesitated. He wasn't sure what was expected of him in a moment like this.

"Do you want to hold him?" Pamela asked.

"I don't know."

"I promise you, he won't break."

Tim reached down for the child, making sure to grab the blankets that surrounded the infant. He placed his hand under the tiny head, careful to support it, as he brought the bundle up to his chest. It was a novel experience, holding a little one as tiny as this, but an experience he was certain he could become adjusted to.

Angela's voice expressed her adoration as she spoke up.

"Isn't he just the most perfect thing you've ever seen?"

"You read my mind," Tim admitted, as he began a slow back and forth motion, gently rocking the child with an unconscious rhythm he was no doubt unaware he was even employing. "You did good, kid," he informed his daughter.

"Don't I know it," she admitted.

"So how'd everything go in here?" Tim asked.

Angela answered for her daughter.

"It was rough there, for a while. It seemed like she just couldn't get the little stinker to move. She kept pushing. And pushing."

"And pushing!" Pamela exclaimed, adding emphasis to the word.

Angela smiled at her. "But she did it. All of a sudden…. Pop, there he was."

Pamela laughed.

"You make it sound as though I delivered a Pop Tart."

"Well, he certainly is a sweet little thing."

Tim rubbed his hand against the baby's cheek, a slow back and forth motion that failed to disturb the infant's slumber.

"He sure is soft."

"And he has all his parts," Angela exclaimed. "Ten fingers. Ten toes. I know, because I counted them. Plus that one special part, that lets us know he's a boy."

"Is Uncle Brian here?" Pamela asked, ignoring her mother's last comment. "After all I put him through – with my morning sickness and everything – he needs to see that it was all worthwhile."

"He's in the waiting room. Along with somebody else."

"Who's that?" Angela asked.

"Bobby Beard."

Pamela showed no reaction; she gave no indication of what she felt regarding the announcement. Angela, on the other hand, scowled and voiced her opinion on the matter.

"What's he doing here?"

"He's the father, Angie. He has the right to see his son."

"Now's a fine time to make an appearance. I don't want him in here."

"Is that fair to him?"

"Who cares whether it's fair to him or not? He doesn't belong here. He's not part of the family."

"I think that decision was made nine months ago, Angie. Whether you like it or not."

"Well, I don't like it," she announced, being certain all present were aware of her feelings regarding the matter. "And I don't see why you can be so calm about this whole thing. Or so nice about it."

"It doesn't do any good to be angry. It doesn't change what happened."

Before Angela could respond she felt a hand against her arm, motioning her to silence. She stared across at the young woman on the bed.

"It's okay, Angie," Pamela assured her.

The new mother's voice was nearly emotionless, as though bereft of any feelings regarding the issue. But she revealed a trace of a smile with her next words.

"I'm glad he's here. He belongs here."

"I still don't like it."

Tim carefully returned the infant to Pamela's arms, tucking in the blanket around one leg that had escaped from the covering.

"I'll go get him."

Moments later Bobby stood in the doorway. He said nothing, just stared at the child in its mother's arms.

"You can come in," Pamela prompted.

He took several steps closer, to the side of the bed, but still said nothing.

Pamela looked toward her parents.

"Can you give us a few minutes? Alone?"

"I don't know –."

Before Angela could progress any further Tim gently reached for his wife's arm, guiding her to a standing position.

"I think they should talk, Angie."

As they exited the room Tim looked back and smiled.

"Let us know when you're done. We'll be right down the hall. I'm sure Brian's pretty excited to meet his new nephew."

As they left Bobby took a step further into the room. He hesitated, reluctant to force himself forward, wondering, in spite of the circumstances, if he truly belonged there. He was still speechless, uncertain on what needed to be said.

Pamela, with a newfound confidence, spoke up.

"I'm sorry, Bobby."

The words surprised him.

"What do you have to be sorry about?"

"The way I've been treating you. Since all this happened. I wasn't very good to you."

"You don't owe me anything."

"Yes I do. I owe you an explanation."

She looked down at the baby for a moment, at a loss for words. Her voice had lost its edge of certainty when she continued.

"There's things you don't know about me. Things nobody knows. That day we were together...."

She took a deep breath, then forced herself to continue.

"I know I overreacted. I couldn't help it. But you have to understand what I was going through."

The baby chose that moment to whimper slightly, and stretch its arms and wave its feet. She held him closer, basking in the warmth the tiny body emanated. For a minute or so he struggled, silently, but at length he accepted the affection and settled down. She smiled through the procedure, amazed with how natural it all felt to her.

"I can't believe you made that," Bobby said.

"We made him, Bobby. You and me."

She smiled, but this time at Bobby. Encouraged by the expression, he returned the gesture.

But it lasted a moment only, as she resumed her recitation.

"Did you know that I was adopted?"

"Well, I didn't. Not until your father told me. Out in the waiting room."

"I was six years old when I went to live with Tim and Angie. My parents – my real parents – had problems. My mother drank. Constantly. It consumed her. My father was violent."

"I'm sorry to hear that, Pamela. It must have been hard for you."

"It was. But that wasn't the worst of it. My father...."

She stopped abruptly, choking back a tear. Bobby approached and sat on the chair beside her, unable to do anything but watch her struggle, helpless to assist but wishing he could do something to ease her pain.

Pamela forced herself to continue.

"My father abused me. Sexually. He made me do things. Things I didn't want to do."

The words were quiet; nearly a whisper. But they fell on the room like an explosion.

"Then I'm glad you got away from him," Bobby told her, uncertain how else to respond to the revelation.

She seemed not to hear him as she continued.

"He used to take pictures of me. Inappropriate pictures. At bath times. When we were alone, together. Any time my mother wasn't around. I suppose that should have told me something. But what does a seven-year-old know? I thought, at the time, that it must have been normal. That it was what all fathers did. I didn't know then what I know now. How wrong it all was."

"That must have been hard."

"It was. It still is. It's something I've had to live with for ten years now. With time I nearly forgot about it. My therapist tells me I blocked it out of my memory. That I had to, in order to get on with my life.

"But when you got your cellphone out, after we had sex, and said you wanted to take pictures of me, I guess all those memories came back to me."

Bobby stood and took a step closer to the bed. He started to reach out, to comfort her, but halted his motion, uncertain what he should do.

"I had no idea," he finally blurted out.

"How could you? How could anyone? It was my secret. Mine alone. It's not the type of thing you can easily share with someone."

She paused, as though finished with her recitation, but something in her manner told Bobby there was still more to come.

So he waited, allowing her the time she needed, and the telling continued.

"And then, when I ran downstairs from your room, and saw your stepfather in the living room...."

287

She stopped abruptly, choking on the words. If anything, the tremor in her voice was even more amplified.

Silence lingered between them, interrupted only by the sounds from the medical apparatus along the wall and the slow, shallow breathing of the baby in Pamela's arms.

Bobby sat again. His gaze wandered the room, as though searching for the words to find.

"I'm sorry I put you through that, Pamela. I had no idea. I didn't think it was that big of a deal. But that's all behind you now. Can't you just forget it and move on?"

"I wish I could. But there's more."

He waited in anticipation.

"Nobody knows about this," the young woman informed him. "Not even my therapist. It's the reason I tried to kill myself. That day on the bridge. The reason I couldn't face going on for another day.

"But somebody needs to know, Bobby. You need to know."

Chapter Fifty-Three:

Alec Sutter wandered the corridors of the hospital, searching for the proper room. His steps were unhurried, as though he had all the time in the world. Or it could have been merely a matter of procrastination on his part, a reluctance to complete his self-appointed task.

He carried a bouquet of flowers with him, purchased at the hospital gift store before heading up to the maternity floor. They hung by his side, nearly forgotten now, consumed as he was by other thoughts.

When he got to her room he paused a moment, taking in the sight within.

Pamela looked so peaceful. Almost refreshed. It was hard to believe the baby had been born a mere three hours ago. She lay in bed, reading a book. Beside her perched a bundle wrapped in a blue blanket. He couldn't see the baby from his position, but he knew what it was.

Alec tapped lightly on the door.

"Pamela?"

A smile was on her face as she peered over the book. The expression instantly became a scowl when she saw her visitor.

"What are you doing here?"

"I came to see you."

"You're not wanted here. I think you should leave. Right now."

"Can't I even see my grandson?"

"I don't want you anywhere near my son. Not now. Not ever."

"You don't mean that."

"I certainly do. I've never been more sure of anything in my life."

"Aren't you even glad to see your father again after all these years?"

"You're not my father. You're a monster that I was forced to live with for the first six years of my life. The most horrible six years of my life."

"It wasn't all bad, Angel."

"Don't call me that."

"But you are my Angel. You always were."

"Was I? If I was your Angel, how could you have used me the way you did? How could you have taken advantage of me the way you did?"

"I'm sorry."

"You're sorry? So everything's okay now, because you're sorry?"

"What can I say? I was stupid. I know that now. I never should have treated you that way.

"But it wasn't all bad, was it? Weren't there good times, too? When I used to read you stories at night. You liked that, didn't you?"

"You took advantage of me. You took advantage of a child. Do you have any idea how much you screwed up my life?"

"I never meant to."

"Well you did."

"And I told you I was sorry."

"I don't believe you. Besides, it's too late for apologies. I think you should leave. Right now."

He hesitated. Then he held out the flowers he had brought with him.

"These are for you, Pamela."

"I don't want them."

"I still care for you, Pamela."

"You never cared for me."

"That's not true. I loved you. It broke my heart when they took you away from me."

"How do you think I felt?"

"So you admit that you missed me?"

She hesitated. Confusion showed on her face as she considered her reply.

"I missed being part of a family," she admitted. "I missed leaving the apartment, and everything I was familiar with."

Sensing an opportunity, he spoke with renewed emphasis. "Then we can start all over again. Get back to the way things were before."

"That's not going to happen."

"But don't you see? This is like some kind of sign. It's like God telling us we were meant to be together."

"God has nothing to do with this. Why would God have anything to do with a monster like you?"

"I'm not a monster."

"Get out."

He refused to admit defeat. His words poured forth, in an attempt to convince her how irrational she was behaving.

"Do you have any idea what it meant to me? Seeing you again, after all these years? When you came down from Bobby's room that afternoon, I recognized you instantly."

"And I recognized you," she admitted.

"Then you felt it too?"

"No, Dad. All I felt was disgust. And shame. And an overwhelming sense of grief and horror over all the things you put me through."

"It doesn't have to be that way."

"Get out."

"Now, Pamela –."

"Get out."

He stopped, considering his options, and realized he had none.

As he turned to leave Pamela called out to him.

"Did Mom know?"

He made no reply.

"I asked if my mother knew? About what you were doing to me?"

"I heard you."

"Well? Did she?"

He stood in silence, head downcast. He refused to face her as he muttered a reply.

"Yes. She knew."

Now it was Pamela's turn to be silent. The shock, the realization of what her family life was truly like, washed over her. The memories of those days came back to her, along with the revelation that everything she had ever felt for her parents was one big lie.

Her mother hadn't just abandoned her. If that was the worst she had done maybe Pamela could somehow forgive the woman. But she had been aware of the horrible things her husband was doing to their child. She had left Pamela with a monster and ignored the fact by turning to a bottle for comfort, while offering nothing to the little girl she had given birth to.

How had Pamela never seen that?

How had she been so deceived all those years ago?

Alec turned to face his daughter once again.

"Your mother was never a strong person. And she was never an... ...affectionate person, either."

Pamela's hands reached up to cover her ears, in an attempt to block the words. "I don't want to hear this."

But he continued anyway.

"She used to drink when we first met. She claimed it calmed her nerves. Then, after you came, she found she couldn't handle the additional stress of raising a child. She wasn't meant to be a mother. So she drank some more. To escape. Which meant I was forced to find other outlets for my needs."

Pamela's head shook violently back and forth.

"No! No!"

He continued with his recitation, heedless of his daughter's reaction.

"She never said anything to me about what was going on. With you and me. But she knew. I could tell, from the looks she gave me. From the way she tried to keep you away from me. But I was your father. She couldn't deny me spending time with my own daughter."

Pamela was livid with her reaction.

"So you screwed up her life, too? You weren't content to corrupt your daughter? You drove your wife into an alcoholic stupor she couldn't recover from?"

"Now Pamela –."

"Get out!"

Her voice, raised now to a shout, disturbed the infant laying beside her. He started to wail, with heavy bouts of breathing interspersed between the tears.

Pamela picked up her child, comforted him, held him to her chest.

A passing nurse, alerted to the altercation, paused in the doorway.

"Is everything okay, Pamela?"

"I want this man out of my room. Tell him to leave."

Alec boldly took a step forward.

"Now, Pamela –."

The nurse interrupted with a stiff grip on his arm.

"You have to leave, Sir. Right now."

He seemed confused; uncertain what to do. He studied both women in the room – his silently crying daughter in the bed and the demanding figure of the nurse by his side – with a bewildered expression.

But there was no way to change things. That time had passed over a decade ago.

Alec Sutter silently left the room. The bouquet of flowers gently slipped from his fingers and landed to the floor with a soft hush of a sound.

Things had calmed down when Tim and Angela entered the room, not five minutes later. As they walked in Angela stole a glance behind her.

"What are you looking at?" Tim asked.

"Didn't he look familiar to you?" his wife asked.

Tim addressed Pamela. "We passed somebody in the hall on our way from the elevator. Angie swears she recognized him."

"I know I've seen him before," Angela remarked. "Somewhere. I just don't recall where. Did you see him, Pamela? Do you know who he was?"

"He was nobody."

She held her baby closer.

"He was nobody at all."

Chapter Fifty-Four:

T HE HOUSE was dark.

A solitary light shone from what he knew to be the living room. It seemed odd that no other lights were on in the rest of the house. Hannah's room was dark. Bobby's room was dark. Usually both kids left a trail of illumination behind them as they moved through the place, oblivious as they were to anything remotely resembling a utility bill, so it seemed strange to be greeted by such an absence of light.

Alec knew it couldn't be his wife. Lisa was still in Nashville. She wasn't due back in Toledo for another two days, when she came home on the weekend to have some family time and unwind from the stress of being away for so long.

But still, the kids should have been there.

He entered through the front door, calling out as he did so. "Hannah? Bobby? Is anyone home?"

There was no answer.

He took a quick peek into the living room, but save for the single lamp that burned in the corner there was no sign of activity. Entering the kitchen, Alec opened the refrigerator, rummaging through the contents for something to eat. Though, in truth, he had no appetite. More than anything he was restless, with nervous energy propelling his actions.

He finally selected a beer, popping the lid and taking a quick swig as he turned around.

He nearly dropped the can in surprise.

"Geez, Bobby. Why didn't you say anything? I didn't think anybody was home."

Bobby said nothing.

The young man stood by the kitchen table, his hand resting on a cardboard box on the tabletop. An assortment of video games stuck out from the top of the container, along with a football nearly buried by the game console. Beside the box sat a pile of folded articles – a few shorts, half-a-dozen assorted t-shirts, some socks and underclothes.

"What's going on?"

"I'm leaving, Alec."

"What do you mean?"

Alec Sutter looked around, as if noticing for the first time that it was only the two of them in the house.

"Where's Hannah?"

"She's at Molly's house. She's spending the night there."

"Then I guess it's just you and me, kid."

Alec took another drink of his beer. His manner was flippant, almost carefree, but it masked a nervousness he couldn't disguise. He refused to look his stepson in the eye, avoiding anything resembling personal contact.

"You're on your own," Bobby answered. "I'm outta here."

"Is that supposed to mean something?"

"I saw the baby," Bobby informed him.

The room went quiet.

"And I spoke to Pamela," Bobby added.

"Good."

Alec uttered the single word, then turned away – much too abruptly – and walked to the sink. He set the beer can on the counter, then looked out the window, both hands resting on the edge of the stainless steel vessel. He seemed captivated by whatever there was to see outside, only there was nothing. The darkness of night concealed the view. The shadows on his face, the dark look in his eyes, matched the environment he looked out upon.

As Alec continued, his voice betrayed his uncertainty. "It's good that you saw the baby. It was the right thing to do."

Bobby stood ramrod straight, not moving, no sign of emotion in his words. "Pamela told me everything, Alec."

His stepfather's shoulders slumped noticeably. A sigh escaped the older man's lips, like he had given up all pretense, yet still he continued with the charade.

"I don't know what you're talking about."

"I know she's your daughter."

"So? She's my daughter. So what?"

"She told me more than that. She told me what type of father you really are."

His stepfather made a waving motion to dismiss the accusation. "Old news. That was in the past."

"Why don't I believe you?"

"Believe what you want. Those things happened a decade ago. They don't concern you, anyway Let's just forget about it and move on with our lives. Okay?"

"How do you expect Pamela to move on with her life?"

"Pamela's fine. Her parents will take care of her."

"Because that's what parents do, isn't it Alec?"

The sarcasm in his tone was thick enough to cut with a knife. Alec failed to respond, so Bobby continued.

"Was Pamela fine last summer? When she tried to kill herself?"

Alec slammed his can on the countertop. The beer within exploded from the motion, splashing the counter, dripping to the floor, and soaking the front of his shirt. He made a light-hearted attempt to wipe it off but his mind was too preoccupied to pay attention to what he was doing. He did little other than to distribute the beer more evenly over his clothes. Eventually he gave up on the attempt all together.

"You can't blame her suicide attempt on me." Alec's voice thundered in the confines of the little room. "I had nothing to do with that."

"Do you really believe that?"

"Of course I do."

"So it's mere coincidence that the day after she sees you – the day after she discovers her abusive father is back in her life – she decides to throw herself off a bridge?"

The older man balled his hands into fists, then took a menacing step toward his stepson.

Bobby stood firm. If possible, he was more calm than before.

"What are you going to do, Alec? Hit me again?"

"I should."

"Go ahead. But know this. I'm not afraid of you, old man. I'm not some seven-year-old girl that you can force to do your bidding. I'm not some drunken woman that is so scared of you that all she can do is drink to keep her mind off how rotten of a person you are.

"So do your best. I dare you."

For several long moments they glared at one another. When Alec spoke at last his voice was calmer, but only slightly so.

"So what are your plans now, hot shot?"

"I talked to Garry. His folks are going to let me crash at their place for a while."

"What about Nashville?"

"I never wanted to go to Nashville."

"Then I guess things are working out pretty good for you after all, aren't they?"

Alec took another swig of the beer, wiping his mouth with his sleeve in an exaggerated gesture of contentment, before continuing.

"What will your mother think? What am I supposed to tell her?"

"I really don't care what you tell her. I'm sure you can make up some kind of lie. You've had a lot of practice with that sort of thing."

"Then get out of here. I'm better off without you hanging around, anyway."

Bobby made no attempt to move. He continued to stare at his stepfather with a venomous look.

"You mean there's more?" Alec asked.

"I talked to Hannah about all this."

The anger flared again as Alec advanced. "You had no right –."

"I had every right! She deserves to know. I told her sometimes people – even parents – can't be trusted. I spared her all the sordid details. She doesn't need to know the trash that went down between you and Pamela.

"But if you so much as lay a finger on her, I'll find out about it. And you'll live to regret it. I promise you that."

Alec paused, considering the words he had just heard. His voice was noticeably meeker as he mumbled his reply. "Thank you. For doing that for me."

"I didn't do it for you. I did it for Hannah."

Chapter Fifty-Five:

PAMELA COULD hear her parents talking before they even reached the room.

"I still don't understand how you did it?"

The voice was Angela's, with just a trace of humor beneath the query.

"Obviously I wasn't thinking clearly," Tim admitted.

"Obviously."

By this point they had reached the room. Pamela sat in a chair next to the hospital bed. She was dressed and looked refreshed, fully recovered from her recent ordeal.

The baby lay on a blue blanket on his mother's lap, his tiny fist held up toward his mouth as though he was considering sucking on his fingers. He was dressed in a yellow one-piece outfit that seemed too big for him; the sleeves were rolled up, while the pant legs spilled over his feet. Overall it made him appear smaller than he actually was.

Pamela rose to her feet as they entered, placing her precious bundle gently on the bed.

"So what's up? I'm ready to go home."

"You'll have to wait a bit longer," Angela announced. "Grandpa here –."

Tim interrupted. "It was an honest mistake."

Angela laughed and began again.

"Grandpa here locked his keys in the car."

"How'd you manage that?" Pamela asked, hesitant to get involved but curious nonetheless.

"There's a perfectly logical explanation," her father offered.

"Sure there is," Angela added, making no attempt to conceal her mocking manner as she poked fun at her husband. "You left your brain at home."

Tim turned toward his daughter, hoping to find somebody more sympathetic to his plight.

"I just wanted to be certain everything was okay," he informed her. "So when we got here I checked the car seat, to be certain it was secured properly."

Angela laughed again. "For the tenth time."

"Twice!"

He held up two fingers, to emphasize the point.

"I checked it twice. Once before we left home, and again when we got to the hospital. Is that so bad? Excuse me for wanting to be sure the baby gets home safely. I had my keys in my hand and I laid them down on the seat. I think they must have fallen on the floor when I climbed in to check the safety harness."

"I guess they must have," Angela added. "Because you can see them there now, plain as day."

Pamela approached, giving her father a quick hug. "I think it's sweet."

In an attempt to distribute the blame, Tim added further information. "And your *mother* left her purse at home."

"I didn't think I would need it!"

"Anyway, Brian's on his way right now. He'll take me home, we'll get the keys from the purse, and I'll be back in a jiffy. Thirty minutes tops."

He made a move toward the bed and peeked at the baby. He reached out, nearly tickled the infant, then changed his mind.

Tim stole a quick look at his watch. "I better head downstairs so I don't miss him."

"Can you believe that?" Angela asked, once her husband had exited the room and was out of earshot. "I've never seen him so excited."

"It is pretty adorable."

"He was in the nursery first thing this morning, doing a final check-up. He wants everything to be just perfect for you."

"I don't mind. I'm glad to see it, actually. I wasn't sure how you guys would be after everything I put you through."

"Don't even go there," her mother admonished, an edge of gravity in her voice. "We're just glad to see you feeling better about things."

Angie leaned closer to deliver a whispered query to her daughter. "You do feel better about things, don't you?"

"Of course I do."

"What about this suicide business?"

"It's all behind me. I promise you."

"Because I'm here. And Tim's here. If you ever want to talk about it."

"I know that."

Pamela was seated by now. As though it was a reflex action she reached toward her son, stroking the infant's back in a slow, gentle circular motion. The baby had been stirring slightly, but the motion seemed to calm him down. Pamela apparently found it soothing as well, continuing with the caressing as she spoke.

"I just wasn't thinking very clearly, Angie. That's all. But it won't happen again."

"How about the father? Bobby looked pretty upset when he left here the other day. Is there something going on there that I need to know about?"

Pamela answered, perhaps a bit too quickly.

"Nothing's going on. And I'm pretty sure he was upset when he left here." Then, as an afterthought, she added more. "But it wasn't about us."

"Us? Is there an *us* now?"

"No, Angie. There never was an us. There was just two teenagers, doing the kinds of things teenagers do. We didn't get to know each other that well. And I don't think we ever will. But who knows?"

She ceased rubbing the baby's back and straightened up in her chair.

"Anyway, this whole thing was just a stupid mistake."

"Not the whole thing." Angela looked toward her grandson and smiled.

"You're right," Pamela agreed. "That's one thing I definitely wouldn't change."

Chapter Fifty-Six:

T HE DINER was alive with activity. Wait staff hustled between tables, laden with trays of food, managing somehow to avoid one another as they made their rounds of the crowded establishment. As soon as one group of customers left their table was cleared and, seemingly in seconds, another party was seated.

Jennifer took a bite from her Chef salad and talked between chews. "I can't believe it's so busy in here. Is it always this crowded at lunchtime?"

Beverly shrugged. "I don't know. I don't go out to lunch very often." She smiled, a mischievous grin. "Maybe if my daughter took me out more often…?"

She purposely left the sentence dangling.

"Come on, Mom. Give me a break. The only reason I was able to do this today is because they're setting up new computers at my office. The IT department has the whole place torn apart."

"Well, I'm glad you thought of this." She looked again at the bustle of activity around them. "And I'm glad we made it here before the lunch crowd."

Jennifer nodded in agreement.

Off to the side, one wall of the diner featured a tropical fish tank. Several large angel fish hung in the water, front and center, as though posing for the customers.

"Dad would have liked this place. The aquarium and all."

"Oh, he would have liked the fish. I'm not sure what he would have thought about how busy it is."

"He never cared much for crowds, did he?"

"No. Russell was content avoiding people. He was comfortable doing things on his own, and being by himself."

Beverly's voice faded with the last of the sentence, as though her mind had wandered off somewhere.

Her daughter, catching the change in tone, leaned forward in her seat. Her voice was quieter. "I'm sorry, Mom. You still miss him, don't you?"

"Of course I do. He was such a big part of my life. So many memories wrapped around him. But that's okay. Life moves on, doesn't it? I keep busy."

"Yes you do. You know, I was talking to Teri a while back. She mentioned something about a suicide. And one of your CASA kids."

Beverly was quick to correct her daughter's comment.

"It was an *attempted* suicide. By a seventeen-year-old. Funny thing is, I represented the same girl ten years ago, when she was removed from her parents. She tried to kill herself a few months ago, but was stopped in time."

"But she's okay now?"

Beverly leaned back in her chair, to contemplate the question for several seconds.

"I don't know," she finally admitted. "The case closed a little while ago. She's back with her adopted parents. So I guess everything is okay. She was even due to have a baby. She might have already had him by now, for all I know."

Jennifer finished chewing on another bite of salad before continuing.

"That must be difficult. To get attached to these kids. And then have them walk away. You don't even know what's going on with them anymore. I don't know if I could handle that."

"It is tough sometimes. But it's all part of what we do. I just hope things work out for this young girl. She was obviously troubled by something. Troubled so much to contemplate killing herself. Who does that? Part of me is still looking for answers to that one. Yet part of me...."

She paused again. Jennifer remained quiet, allowing her mother the time she needed to compose her thoughts.

"Part of me hopes I never hear from her again."

"Why would you say that?"

"Because the only time I hear from her – the only time I'm involved in her life – is when something goes wrong. I don't want something to go wrong. The poor girl's gone through so much already. I think she deserves to get a break out of life for a change."

"We can all use that, that's for sure."

For several minutes the lunch continued, both women absorbed in their own thoughts. The moment was interrupted by the chiming of Beverly's cellphone.

"Do you have to get that, Mom?"

She considered a moment, then waved the notion aside. "They can leave a message."

Jessica, noticing the indecision in her mother's tone, offered her an out.

"It could be important."

Beverly hesitated another second.

"Do you mind?"

"Of course not," Jessica responded. "Take the call."

Beverly removed her phone, glancing at the caller ID displayed on the device.

PAMELA WATKINS.

The name startled her, especially considering they had just been talking about the young woman.

"It's her," Beverly announced, a bit breathless in anticipation. A worried look crossed her face.

"Maybe it's something good?" Jennifer suggested.

Beverly was pretty certain she didn't believe that, but she took the call anyway.

"Hello. This is Beverly."

"Hello Beverly. This is Pamela."

"How are you doing, Dear? Is everything okay?"

"Everything's great. I just called to tell you, you were right."

"About what?"

"When we talked about giving birth. You told me it would be painful. But that it was worth it. Well, you were right."

Comprehension dawned on Beverly.

"You had the baby?"

"Yes. I had the baby."

"That's wonderful. How is he doing?"

"He's doing great. We're all doing great. He's eight pounds three ounces, twenty inches of pure joy."

"That's wonderful."

"And there's something else. When you were talking to me earlier, you mentioned your husband. And how much he loved children. He sounded like a wonderful person."

"He was."

"Well, I just thought you should know. I named my son Russell."

Beverly was still smiling after the call was completed.

THE END

Keith Julius

Afterword:

THE COURT Appointed Special Advocates Program –
CASA – began in 1977 in Seattle Washington. In the forty-five
years of its existence it has grown tremendously into a truly
national organization, with 49 states now enlisting the aid of
volunteers to help children in need. Nationwide, over 97,000
volunteers in nearly 1,000 CASA programs speak up on behalf
of the more than 280,000 abused and neglected children they
work with each year.

CASA volunteers deal with issues of domestic violence
and child neglect. They work with families whose parents suffer
from a dependence on alcohol, or struggling with addictions to
prescription pills or narcotics. The children they serve come
from all walks of life, covering the spectrum of society, though
many of the children they deal with live below the poverty level.
These are children who go to bed each day hungry. Or cold. Or
alone.

Many of the children who get involved in the juvenile
courts, and subsequently represented by CASA volunteers, do so
as a result of sexual abuse.

Obviously this is a difficult subject to quantify, due to the
very secretive nature of this most personal of violations against
these children. Numbers vary greatly, depending on the source
material reviewed. One report from a decade ago stated
"During a one-year period in the U.S., 16% of youth ages

fourteen to seventeen had been sexually victimized." Another report states a much more conservative figure of 1.6%.

Either figure is alarming, particularly when you consider the nearly 17 million U.S. children in this age group. Even at 1.6%, that translates to over 270,000 children who are victims of childhood sexual abuse, with the numbers being as high as 2.7 million children involved.

Each one of these children has a lifetime ahead of them to deal with the traumatic scarring that results from this type of mistreatment. Each one of them will undoubtedly exhibit emotional, as well as physical, difficulties resulting from this trauma.

And what is perhaps the most frightening aspect of childhood sexual abuse is the fact that the National Institute of Justice reports "3 out of 4 of these children were victimized by someone they knew well." It has been reported that in as many as 40% of child molestation cases, this abuse was at the hands of their parents, the very people who should be the most concerned about their children's safety.

Thankfully there are CASA volunteers, Children Services personnel, caring foster families, and medical and psychological professionals who are doing their best to assist these children. As difficult as it is to write about this subject – and to read about it – just think how much harder it must be to deal with this on a daily basis. But these children require our love and attention and, through our perseverance and assistance, an opportunity to move past the hurt.

This book dealt as well with the issue of teenage suicide. The statistics presented in the story are, alarmingly, true and accurate. *Suicide is the second-largest cause of death for ages fifteen to twenty-four in the United States. Over 9% of people in that age group have actually attempted suicide.*

Pamela's case is indeed an extreme one, due to the horrendous backstory of her early childhood. But any suicide, any attempted suicide, by a child is a tragic occurrence. These are issues that cannot be made light of and should not be ignored.

The best defenses against suicide are awareness and maintaining an open dialogue. Be on the lookout for changes in your child's behavior. Keep conversations alive and stay attuned to what they have to say and, perhaps even more importantly, what they don't have to say. If there is any chance that your child is depressed or needs consolation then don't hesitate to act.

Because if you wait a day to do something about it, you may find that it's already too late.

Author bio:

DRAWING FROM nearly a decade of personal involvement working with troubled youth, author Keith Julius creates intense stories that pull readers into an emotional landscape of hopes, fears, and brutal realities.

Growing up in a large family, and raising two sons of his own, Julius has always had a compassion for children. Realizing not everyone has the stability he's been able to create for his own family, it has become his mission to provide a voice for the children in our society who need it the most. This led Julius to discover the CASA program. Founded in 1977, the program enlists volunteers to represent children in cases of child abuse and child neglect. CASA volunteers work closely with families to assure the children in these traumatic situations are placed properly and are well cared for.

In 2015 Julius released his first novel, the suspense thriller REMORSE BY DEGREE. This was followed by his series "The CASA Chronicles," which currently stands at four volumes, including the 2023 release A DECADE ABORNING. Each book focuses on a different family struggling with some of society's most challenging issues, including addiction, mental illness, human trafficking, teenage suicide, and childhood trauma.

Though his books are fiction, the writing brings a compassion and understanding to the stories that can only come from personal experience. These realistic portrayals allow the reader to join with mothers and fathers, and of course the children involved, as they face life's adversities. The author invites you to share in their triumphs, and sorrow in their failures, as they confront their struggles with dignity, determination, and the promise of a better future for their children.

Daniel Jameson was living the American Dream. With a secure job, a house in the suburbs, and a wife and two children, he seemed to have everything he ever desired out of life.

His storybook existence is thrown into turmoil when he witnesses a tragic accident at his workplace. Following the event Daniel begins to question aspects of his life he had long taken for granted. He manages to become separated from his wife Becky and on his own, aimlessly adrift and uncertain of his future.

A chance meeting at a restaurant introduces Daniel to Jackie Somerset, a younger woman to whom he is immediately attracted. His infatuation runs counter to the wishes of Jackie's boyfriend, Brad Wilkens, who unleashes a torrent of violence - beginning with a brutal attack against Daniel - that soon escalates to much more.

Daniel finds himself involved in situations and events he could have never imagined, fighting not only for his peace of mind but for the life of his family as well.

Aleisha Turner is young and attractive, a wife and the mother of three beautiful children.

Aleisha is also an addict.

Following a heroin overdose that nearly takes her life away her children are taken from her. Aleisha finds herself in a rehab center, the first step in what will prove to be a difficult recovery. She faces a long road ahead to restore normalcy to her life and bring her family back together.

Beverly Stone works as a CASA volunteer, a Court Appointed Special Advocate. Her responsibility is to see that Aleisha's children are living in a healthy environment conducive to their welfare while encouraging their mother to break the deadly habit that has come to monopolize her life. Along the way Beverly must immerse herself in a world far different from the one she is accustomed to, experiencing life from the perspective of the people who reside in inner city America.

When nine year old Aaron Reed has an accident at a local playground it seems like a routine emergency room visit. The case becomes more than routine when signs of child abuse are discovered. The young boy and his family find themselves embroiled in events that threaten to tear the household apart, as suspicion deepens and trust disappears.

Court Appointed Special Advocate Larry Kendall arrives on the scene to discover things are not always what they seem, as the secrets behind the family slowly begin to unravel. The truth, unsuspected by all, at last emerges. It is an ordeal that will test the bonds of family and the strength of faith.

A young girl's life is thrown into turmoil following the death of her older brother.

Fifteen year old Rosaletta Guiterrez finds things turning from bad to worse after witnessing the tragic accident that takes her brother's life. Estranged from the only family she's ever known – removed from a verbally abusive mother who has no concern for her daughter's well-being – Rosaletta is sent to a foster home, to live with a couple she can't relate to as she struggles to get on with her life.

Court Appointed Special Advocate Melanie Cox is assigned by the juvenile court to safeguard the child's interests, a task made more difficult due to the trauma that has infected the youth's thinking.

Desperate for change, seeking liberation from the loneliness that refuses to release her, Rosaletta runs away. But the escape she seeks becomes a nightmare, as the teenager becomes entangled with people and circumstances she could have never anticipated.

A suicide attempt by teenager Pamela Watkins leaves the young girl's family concerned regrading her state of mind and what could have driven her to contemplate such a drastic solution. No answers can be found from Pamela herself, who has withdrawn into doubts she refuses to express to others. As answers begin to reveal themselves Pamela's life spirals further downward, complicating the situation further and driving her closer to tragedy.

Beverly Johnson, a Court Appointed Special Advocate, is assigned to the case. Meeting with the teenager brings up unresolved issues form both of their pasts, with the clues to Pamela's mental health and Beverly's recurring doubts buried beneath ten years of family complications and unresolved issues.

www.ingramcontent.com/pod-product-compliance
Lightning Source LLC
Chambersburg PA
CBHW060402260626
47160CB00006B/2401